So Below

(An M/M Demon Angel Romance)

Julie Mannino

Published 2023

Author's Note

This novel is intended for mature readers only. Demons and angels aren't made of rainbows and fairy dust. A full list of cw can be found in Castle Village on the pinned post or on GR.

This trilogy contains a HEA.

Castle Village

For info on the latest books, sign up here for the Newsletter

Prologue

Eren jumped when he heard something crack in the distance. It was too late for Riley to come, so he started climbing a tree. Other humans were dangerous and not to be trusted. The book had said they hurt and killed fairies.

Crouched among the branches, he scanned the area as he wrapped his tail around his leg for comfort. The forest seemed empty, but after a couple of seconds, he caught the chirp of a bird. Animals were usually scared of humans too, so if one made noise, that must mean it was safe. Still, he remained in the tree as he watched and listened.

No human adults came running with pitchforks and torches. Nobody prowled around for a fairy child. Eren wished he had parents to keep him safe. Riley said most human kids had those, except for him. He had an Uncle, but that was just as good.

Eren had no family. He didn't remember anything from *before* except for his name when he woke up in the forest one day in a clump of bushes with a few books. The books told him what he was and what to watch out for, but they were gone now.

Since it seemed safe, he climbed down. Without Riley to play with, Eren could entertain himself. He found a good patch of dirt and cleared away some weeds and leaves. With a twig in his hand, he lay on his stomach, kicked up his legs, and drew in the dirt.

For a house, he made a square with a triangle on top because that was how Riley drew homes. He added a little rectangle with squiggles at the top for a smoking chimney. More squares and another rectangle became windows and a door. Next to it, he drew two stick people who were holding hands. One was a human, and the other had a tail like Eren. A circle with sticks and tiny triangles on top was Riley's pet cat, Kitty, who didn't like to go exploring. He preferred to be lazy at home.

Eren decided that one day when he was grown up, Riley would be too, so they'd make their own house and live in it together. Surely, Kitty wouldn't mind if they got a puppy because Riley said they were fun. No other humans would find them, and Eren would keep Riley safe forever.

The light grew dim as the sun sank lower, but Eren could see. He was pretty sure humans couldn't see so well, and that was why they didn't usually go out at night. Riley had to stay home and couldn't come to play in the dark.

He was doodling swirls and squiggles in the sky above the house when he heard a rustle behind him. With his focus elsewhere, he hadn't registered the silence blanketing the woods. He jumped up, saw a cloaked figure behind him, and was ready to run until he noticed horns sticking out from under the hood.

Humans didn't have those.

"Eren, I've been looking everywhere for you." The figure pushed its hood back to reveal a woman with long black hair. Her smile showed fangs like his, and she had purplish blue eyes.

Eren tilted his head as his heart still pounded. "Who are you?"

"I'm your Mother. Don't you remember me?"

He shook his head, almost too stunned for words. "I don't have a Mother."

She smiled and approached him. "Everyone has a Mother. I've been looking all over for you. I thought you were lost forever."

"Why?"

"I had to put you here for a bit because it was dangerous at home, but we can go back now."

He squinted at her because that made no sense. Why couldn't he remember her or anything from *before*? But if she was his Mother, that meant she was a fairy too, and others of his kind could be trusted. He'd also be getting his wish to have parents.

"Where's Father?"

"He's at home, waiting for you. We have to go now."

But if Eren went home, wherever that was, what if he couldn't see Riley anymore?

"Can't we stay here? I like it." He figured Mother could keep them safe because she was an adult, and Father could come here too. The bushes where Eren usually slept were roomy enough, or they could build a house.

Mother blinked her nearly black eyes. "Why would you want to stay here? We'd have to stay far away in the forest because of the humans."

“I have a friend. He’s a human child, but he’s nice. He plays with me every day.” Eren's throat tightened at the idea of never seeing Riley again. "I want to build us a house someday."

“Oh, well, if you have a friend, I suppose you can come to visit every day, but at night, you must come home because children have to obey their parents. You’ll like your home.”

Riley always went home before it grew dark, and he had to listen to his Uncle, so that made sense to Eren. They could still play, and one day in the future, they'd have their own house together.

Mother put out her hand. "It's dark, so you have to come home now."

"What's it like?"

"You'll just have to see, won't you? Your Father wants to see you too."

Excitement flickered at the idea of having a family as he took her hand. He couldn’t wait to tell Riley that he had a Mother with horns. He’d describe his home and what the other fairies looked like.

Maybe Riley could one day visit.

"Are there lots of other fairies too?" he asked as Mother gripped his hand.

"Of course."

She reached into the collar of her dress. Eren flinched at the faint squeezing sensation that quickly vanished as they appeared in front of a cave. The rest of the forest looked different.

Mother led him into the cave. The enclosed space, the room that moved, the dank tunnel, and what lay beyond two large doors didn’t seem like home. He’d imagined something brighter, and the box at one end made him shiver.

Did all fairies live like this in caves to hide from humans?

Mother’s grip had grown too tight. The hand holding his was now skeletal with grey, taunt skin. Every ridge of the bones underneath looked ready to burst out, and he froze when he looked up. Mother’s face was a skull with the same tight skin, and the eyes were pure grey. No iris, no pupils, no feeling. The horns were gone, and matted hair hung down.

Before he could try to run or do anything, other skeletal hands suddenly gripped Eren, and he screamed as they started dragging him toward the box. To one side, he noticed Mother again, but she was grey, transparent, and did nothing as the cloaked skeletons forced him along. How did she get over there? How did that other thing get him?

"Mother!" he shouted as his eyes blurred with tears.

"So sweet and innocent."

The thing that rose from the top of the box made him close his eyes as his stomach seemed to drop. Its laughter rang in his ears as something touched his face.

"It won't hurt for long," it whispered near his face. "You're so sweet and trusting, it's almost a shame."

Eren opened his eyes in time to see the top of the box sliding away to reveal a black gap. Mother still did nothing as the cloaked figures shoved him in.

"I want to go home! Please just let me go home!" Eren struggled as the bony hands pushed on him, but his strength was no match for them.

"You are home," rasped the thing.

Eren hit the bottom, and the top grated as it slid shut and trapped him in the tiny, dark space. He kicked and hit the stone which scraped his knuckles. He wanted the woods, Riley, and his drawing back. This wasn't home. The space was too small, and the darkness pressed like a weight and crushed the air from his lungs as a sharp pain stabbed through his skull.

Just that morning when they had been climbing trees, Riley had grabbed Eren's arm before he slipped off of a low branch.

"I got you," he'd said.

Eren pounded on the stone as the agony ripped through him. "RILEY!"

Riley didn't come.

Chapter One

Riley threw down the red feather. It fluttered to the bricks as he reached under his shirt and strained to grab between his shoulder blades.

"Get this shit off me!"

The angel grabbed his shoulders. "Stop! Calm down for a second."

"I have something growing out of my back! Don't fucking tell me to calm down."

Other demons came running. No. Angels. He wasn't on the demon side of this realm anymore. Riley ripped out another feather, mindless of the pain. He'd rip every fucking one out and remove whatever had been done to him.

"Don't rip them out!" shouted the angel. "You can't stop what's happening. Do you want some ugly, bald wings?

"I don't want wings at all!"

"That's a cambion," someone snapped. "Why would you bring that here?"

"He's both," said the angel who had saved Riley. "See the feather?"

"Look at his damn neck," someone else said. "One must have kept him as a pet. They bit him."

"Poor thing."

"He's not a poor thing if he's both. Who the hell fucked a demon and made a damn baby?! That's disgusting."

The angel that saved Riley forced him to sit on the cobblestones and grabbed his hand. "My name is Giasone. Lord Erebus called you Riley, so we know yours. You're in Life City. It's safe here, and the demons would have a hell of a time to get this far, so we're not about to be overrun. We're far away from the Point, and nothing can hurt you now. Got it?"

Riley trembled and clenched his fists to keep himself from reaching back to rip out more feathers. "I don't know what's happening to me."

"You're not a cambion. You're a nephalem, so that means you're part angel and demon."

Riley stared at him. He couldn't be. He was supposed to have a human parent.

If I let go of your hand, will you stop trying to rip out your feathers?" asked Giasone.

"Yes." For now anyway. "It itches."

"That's normal." Giasone released Riley's hand. He had blood spattered on his armor, one wing was still cocked, and his nose released another trickle of blood.

"Giasone, if you're here-" The angel cut off. "Can we take back the Point?"

Giasone pressed the back of his hand to his face under his nose for a moment. "It was bad. The Point is destroyed, the Nevyyn worked, and there's nothing to take back. We'd have to rebuild it, and that would mean pushing the demons back."

"We pushed them back before."

"Not from there, and..." Giasone pulled a cloth from inside his armor. "Fuuuck."

The other angels exchanged looks.

"I'm pretty depleted," said Giasone. "I used up a lot to save him. He was running and...I'm tired."

The angels looked at Riley who felt like he had been put on display again. Like the demons, they had odd features, and strange colors. One had a fluffy black tail like a cat.

One huffed. "Riley, you don't know shit about yourself do you?"

"I-"

"What did demons tell you?"

"Shut it," said Giasone, who had finally gotten his nose to stop bleeding. "For God's sake, he's traumatized.

"Don't swear like that."

"He's in shock, and I'm worn out. Come on, Riley. There's a spot we can go."

Someone else suddenly appeared about ten feet away, stumbled, and nearly fell. Blood glistened all over their armor. "The Point has fallen! The others are retreating to Fringe."

"Come on." Giasone tugged on Riley's arm. "Up. Someone get info from him. I'll deal with Riley."

In a numb haze, Riley followed Giasone. A doorway led outside of the courtyard and down a brick-lined path. Much further out, a wall surrounded the area, and he heard noises like that of a city beyond it. A few buildings were scattered about, and there was a training yard. In the center stood a huge statue of a woman with wings who was looking at the sky. Her robe was belted at the waist and had ripples as if a breeze was blowing. It sat on a stone plinth.

Giasone touched the foot of the statue as they went by. Riley didn't, but he stared at it, wondering who that was. He wondered about a lot, but a part of him just wanted to curl up and never think again. Or feel. He'd felt too much in the past days.

"This isn't my house. The guy who lives here is stationed elsewhere, and he won't care if we crash here. He usually trains others."

Riley grunted. The words meant little. The tiny stone house was just one room and had the bare amenities. Giasone turned to him as Riley stood in the middle, clueless about what to do.

"I guess…the demons probably raped you. Or Lord Erebus did at least." Giasone's tone was gentle. "They usually take good enough care of their pets, but you look like you've been through shit." Riley's wrists still bore marks, and his eyes lingered there. "Do you have any injuries that need dealing with right now?"

"No."

"Are you sure? You don't need to be embarrassed even if Lord Erebus did something terrible to you."

"No, and he never raped me."

He had kept his word only so Riley would eventually come to him in that regard. The betrayal still felt like a knife. He had been so stupid to keep allowing more and more, thinking they had something special. Thinking that Eren felt something more for *him*. He'd just been a source of energy and a cum midden for Eren to dump himself into.

Giasone frowned and didn't seem to believe him. "If you want to check your back in the looking glass there, you can. What's happening can't be stopped. You were glamored, and it's coming off. I'm guessing you lived on Earth?"

"Yeah."

"That explains it. You wouldn't have any magic and skipped normal puberty."

Riley headed for the looking glass to gaze at himself. Dark shadows loomed under his eyes, and his skin had a whitish sheen. When he wiped at it, it smeared and felt gritty, so he guessed that it was stone dust. He took off his filthy shirt and slowly turned.

Between his shoulder blades, a few red feathers were emerging, and a little blood had dried on his skin.

"Fuck."

"It's not so bad. You'll be able to fly once they fully come in."

"I don't want to fly. I just want to go home. I don't want to be here anymore. I never wanted any of this. I was taken by a cart, and given to Eren, and everything he said was a damn lie."

Giasone headed for a cupboard. "Technically, I could take you home. Or someone else could. But that's not a good idea-"

"Fuck you! I'm not going from one Master to another! I'm not going to be your hole to fuck just because of my parentage!"

Giasone pulled out a case from the cupboard. "I'm not your Master. No one is keeping you here, and we don't lure humans or anyone to enslave. If you want, you could walk right out that door, although I'm pretty sure someone would drag you back after a bit or to someone in charge because they'd be wondering why a lost nephalem is wandering around. Nobody is going to rape you or use you for energy. We're not demons, and you're not a pet here."

With his hurt wing out, Giasone sat on the edge of the bed, pulled a vial from the case, and popped the cork. He drank the glowing, pale blue contents, squinted, and his cocked wing seemed to fix itself. He set aside the case and the vial before flopping back with a sigh.

"God, I'm still drained, and there's no more. I can heal you in a bit, but I need to fuck someone before I do. Or get more vials. I can barely take care of myself right now. You have no idea how hard it was making that shield to protect us both. Even with glamors, I can sense if someone is human, angel, or demon, and that's why I got you. Whoever put that on you had a rare ability."

"Thanks. For saving me, I mean." Ashamed from his outburst, Riley stared at the feathers on his back in the looking glass. Questions wanted to tumble from his lips like why a glamor was on him, but the urge to sleep and not feel or think was stronger.

And then he realized he could never go home. Not like this. Humans didn't have wings, and this was the only place he could stay.

Unless someone decided that an abomination like him couldn't be allowed.

Chapter Two

Eren's heart thudded behind his ribs as the small room moved down. He kept his wings tight and close to his body to keep them from brushing against the walls and further reminding him of how tiny the space was. His tail lashed, and his breathing grew ragged.

He had failed.

The room shivered to a stop, and he heard nothing for a second. That tiny fragment of time always made his terror spike as he imagined the wall refusing to open and leaving him forever trapped in the dark space. No one would miss him for ages, thinking the demon lord was out on business. After all, his life was his own, and no one could order him about, right?

The wall finally slid down, and the sound scraped on his frayed nerves. He was already scrambling over it in his panic to get out before it was halfway down, and he nearly tripped in the dank hallway.

To put off going through the door at the end, he walked to the shelf in the corner that held old junk, including the books he'd had as a child in the forest.

He flicked back the ragged cover to reveal a picture of a little group of "fairies" who had tails like him. How gullible and naive he had been, thinking he was a fairy and lost among the humans. Some of the fairies had horns, and others had wings. It was easy to tell they had been drawn in haste with the sole purpose to entertain a little boy and fill his head with lies.

It was only after he'd been brought back and tortured in the box that he was made to remember who and what he was.

He opened the other one which showed sketches of evil, adult humans. They fought, robbed, and murdered each other. Anything unlike them wasn't to be treated with kindness either. A drawing showed humans standing over a dead fairy with their weapons drawn and pleased expressions.

In a way, the book hadn't been entirely wrong. Plenty would have killed Eren with his devilish tail if they had seen him. He'd made sure to stay away from civilization but that one little boy had drawn his attention.

They'd both been small, and the books never mentioned little boys and girls as being dangerous. What harm would one friend do?

He caught the figure at the end of the hall in his peripheral vision.

"Athena," he whispered.

She said nothing as usual before she turned and went through the door like it wasn't there. Waiting would only push off the inevitable and make it worse. He straightened his coat and tried to calm his tail before walking to the door with his head up.

The room beyond was lit with a massive chandelier, although its glow wasn't enough for the entire chamber. The blue fire, an angel invention, flickered as usual and illuminated the large table covered in a white tablecloth and a dinner set for one.

"Eren."

The nickname his parents had given him sounded so wrong. He forced his lips into a smile as he sat.

"You lost him. He's with the angels."

Eren shook out the cloth napkin, knowing that denial was pointless. A crow swooped by the table and landed on one of the chandelier's delicate, curved limbs, causing it to jiggle and throw wild shadows about.

"He tricked me and his new owner," said Eren.

"I know what happened. I saw enough. I wasted magic to send out the crow only to see him get away."

Eren lifted the cover from the plate. It was a farce. The food was already cold and congealed, and wraiths weren't good cooks. This whole hospitality was a joke, and he wished he didn't have to bother eating the disgusting food. It wasn't like he was making a deal and discussing terms with someone, in which dinner would be appropriate.

It was take, take, take, and he was supposed to pretend to be grateful for this. Fury sparked in his chest, but like every other time that happened down here, he forced his expression into a neutral one and picked up his fork.

"You should have sold him directly to someone who wouldn't be tricked by a pet."

"I promised I'd find him, and I will. Even there, he can't hide forever." Eren poked at a piece of meat. "We got past the Point with the Nevyyn, and when we get over the river, we can make another. The Tree of Life will be ours too."

The laugh was hideous as Eren forced a bite into his mouth. He wrapped his tail around the chair leg although it was a poor substitute for Riley's leg. He'd cut off his pinky if he could have five minutes to kiss up those strong legs like he had before. Of course, his pinky could grow back, but he'd still do it to have Riley in his arms and his cock up the nephalem's ass.

No energy had ever tasted quite so good.

The laugh died out. "You better. Once I grow stronger, you won't even need to come here much. That'll save you time, eh?"

Like Eren cared. The torture would never end.

"Eat your carrots, boy. They'll make you strong."

Eren ignored the snort and glanced at the pale figure in the back. It was a struggle to keep his expression steady as he inserted each bite, trying to get the food over with. Athena glided around the tomb and drifted closer while watching them.

He never understood why she was here. Ghosts weren't real. Or at least they weren't here in this realm. He was sure she didn't seem quite as solid as she did when he was a child.

"You failed me, and you'll be punished, but I'm merciful as always. Aren't I merciful?"

"Of course, Grandfather."

The first lord of his line peered across the table at him, and his one red eye shimmered. His skin was still dry, and he appeared brittle as if he'd collapse if a strong wind blew, but he was stronger now than when Eren was a boy.

"I'll let you have him if you like once this is over," Grandfather rasped. "A reward. But you cannot fail me."

Eren swallowed a bite of bland, diced carrots. "Thank you."

"Drink your wine."

Eren pushed back the plate and picked up the spiked wine. He could taste the faint, bitter tang as each sip slid down his throat, and the poison clung to his insides. It was stronger than usual, and he knew why.

"A week for such a failure," Grandfather declared.

Eren's wings twitched. "Grandfather-"

"You lost the only nephalem in existence. It should be two weeks."

Grandfather's glare bored into Eren who tried not to let the wineglass shake in his hand.

Grandfather's fangs showed as he smiled. "Finish it, and come here."

Eren unwrapped his tail from the chair leg as he forced down the rest of the wine. His heart rate was already increasing as he stood and swayed slightly. The weakness shamed him as he approached Grandfather and kneeled to the only being he'd ever bend the knee to.

Grandfather stared at his bowed head. When he held out his hand. Eren had no choice but to take it and kiss the ring the first of his line still owned. Its iciness made goosebumps erupt on him, although maybe that was the poison that was now twisting his guts.

"Go. I need to feed."

If he refused, Grandfather had help. He rarely ever used any magic and preferred to keep it stored for his personal use so he could grow in strength. Eren caught the other shapes in the corner as Athena moved away from the stone tomb. Even now, he could still remember the feel of those skeletal hands.

Of course, he couldn't die in the tomb, but it always seemed like he would, and he almost wished he could. It would be a relief if he didn't have to worry about his future heir ending up in there one day.

The fact that he had to willingly get into the thing he hated most made it far worse. He'd spent a week in it once as punishment for something, and he still remembered it.

The top was indented like a body, but it was empty. The one that permanently belonged on it lurked behind him, hungry and greedy as usual. The top slid aside and revealed the dark space that Eren had to crawl into, and he froze as his mind went utterly blank with terror.

This was worse than the room to see the children or the room to get here. That space was hell, and his mind had been warped to fear tiny spaces more than anything else. Being forced into it as a child still haunted his nightmares.

"Grandfather, please," he begged.

“I need the energy that you collected for me. Even after the battle, I know you're brimming full of betrayal energy. Get in. Now. Or I’ll make it longer for your failure *and* your refusal. You only exist because of me, and you should be grateful to serve me. Or are you not?”

The blank gap took up all of Eren’s vision. “Of course, I am.”

Grandfather’s touch on his back made him shiver. “You’ve been loyal, and after me, you’ll one day be the most powerful being below the heavens, so don’t let your fear control you. Give it to me.”

The slight shove told him he better do as he was told. The stone was like ice as he crawled in. He was barely in all the way before the stone grated. It slid shut and trapped him in the dark space.

All around, he could feel the cold stone pressing on him. His heart raced as he shook, panic erased all logical thought, and he pounded the sides and the top even though it was futile. In fact, he was sure the space grew smaller as the pain stabbed him.

He should have said the words before it was too late.

He knew Grandfather was on top of the tomb and absorbing all he could, uncaring of the agony Eren suffered as his mind was raped of energy. Eren always told himself he wouldn’t make a sound. He’d remain silent throughout, retreat into himself, and feel nothing. He’d let the pain drag him into oblivion, but the poison pumped through his veins and kept him present.

He kicked at the unyielding space, scraped his knees on the stone, and screamed.

He was still awake after a week when a wraith dragged him out with its frigid, bony hands and dumped him on the floor. For a moment, Eren still thought he was in the tomb, just joined by something else, but the light from the chandelier flickered across his vision as Mother’s grey dress swept by.

"Your loyalty makes her proud."

Eren finally blacked out.

When he woke up in the hallway, he knew Grandfather was done with him. The poison had worn off since he was out of the tomb. The dark room waited like a gaping maw at the end, and he knew he had to go. Lingering might result in him ending up right back in the tomb, although there was nothing left to take unless Grandfather simply felt like feeding off of his torture.

The grim light from the orb above him was agony to his eyes as his skull pounded so hard, it felt like it would splinter. He had to crawl into the dark space, and even the rustles of his hands and knees on the stone were too loud. Once he collapsed in the center of the dark room, the wall closed and trapped him again. He trembled as the room started to move up.

The grating sound pierced his brain as he struggled to keep a cry of pain locked behind his lips. It took an eternity, but the room finally stopped. The side opened, and he dragged himself through the cave. He only stopped once he was in the grass where he covered his face to block out the light and remained huddled there until he threw up all over the ground and himself.

He fumbled for the leather cord around his neck and squeezed the stone on the end. In a blink, he was outside of Hell City in a barren field.

The short flight back to his home was torture. He could barely see through his slitted eyes as the sunlight rammed daggers into his head. He stumbled and fell when he landed in the courtyard, which sent further pulses of pain through his skull.

Something watched him. Green and blue.

"Riley," he whispered.

It whimpered and licked his face. It wasn't Riley, but Buddy. Eren had stupidly left a window open in the house and found that the drog had run away shortly after the battle at the Point.

How had he made such a big trip alone and gotten in? Why not try to find Riley? Nagorth and Eedwa didn't seem to be around, but they must have let Buddy in earlier. He'd grown so much bigger in such a short amount of time, and his wings stretched as he gripped Eren's sleeve and tugged.

He should have hated Eren. Buddy was bonded to Riley, so why would he be here?

Instead of trying to rip out his throat, Buddy dragged Eren across the grass to the door. It was bad enough that Nagorth and Eedwa knew of his migraines, not that they understood where they came from, but he didn't want them to find him collapsed in the hall with vomit on his coat.

He had to hold onto Buddy to get upstairs, down the hall, and to the doors. Another eternity.

As soon as the doors were closed behind him, he dropped to his knees and cried for the first time since he was a boy and knew what had a hold on him.

Buddy whined and licked his face again. Half-crawling and half-dragged by the drog, he made it to his bedroom. The darkness was finally welcome, and he managed to get into bed. Holding onto Buddy, he sobbed into his fur until he finally slid into unconsciousness.

Even there, he couldn't find the touch that he wanted.

Buddy was gone when Eren was finally able to get out of bed three days later. Nagorth and Eedwa had come to give him rewek while he'd lain helpless in the dark, unable to even remember where the bottle was. He had no memory of Buddy leaving him.

Eren almost wondered if he'd imagined the drog, but there was fur in his bed and on his clothes. Nagorth confirmed that the drog had been there, and he'd simply flown into the courtyard one day. Eedwa nodded.

Eren almost thought they were joking. Drogs weren't supposed to be able to fly, but Nagorth insisted Buddy had and that he was so much bigger now.

When Eedwa asked where Riley was, Eren snapped at them to get the fuck out which sent them scurrying.

Once he washed, he skipped a shirt to spare himself the itchy feeling that was brought on by hiding his wings even if it was quick.

He'd noticed Riley occasionally scratching at that space between his shoulder blades a few times. It hadn't seemed to bother him since he never mentioned it.

That was always a sign, and it usually started several months before the wings would come in. Eren remembered it from when he was younger. It grew much worse before they finally broke through. Of course, Riley's would be a bit faster. Intense stress and trauma could hasten the process if the victim was old enough, and Riley was far past the age when demons matured.

He had some vials of stored energy that he drank even though it tasted nasty and stale. It was time to go downstairs and present the image of a hard lord who was ruled by no one.

The spot by his throne was empty as he hurriedly dealt with petty things and sentenced criminals. The vials hadn't been enough, and he wanted fresh stuff, so once the Hall emptied, he decided to visit the prison and pound someone's ass.

As soon as he stepped into the prison less than an hour later, he could taste the energy. He walked down the large tunnel that led to the underground house of horrors for human souls. Once he had taken a separate hall to his private entrance, since being the lord had perks, it was like jumping into a lake full of energy.

Riley would think he was disgusting.

He slowly walked by the windows that allowed him to see into various chambers, although nobody could see him. They let the screams through quite nicely as humans suffered in each room. By the tenth window, he was sure Riley would have thrown up by that point if he was here.

Being trapped in the human world for so long had made him too human. Eren wondered what his halfling would look like once the glamor wore off. Probably not too different. Angels were typically far more human-looking since their side hadn't liked mating with animals that much before the flood. They hadn't been so keen on seeing what they could create. He'd probably look even more exquisite, and angels would lust after him.

Riley would probably get on his knees for one. It might take a bit, but he'd find one he liked. He might already be on his knees right now, hoping the touch of another could make him forget Eren.

The thought grated on his nerves so much as he watched a human take a hot poker up his ass, he wanted to take the poker and shove it up the ass of whatever angel dared to touch Riley.

There was only one that Riley should be willingly submitting to and getting on his knees for. Eren wanted his energy now, and only his, but he forced himself to sit and watch the human suffer other unimaginable agonies in his cell. The halfling wasn't an option, and Eren needed to start piling energy in now.

Bones cracked as he sighed, leaned back in the chair, and damn near salivated as he tasted it. Thoughts of the tomb threatened to invade his thoughts, but he shoved them back. If he dwelled on that, he'd have already gone utterly insane years ago.

Further distraction was needed so he snapped his fingers.

A naked shaper was at his side in about five seconds flat. Eren glanced up and down its pale, nearly featureless body before he imagined what he wanted.

The demon made no comment as he shimmered. For a moment, his skin looked like melted wax before he reshaped to match Eren's desires. It probably wasn't the first time the shaper had been made to take on a human's appearance. There were demons with fetishes for them.

The shaper was smart to keep his ass stretched and oiled. Eren wasn't in the mood to be gentle or make sure the other was ready. He dragged the Riley copy into his lap and purred as he ran his hands over its torso. The demon rubbed his body on Eren.

It was pretty damn close, although the eyes never changed to match. A shaper couldn't change them.

"Watch."

Eren roughly spun the demon in his lap, undid his trousers to free his cock, and rammed it home. The demon gasped and even sounded like Riley. Eren dug his fingers into the copy and slammed him down over and over while he watched the human prisoner suffer.

"Fuck me harder, Lord Erebus," the copy gasped in Riley's voice.

"That's Master," snarled Eren, despising the sound of his real name on the copy's lips. Riley had never called him that when they fucked. It was always Eren, and occasionally Master when he was in the mood to be particularly good. "Better yet, keep your mouth shut."

The orange smoke built while he rammed his tail into the copy's mouth and fucked his throat so hard, he was probably ready to pass out from lack of air by the time Eren came in his ass. Not that the copy would dare complain. Not-Riley went limp on him as he came too, and the pearl formed. Eren pumped out the last dregs and shoved him off of his lap.

"Get out of my sight."

The shaper shimmered and melted back to his usual self as he gasped and hastened to crawl away. Eren plucked the pearl from the air and ate it.

It was sweet, but it just wasn't the same. He needed the real thing writhing and panting under him, and he'd have it again no matter what. Riley was his, and he better remember that even if he was currently in an angel's bed and shouting someone else's name.

The image made Eren see red.

Chapter Three

Riley didn't feel so physically bad after a couple of weeks. Lots of sleep helped at first, and he stayed in the house with Giasone while he tried to come to terms with things. No one was to bother him, and Giasone said he'd broken the news to others so the concept of a nephalem among them wouldn't be so shocking.

His feathers had come through a little more, and it took a special balm to make the itching and burning stop. The bleeding wasn't an issue after a few days. Mentally, he was beyond tired while two angels interrogated him and made him recount everything that happened during his time from start to finish. He thought that would be enough, but they wanted more. Demon names, the layout of Eren's home, and anyone who seemed important.

They also wanted to know where the children were kept.

That was something Riley left out. Even though he despised Eren with every fiber of his being, and most of the other demons could all fuck themselves with pitchforks, he didn't say a peep about the children's location. Even though Eren was a liar, a couple of things he said were likely true, and the fact that the children were kept hidden behind a magic entrance proved that.

He wasn't sure if these angels would spare tiny babies and children like Kyrian who hadn't had a chance to grow up and do anything bad yet. Children were often casualties of war even on Earth.

He was too afraid to ask what they'd do, and he didn't want to push his luck here since he'd been treated so well. Overall, the angels didn't seem bad. Nobody hurt Riley or tried to use him for sex. Besides that, the angels were a little disappointed with the info.

"Do you think Lord Erebus would really tell his pet every secret of the demons? War plans? Anything?" Giasone lounged on the bed and rolled his eyes. "You've already been through this stuff with Riley in every way you could imagine."

One of the angels in a chair huffed as he wrote notes. “We still have to check. If Lord Erebus slipped up even once, anything could be important.”

Riley suppressed a sigh as he sat on his cot. “He didn’t want me to know anything that was important.”

“If you remember anything else at all, let us know.” The two angels stood and finally left to Riley’s relief.

“I’m sorry.” Giasone started gathering his dark curls into a ponytail. “I know that was exhausting, and we didn’t expect much, but we had to ask. Even something that seems silly and unimportant to you could be crucial if we get that far. We will…someday.”

Riley tilted his head. “You just lost a crucial place and plenty of soldiers.”

Giasone flushed. “I know, but it’s not over yet. The Queen says she's working on a plan.”

“Like a Nevyyn?"

Giasone quirked his mouth. “Honestly, I have no idea what. She won’t tell me, and she usually tells me everything.”

“Oh?”

“We’re friends.”

“So…what happens to me now?”

“You can stay with me. If you want, you can learn to fight later. I don’t think going home would be a good idea even when you learn to hide your wings. You’ll always be different with your long life, and your eyes glow in the dark. You also never know if someone might come knocking on your door one day to get you. Lord Erebus must be furious that you got away, and he’d probably send someone to look if he thought you were on Earth.”

Riley stood to look at himself in the mirror, and he noticed the few tiny changes that had already started besides his crimson wings. His black hair had a few reddish highlights near the roots, and in the dark, his eyes had a faint glow. He could also see a little better with less light. Maybe he was imagining it, but he was sure his complexion seemed a bit brighter too.

Luckily, he wasn’t growing horns or a tail.

As a child, he should have had glowing eyes and highlights just like Eren. A damn good glamor placed on him at birth had hidden those features. While living on Earth, any demon or angel would lose their energy over time. Riley, not being exposed to any, had kept the glamor, and it had suppressed his wings. He'd gone through the human version of puberty late and dealt with the other effects that demons, angels, and humans all shared such as the cracked voice and hair growing in mysterious places.

His lifespan would have been the same on Earth, but he would have appeared normal overall except for one blue eye and one green eye. Glamors were hard to create, and they usually only went so far. Whoever had done Riley's had an excellent and rare ability, although it hadn't fooled Giasone.

After being exposed to energy over time in this world, a glamor would slowly start to peel away, and they'd be able to feed again. Giasone said that insane amounts of stress and trauma could force puberty. Eren had certainly traumatized him.

Riley thought of all the times Eren had fucked him, the energy they had made, the pearls, and the fact that Eren had given him blood a few times. Even if he hadn't been able to feed on energy, all of that had been affecting him.

The Nevyyn exploding so close had finished the job a little faster.

Since Riley would basically be going through a second puberty, he would soon be able to feed, do spells, and fly. Giasone said that once Riley had changed and it became apparent that he was more than a cambion, Eren would have rushed to take him back and kept him as a sex slave. A cambion was one thing.

A nephalem was quite another.

Besides being the fanciest pet imaginable, Riley wouldn't have been permitted to learn spells, but if he had a special ability, Eren could have possibly used it. If Riley refused him, he would have likely suffered worse conditions as the demon lord's sex slave.

It made his stomach twist in revulsion. He'd never been more than a hole and a fancy thing to lord it over in Eren's eyes.

"Riley, stop staring at yourself," said Giasone. "I know you don't like this, but you can't will it away. Come sit with me."

"It hurts."

"Do you need balm?"

"No. What he did. I'd rather be on Earth and hidden under a glamor. At least I felt mostly normal." Riley sank to the edge of the angel's bed. "Who the fuck decided to betray their side and go fuck the enemy? I guess I was a shameful thing to have around, so I had to be dumped off."

Giasone bit his lip as Riley sat next to him on the bed. "Your angel parent might be dead. Even if they're not, they might not be willing to claim you. I mean, who wants to step forward and say they got down with a demon? They'd end up in prison for such an interaction with the enemy. We don't allow that. Imagine if two enemies have been fucking, and they let a secret slip?"

"But you won't imprison me?"

"No. You didn't ask for this."

"How will I know what my ability is?"

"It's like instinct. You'll just know. You might have more than one or you might not have anything in particular. Maybe you'll be a healer like me!" Giasone brightened at that idea. "Even if you don't have a special ability for it, you could still learn to be one. My powers are stronger and faster. My shields are also better."

"Oh. I don't know what I want to do later. This is…it's a lot."

"It'll get better. Nobody's making you pick a job now anyway. It takes a while to set spells, and you have to work up to those."

Giasone had told him it would get better a lot over the past couple of weeks, but it didn't help. Riley was sure the pain would never get better. His heart had been wounded too many times now. He'd already decided he'd never love another. There was no way he'd risk himself again and hand over something so valuable.

The sick thing was that he missed Eren. He missed what he thought they'd had. He wanted the version he thought he knew. But it hadn't been real. It had all been a pile of lies for the sake of betrayal magic.

"You need to get out of this house," said Giasone. "I don't normally stay here for so long, and we can go to my house in the city. It's bigger, my stuff is there, and you can stay with me. The Queen put me in charge of your care anyway."

Now Riley knew where the angel had gone a few times. Probably to go talk to her. "Don't you have to go back to war?"

"We're regrouping and planning defenses. Besides, I'm not the only healer, and we don't want you tossed out in the city on your own while with no guidance or help. You already know me anyway now, so why not stay with you?"

"I won't be a bother?"

Giasone smiled. "No. I don't mind helping you. Oh, and Queen Nyla wants to meet you."

Great. Riley would probably be treated like a spectacle since he was the only nephalem in existence.

The angels certainly stared as he walked through the streets the next day. Word of his appearance must have gotten around. Some were too busy with whatever to notice him, but plenty did.

Riley tried to ignore it as he looked around. Overall, the place wasn't much different from Hell City. Most places were built from stone, the streets were paved with cobblestones. They had shops and homes just like demons.

Of course, sex seemed just as popular. No humans were being lugged around naked or clothed, but he spotted a naked angel being led on a leash. Perhaps he got off on that. A whorehouse had silhouettes painted on the window. It was clear what the one on his knees was doing for the one standing in front of him. The standing one held what looked like a paddle.

They passed an alley where two were loudly fucking on the ground and making an orange pearl. Riley quickly averted his eyes even though he should have been used to such public scenes now.

Ahead, a tower rose in the distance. Riley hoped they didn't have to climb all the way up to meet Queen Nyla because he didn't feel like it. The place didn't seem bigger than Eren's home, and Giasone's house was right next door which was handy. Riley would have his own room.

They went next door after Giasone showed him around. Riley had to wait in the Hall while the angel went through a side door to find the Queen.

He looked around, noting the burgundy cloth carpet and the bronze trim on the walls. Paintings of nature scenes lined both sides. It seemed that the Queen had wanted a personal touch where Eren's place was devoid of that stuff.

Probably because that soulless beast was devoid of feeling. For a moment, he remembered Eren's office, the only place that had a feeling of being special.

No. He could not start imagining that Eren was some lonely thing born into a war. Everything he said was a lie. He had no heart.

The door opening startled Riley. He had expected the Queen to be some tall, grand figure with huge, gold wings. Maybe she'd even have a halo, although no one else had those. Instead, the angel's ruler was a slip of a thing who probably weighed ninety pounds while soaking wet and couldn't have been more than five feet. She had red hair done in a braid, and her dress wasn't quite as fancy as he expected either. Judging by her young face, she was probably around his age. Her yellow wings were tucked close.

"Oh, um, hello, Queen Nyla." Riley gave her a bow while she curtsied.

"Hello," she said. "Giasone, you didn't tell me that the halfling was so attractive."

Riley's face burned as Giasone shrugged. "You were going to see him anyway."

"Riley, you can call me Nyla in private. In public, if you speak of me to others, use my title."

She approached Riley who started wishing he'd worn a shirt even though the press on his sprouting wings was uncomfortable. He couldn't magic them away yet either.

She peeked around him to see the feathers. "The red is pretty. I got yellow like my Mother." She sighed like that was horrible.

"I think yours are pretty," he said. "It rather fits the image most humans have of angels. Gold, yellow, white…that sort of thing."

"I don't think it looks good with my hair."

Giasone snorted. "I've told you it doesn't clash, but you won't believe me."

She wrinkled her nose at him and flexed her wings before tucking them close to her body again. "Giasone, I know you just got Riley, but I've decided something, and I can't wait much longer." She sat on the edge of the dais. "Maybe I should have decided on it far earlier, but I thought the Point would hold."

"We all thought that," said Giasone.

"Since it didn't, things will get worse as the demons advance. I don't want more of my people hurt."

Giasone tilted his head with a suspicious expression. "Nyla-"

"I'm going to offer myself to Lord Erebus as his wife."

"What?!"

Riley stared at her and forgot who he was speaking to for a moment. "Are you fucking insane?"

"You can't offer yourself to that slimeball!" shouted Giasone. "When you said you were planning something, I thought you meant a smart strategy or-or maybe a meditator came up with something, but you just drop this on me?"

"I'm the best bargaining piece we've got."

Giasone turned red. "Over my fucking dead body! I'll tie you to a chair and lock you up in a room until you come to your senses."

"No, you won't." She straightened her legs out and clasped her hands in her lap. "Nobody has been able to create anything like the Nevyyn. I mean, maybe we could since we have the Tree of Life, but that's like a human pissing on the Bible and burning it. We can't use that for violence."

Riley realized that was for him in case he didn't understand that the Tree was special.

"Back and forth we've gone," she said. "We never get anywhere, and when one side finally manages it, we're on the losing side. Do you think I want to die in my old age and simply pass this on to my children? Or maybe we'll finally be overrun? They can create more Nevyyns if they get past the river and take Fringe. They could make a hundred from the Tree! If I marry Lord Erebus, it'll unite all of us and stop the war."

Giasone's face appeared ready to explode, and Riley spoke up. "He won't marry you. I'm pretty sure he only likes dicks."

Nyla bit her lip. "He might like both. Plenty of demons used to like both before women became rare."

"Does he?" asked Giasone. "You spent the most time with him."

"I'm pretty sure he won't go for her."

"He might not because he's interested in my snatch but for the power," said Nyla. "We'd have to word the contract properly, but he'd likely require the majority of the power over both sides to agree."

"I'm not kneeling for him." Giasone folded his arms.

She hardened her eyes. "Even to save countless lives?"

"Do you know what he'd do to you?" he asked. "Demons love torture. Who knows what he'd do to you? And he might go back on his word and have angels slaughtered."

"If we sign it in blood, he can't go back on his word. You know that."

"I wouldn't put it past him to make or find some loophole. And that means you'll have to do whatever he says. Do you think he'll accept a deal written solely by you with only angel interests included? He'll have demands too, and I'm sure that will include you being in total obedience to whatever sexual stuff he wants."

Nyla swallowed. “I’m willing to do it if it ends things. I won’t do it if he makes a ridiculous demand like all angels being turned into pets and slaves or something like that, but if I have to accept some less-than-desirable things, I’ll agree to end this.”

Riley knelt. “Nyla, I barely know you, but even I think this is a bad thing. How old are you?”

“I’m thirty-eight,” she said with a slight edge to her voice. “I probably look like a teenage girl from Earth to you, but I’m an adult, and this isn’t something I decided on a whim one day.”

“I’m sure you’ve put thought into this, and I see you’re reasoning, but I lived with him. He betrayed me. Right before he was about to finish the last time we had sex, he admitted he was going to sell me, and that he was done for me. He used me for betrayal magic."

"Giasone told me."

"He spent months making me think we had real feelings growing, and then he betrayed me for a magic boost. If he’d do that to a pet, he’ll treat you like shit. Hell, he’d probably make you act like a damn pet and-and he might keep you collared and naked in public. He’d probably cane you bloody, and he wouldn’t give a shit about whatever you like. He might keep you inside forever. You have a very long life ahead of you. Do you want to spend it like that?"

“Do you want to spend it as a shell if he breaks you down?” asked Giasone. “Even the strongest have a limit.”

“He might make allowances and not be cruel to me if it means he’d rule over both sides,” said Nyla. “I’m sure he wouldn’t accept us co-ruling as total equals. I’ll attempt to get that, but I doubt I will. If I end up miserable, it’ll save a lot of angels from dying and losing loved ones.”

“Nyla, no!” exclaimed Giasone.

“What if you go to fight one day, and you don’t come back?” spat Nyla. “You think that won’t make me miserable knowing that some damn demon killed you?! Your Father died in this war too. How many others are going to lose loved ones? This might be the only option.”

“It sounds like you’ve given up!”

“I’ll regret it more if I don’t try this, and if we’re overrun, he'd kill me for sure. If he says no, the war goes on. I have to at least try while we still have time.”

"Your Mother would say no."

"She's not here anymore. It's up to me to think of what's best, and this is an option. Even though Lord Erebus is a demon, I'm sure he would like to end this war too."

"He likes killing," said Riley. "He told me he's killed angels, and he looked gleeful about it."

"Yes, but his parents died fighting too," she said. "I'm sure he enjoys killing, but he knows he could die in the war too. He knows there's a possibility that his side could lose and be wiped out even though they destroyed the Point. No one is invincible. Regardless of what you say, Giasone, I'm going through with it. I'd rather you be on my side than against me."

His face tightened, but he nodded. He wasn't the ruler, and it wasn't his choice. "Fine."

"As for you, Riley, I'd like you to come with me when I ask for a meeting with Lord Erebus."

"Why do you need me? He'll want to drag me back! He swore he'd find me, and-"

"It's not like we'd let him have you, but since you're a nephalem, I think you'd make a good person to act as a go-between if this goes through. I'll put in the contract that you're not to be harmed in any way, shape, or form. With a contract signed in blood, he couldn't go back on his word and enslave you. If he dared to do that, he'd die."

"Okay, but I'm not from his world. I've learned some stuff, but I'm not fit for a job like that. I can't even absorb energy yet. I'm like a baby here, and I still barely know shit."

"But you'll learn about this world, and you'll be like any other angel soon," said Nyla. "Even if you're part demon, you're more like us anyway, and I think the citizens of both sides would appreciate having someone like you taking care of little details. You could settle minor disputes and issues, especially in the beginning. Things that a lord might not want to deal with."

Riley felt a slight tension in the back of his head, which probably meant a headache was coming on from the stress. If he was acting as a go-between for both sides, he'd surely have to see Eren sometimes. What if there was an issue that was out of his range of power, and he had to go report to Eren? He'd promised himself he'd kill the bastard, but he couldn't do that without risking peace if Nyla married him.

For a moment, he wanted to tell her absolutely not, but then again, it might not be so bad. If he had a position of minor power, he'd live decently. He wouldn't be some starving beggar or a powerless pet at someone's whim. Eren wanted to keep him down and use him, but Riley would be his own person and protected by the contract. Eren could live and know he'd never truly dragged Riley down.

Besides, he might as well do something useful. The angels took him in without hesitation despite his demon parentage, and this would be a way to pay them back. Growing up as a human, they probably figured he wasn't too close to either side, so he'd be able to decide on issues with fair logic instead of favoritism.

He probably wouldn't have to deal with Eren that much. Hell, he could probably write a letter if needed and avoid any face-to-face interaction.

"Okay," he said. "I'll do it."

Chapter Four

Thanks to the stress and the magic of the Nevyyn, Riley's wings were coming through faster than most. Two days after meeting Nyla, he even started to taste energy for the first time. The residue that was often in the air was undetectable, but he walked past a whorehouse with Giasone and caught a bit.

It was like he was tasting something in the back of his throat while a faint warmth gathered in his chest. The first thought in his brain said to go find the source to gather more and join in whatever was happening. He needed it.

"Yooohoooo!" Giasone waved his hand in front of Riley's face.

"Huh?"

"You stopped dead in the street."

"It tastes sort of like…fruit and sweets and honey all mixed, but better."

Giasone laughed. "Oh, you feel energy? It's good, isn't it?"

"It's fucking delicious." Riley turned toward the whorehouse and started wondering how much they charged.

"No." Giasone took his arm and tugged him along the street. "You don't want that one. It's a shithole. Do you want your first time feeding to be with some dirty whore who probably hasn't washed his ass since six customers ago?"

"Ew!"

"Yeah."

"Wait, do sexual diseases exist here?"

"No. We're immune to that. Good thing, right?" Giasone snorted. "The war wouldn't be an issue because we'd all be dead from something else. Or our dicks would fall off."

"If I masturbate now, I can make my own energy?"

"Of course. It's not a lot, but it's something. You'd make more with someone else, and that's the only way to get pearls too."

Giasone gave him a quick glance, and Riley caught a bit of energy again. He realized that he could probably tell when someone had a dirty thought about him if he wasn't picking anything else up. His face warmed.

“You know, plenty are probably going to start wondering what it’s like to be with a nephalem.”

“Uhh…”

“And since you can feed, it's time to start learning spells!”

“Oh, fuck.”

“What? It’s fun. I still remember my first spell.”

Masturbating became Riley's favorite activity for a few days since he could taste his own energy while he did it. Giasone was right when he said it became easier to not be so enraptured by it. It was like trying a new, exquisite food. It didn’t seem like the best thing ever anymore after several servings. It was still pretty damn good, but the newness wore off.

Giasone set him to memorizing spells from a book that was as thick as Riley’s thigh. He wanted to learn something awesome like how to throw a fireball, but Giasone said he had to start with the beginner stuff, and there were no exceptions even for a nephalem.

“Also, I don’t want you tossing fireballs in my house. Go out back and use the stone wall for that stuff.”

As Riley’s wings came in, which was an itchy, burning nightmare unless he slathered on balm, he began to notice another feeling that he wasn’t sure how to put into words. He could detect how much energy he had. It was partly like a second hunger in the back of his brain, but instead of wanting food, he wanted sex. Or to watch. Or to masturbate. Whatever it took to satisfy it, he wanted it. It made masturbation even better, and he damn near gave his right hand a cramp one night.

Another night, he started catching bits of energy that weren't his, and he had a feeling that Giasone was jerking it in his room. He wasn’t interested in the angel, but the idea they were both rubbing one out somehow made it better.

Not that he’d ever dare to admit it. He also didn’t want to start anything with Giasone or anybody for that matter. Not with Eren’s betrayal still sharp and lurking in his brain.

He also didn’t need to eat anymore. He had in his first days here, and angels had food since eating was enjoyable for some. His hunger had lessened, and he didn’t require it now. Sometimes, he thought to eat at certain times because it was a habit, but he’d grown used to it surprisingly fast.

It was rather a relief in a way since it wasn't a requirement for life now. Since he didn't need food or water, that meant no trips to the privy.

When Riley woke up one morning, he realized his wings had grown more than a foot overnight. He stood in front of the large looking glass in his room while trying to get used to the fact that he'd have these extra appendages on his body forever.

Flight seemed exciting, but he felt a spark of anger at his parents for doing this to him.

He wondered if they had been ashamed of him. Sometimes he had the horrible thought that his demon parent raped the other and caused them to want to be rid of the permanent, living reminder. He had no way of knowing which one had been angel or demon.

What if they had loved each other but hadn't been responsible, ended up with an oopsie baby, and had to hide him to avoid trouble? Either way, he had to deal with the consequences.

He stepped back from the looking glass and spread out his wings. The crimson feathers gleamed in the light coming through the curtains over the window. Surely, they were done growing by now.

Despite his misgivings about having two extra appendages, he couldn't deny that he was slightly enthralled with them. He'd spent plenty of time examining them as they came in. The arches supporting them were light and strong. The skin under the feathers was sensitive and a paler red. Plucking a feather hurt. He'd lost a couple that didn't hurt at all, and they had simply come loose.

In their small, fenced-in yard, he'd tried flapping a little, but Giasone warned him to not try flying just yet before they were full-grown.

He could now.

Nyla had a large courtyard, so he tried there with Giasone while the Queen sat under the walkway covering to watch.

"They'll probably get tired pretty quick," he warned Riley. "Wing strength is like arms and legs. You have to build it up."

On the first few attempts, he only got a few feet off of the ground. It made his stomach lurch because it was higher than he could jump, and he had the urge to grab something so he could hold on. After a few more, he managed a half-decent glide across the courtyard, although he stumbled and fell when he landed.

Eren and everyone else had always made it look so easy, but probably everyone had to practice at first.

On his next try, he managed to gain more air. For a moment, he thought he'd end up out of control and smash into the roof covering the walkway, or he'd overshoot and land in a heap somewhere. Fortunately, he managed to land on the roof, and he tried to look confident like he'd been in total control the whole time and not worried at all.

"You looked ready to piss yourself!" Giasone laughed, and Nyla giggled.

"I'm not."

It was kind of exhilarating too. Riley turned to look out, and he noticed something flying in the distance. Just another angel. He was about to jump off and glide into the courtyard to try again when he thought he heard a shout.

And then another. And another.

Someone in the nearby street screamed. "What the fuck is that?"

Riley whirled around to see the thing was much closer and coming in fast.

"What the fuck?!"

Buddy slammed into him and knocked him right off. They fell in a confusing tangle of wings, limbs, and drog slobber. Riley expected to feel a bone snap when he hit the ground, but it was no worse than falling a couple of feet. Buddy jumped up first and spun in a circle.

"Buddy!" he exclaimed. "Oh my God, what are you doing here?"

Nyla screamed like the Devil had just landed in her yard.

"Wait!" yelled Riley. "It's okay! He's mine! This is Buddy. Remember, I said I had a drog."

"Why the hell is it so big?!" Giasone had backed up like he expected the drog to blast fire at them all.

"I guess you don't have them here?" asked Riley.

"No! That's a demon pet."

Buddy had grown, and his head came to Riley's chest now. His wingspan was bigger too, but he was still his usual excitable self as he practically knocked his owner flat again while attempting to slobber on his face. Riley flung his arms around him, overjoyed that Buddy had somehow learned to fly and came to find him.

"Sit, boy. You're going to smush me. How did you learn to fly?"

"I guess he got past Fringe since he's an animal and not a demon," said Giasone.

Buddy sat and trembled with suppressed energy. Riley finally got a proper look at his face and froze. Giasone said something else, but he didn't hear it as he stared. This wasn't right. There was no way Buddy could have done that. And why would he? He had no damn reason, and he wasn't supposed to be able to anyway.

"Riley?" asked Giasone.

"Huh?"

"He won't bite us, right? I like having my fingers."

"No, no, no."

"What's wrong?" asked Giasone.

"Fuck! Look at his eyes!" Riley pointed, and Buddy tried to lick his finger.

Giasone came closer to see. One of Buddy's eyes was half green and half blue, showing his bond with Riley. The other was half silver and half purple. Somehow, in the time he'd been away, he'd managed to do the impossible, and worse, he'd bonded with the one Riley hated most.

"What the fuck? He bonded with Eren? He's not supposed to bond with two people."

Giasone stared at the drog who let his tongue loll out of his mouth.

Nyla crept forward. "That's impossible."

"Come look at his eyes! What is that supposed to mean?"

"I don't know," said Giasone. "It's supposed to be impossible for them to bond with more than one person."

"Traitor," snapped Riley.

Buddy ducked his head and looked so ashamed, that Riley instantly felt guilt punch his gut. It wasn't Buddy's fault that this happened. He was a good boy, and Eren must have somehow figured out how to do this to be a conniving bastard and fuck with Riley. Buddy was so sweet, he probably didn't comprehend how bad Eren was.

Riley dropped to his knees to hug his pet, grateful that he'd gotten so far without being hurt. "I'm sorry. It's not your fault. You're still a good boy."

Eren could go fuck himself. He might have figured out some way to bond with Buddy, but the drog had come to find Riley instead of staying with the demon lord. Buddy had proven who he loved more.

"I know you didn't do it on purpose, and you can't help it. It looks like that bastard didn't hurt you, so I don't have to rip off his balls and make him eat them. Actually, maybe I will anyway, but for other reasons."

Nyla cleared her throat. "If you do that, make sure it's after we ask for a marriage contract if he says no."

"He's welcome as long as he doesn't pee on the floor," said Giasone.

Riley suddenly realized once he got the flying thing down, he could fly with his pet.

"Look, Buddy!" Riley stepped back and spread his wings. Buddy barked, let out smoke, and spread his wings as if to show off too.

"I'm sure some angels saw him, so I better go make sure no one is panicking," said Giasone.

Over the next few days, Riley got better, and he managed to fly around the tower without crashing. It was tiring at first since his wings weren't used to it, but with practice, they grew stronger. He'd never imagined that he'd be able to soar in the air like a bird, and once the unease wore off, he quite enjoyed it. Buddy flew with him, and other angels were awed by his pet.

Drogs weren't supposed to fly, but Riley said his was simply special when someone asked. Most angels stared at him in awe too or with lust like they wanted to mount him right there. Riley was sure his dick wasn't extra special due to his parentage, but at least he got to taste the energy.

Unfortunately, it turned out that not everyone liked him. He'd caught nasty looks a few times, and one day, a bright pink thing that looked similar to a cabbage came flying at him when he was walking down the street with Buddy. It missed his head by an inch.

"Freak! Go back to Hell City, or better yet, go to the real Hell!"

A few angels yelled at the thrower. Buddy took off after the angel who screamed and ran.

"Buddy! Get back here!"

The drog returned to his owner while practically frothing at the mouth in his fury.

“You can’t run after someone for petty shit like that,” said Riley, and Buddy growled before he puffed out smoke.

Someone asked if he was all right, and he said yes, but he knew some from both sides might hate him for having a parent from the enemy. Most seemed to get that his parentage wasn’t his fault, but not everyone would follow that line of thinking.

Giasone got him a sword to wear at his side after that. Buddy was good protection, but it was better if Riley had something himself too. He still caught some leery glares a few times after that although nothing happened. They probably thought Buddy would eat their limbs.

Someone else tried to proposition him right on the street too. The taste of the stranger's energy was beyond tempting. Riley hadn’t truly fed from anyone yet, and there was nothing wrong with a quick fuck. It wasn’t like he had to marry the pretty angel before him with lavender eyes and midnight blue skin.

The word yes almost tumbled from his lips, but guilt nagged at him.

“No, but thanks.”

The angel gave him a pouty, disappointed look but didn’t push it. Riley continued on his way while picturing Eren and utterly hating himself. This was absolute bullshit. It wasn’t like he owed Eren anything, and they weren’t together. They never had been since the demon had simply been using him, but he couldn’t shake off the guilt for some reason.

“Fuck,” he muttered under his breath.

Giasone sat at the table in the sitting room the next morning while Riley practiced making sparks shoot from his fingers. They were dim and pretty useless, but he had to set the spell or he'd never be able to learn stronger stuff like fire.

“You need to start making some pearls,” said Giasone. “I mean, maybe I’m wrong, but when you go out, you’re never gone for that long, so I bet you’re not fucking anyone. Wanking in your room isn’t creating that much energy.”

Riley felt his face redden. “I’m not in the mood for sex.”

Giasone frowned. “Are you still upset over Lord Erebus?”

“Yeah.”

“In the few times you’ve mentioned him, you always call him Eren. Any reason for that?”

"It's just a nickname." Riley hadn't even noticed. He had usually called the demon Lord Erebus if he spoke of him to someone else in Hell, but here, he'd completely forgotten.

"I figured, but it's kind of weird to call him by a nickname when you hate him, and you're not around him anymore."

"It's just a habit," said Riley. "I got used to it."

"Oh."

"How do you get someone's claws out of your brain?" he asked, finally deciding to admit his issue. "I'd be glad to see him dead, but at the same time, I feel guilty about screwing someone else. I know it's stupid because he didn't give a shit about me, but it just..."

"There was this guy I was with once," said Giasone. "He said he wanted us to bond, but I found out he was fucking two others on the side. He didn't give a shit about me and just said what I wanted to hear. It takes a bit of time for hurt like that to go away."

"Is there any way to hurry it up?"

"Not really. Once you see him again, you'll be reminded of what a shitpile he is. Nyla's pretty sure he'll take her offer, so I'm sure you'll see him gloating over that."

Riley cringed at the idea of Eren basically winning, ruling over it all, and getting a spouse, not that he'd really care about that last bit.

"I hate this idea of hers," Giasone continued. "We've been friends since we were kids, and I'm supposed to just watch her go away with that asshole if he accepts?"

"Are you guys close like-"

"We wouldn't bond. She likes men, but I do too. I'm not into ladies, and we've never had sex even for energy. I know she's doing this for everyone, including me, but I don't see how I can stand this if Lord Erebus says yes. The angels won't have a choice over it, and they won't be happy. They'll get her reasoning, but it's hard to suddenly have the most hated bastard ruling over you. This isn't going to be an entirely peaceful transition either. She already sent a crow, and I can teleport us to Fringe when it's time to go, but I almost don't want to go. It's practically like delivering her to the enemy even though they won't bond right then."

Riley slumped back in his chair. "Can I bring Buddy?"

"Yeah, but you gotta hold onto him when we teleport, and he'll have to stay back in Fringe."

Riley would have to see Eren again.

Fuck.

It took him ages to get to sleep that night. At least he'd gotten used to sleeping with wings, and he could lie on his back too. He found himself back in the woods where he played with Eren as a boy, but instead of the demon being there, Giasone stood next to him.

"What the heavens are you doing?"

Riley blinked at him. "Not much."

Giasone narrowed his eyes. "Are you aware of this?"

Why the weird question? "I'm lucid dreaming."

"It's rude to drag someone along into your dreams without asking! What the hell? Wake up."

"What?"

"Wake up right now. I'll talk to you afterward."

"Erm, okay."

Not once had anyone spoken to him as if aware that this was a dream and not real life. They were supposed to be created from his mind.

There was no way...

Riley closed his eyes tightly and woke up in his bed. Barely a second had passed before he heard footsteps thudding through the sitting room. Giasone barreled into his room without knocking and ran up the bed which made Buddy bark.

"Why didn't you tell me you could lucid dream? That's such an amazing ability! But it's rude to drag me along with no warning whatsoever. I had just barely dozed o-"

"Are you serious? I pulled you in?"

"How could you not know?" Giasone turned away to leave.

Riley followed him into the sitting room. Buddy jumped down from the foot of the bed and followed him. "Why are you all freaked out? It's just lucid dreaming. I've been doing it for years."

Giasone turned around in front of the fireplace. "You've been doing this for years, and you didn't even say you already knew of your special ability?"

"I don't think that's my ability. Humans can do it too. I only know because I asked a wise woman why I could sometimes control my dreams. When I was a kid, I kind of had a stage where I wanted to be a wizard after I read a book about one who had to find a spell to save his kingdom from an evil wizard, and-uh, you probably wouldn't know it. But she said it didn't mean I was a wizard."

"Uh-huh."

Riley gestured with his hands. "I asked her because some of the local kids said she was a witch. She wasn't, but she told me she could lucid dream too. That's all."

"And you've been doing this for years and years whenever you feel like it?"

Riley shook his head. "No. It just happens once in a while. It's not a nightly occurrence."

Giasone poked at the blue fire with the poker to make it grow brighter. "So you control everything in them?"

"Yeah, but sometimes, things just happen, and I go along with it. I think it's what I do in real life or maybe something I want in the back of my head that affects it if I'm not purposely making stuff happen."

"Like what? What did you do as a kid?" Giasone plopped on the couch.

"I played outside, or I'd go to town and do stuff like sneak into people's houses just to be nosy, but I'd only find what I expected. Once, I danced on a table in a tavern even though I'd never do that in real life. All of the patrons yelled at me, but it wasn't real, so I didn't care. When I got older, I've occasionally, erm, had kinky sex with guys in my dreams."

Giasone laughed. "Did you get off?"

Riley felt his face grow warm as he sat on the couch. "Yeah." A few times, it had made him ejaculate in his sleep, which he hated because waking up with cold, sticky cum in his drawers wasn't fun.

"Can you find out things? Could you go into a place, read a book, retain the info, and come back with it?"

Riley shook his head as he patted Buddy's head. "No. If anybody says or does anything, it's something I know, have seen, or expect. Or I make them do it. I rode a purple unicorn through a town I lived near once, and that was fun, but it's something I imagined. Other weird stuff has happened, and it was stuff my brain made up. I think if I picked up a book, it would only have what I expect to find inside or maybe nothing. I can't read new things because I haven't done it in real life."

When he asked Eren questions in the dream, his subconscious filled in the blanks. He'd wanted more, and that made dream Eren say they could have been lovers if they had grown up together. What an idiot he'd been.

Giasone rubbed his chin. "Hmm. You just dragged me in. Normal people might be able to lucid dream and control things, but they can't bring others along for the ride. Even if two people were lucid dreaming at the same time, and they were able to imagine the other person, when they wake up, the other won't know what their buddy dreamed or did."

"Oh..."

"You just did," said Giasone. "I think your ability wasn't fully masked as you were growing up because it's inherent. Those don't always go away completely. Even if you're bone dry on magic, you could do it. It's more powerful now since you changed."

"Oh, that's neat. That's also kinda useless like sparks flying from my fingers or that one to make cum gold."

Giasone sat up straighter and turned to him on the couch. "That's not useless at all! Don't you realize what you could do with that?"

"Er, we could ride pink ponies together?"

"No. You could take someone and show us the demon side of the realm and their defenses."

Riley's eyes widened. "Ohhh. But the world in my dreams is just made up of what I've seen before."

"Okay, but you've seen enough, and even if something is a few weeks old, it's probably similar. For example, Eren wouldn't have moved his whole house somewhere else. The layout would be the same. You could imagine it."

"So you could see the walls I passed by?"

"Yeah!"

"That could be kinda helpful, but I'm sure you guys know most of the defenses. As far as I know, the Nevyyn is the only new thing created."

"That's true, but never discount something completely just in case."

"Mmhm."

Riley's mind was wandering back to the night Eren had almost raped him. The guilt had been faked, of course. It was much easier to get Riley wrapped around his finger by not doing such a horrid act. Riley had thought the guilt had been keeping him up, and that was why Eren had taken rewek to sleep.

But since the bastard couldn't have been guilty, perhaps he'd had trouble sleeping that night for no particular reason. The problem was that Riley had lucid dreamed when he finally managed to fall asleep. Eren had been there because Riley had accidentally dragged him in.

The real Eren had come storming in, ranted about "what he did," and backhanded him across the face for it. Riley later thought Eren was furious because he'd been made to feel guilty, but now he knew differently.

"I think-I think I might have dragged Eren into a dream by accident in the beginning," said Riley. "When he woke up, he flew into a rage. I didn't know what he meant when he said I better not ever do it again. He must have thought I knew about my power, but I didn't, and when he realized that, he didn't push it."

Eren had never exactly said what Riley did. Later, Riley dragged him in again by accident, and Eren took advantage of it by saying that they would have been lovers if they had grown up together. He hadn't been created from Riley's mind that time, and Eren had manipulated him.

If he had figured it out, that meant he probably planned to use Riley's ability for something else later on.

"Wait, you said you've been doing this as a kid too?" asked Giasone. "Before you went through puberty? We don't get our abilities that early."

"I remember doing it as young as five."

"Hm. That's strange. I wonder if being a nephalem means getting your ability earlier. There's nothing about that in books."

There also weren't any other nephalem to compare Riley to.

"You should see a meditator," said Giasone. "Usually, they only help people who have blocks or issues with magic because there's no point in rushing an angel's powers, but I have an idea, and you need to have more control now."

Chapter Five

Eren spotted the crow as he flew toward his tower. It had a parchment roll tied to its leg, and he assumed it was from Banna or someone important like that until he noticed its bright green eyes.

The angels weren't in the habit of writing to him.

He landed on the roof of the tower and let the crow perch on his wrist. To the bird, Eren was just a recipient, not an enemy or a lord. He plucked at the string and freed the letter. The crow moved to sit on his shoulder while Eren unrolled the parchment.

The writing was small, neat, and rather delicate. His eyes went right to the bottom where the angel's Queen had signed.

Nyla wanted to arrange a meeting outside of Fringe by the river. He could bring guards if he wished, although the meal would be private. Eren curled his lip at the mention of a meal. Was she expecting to ask for a peace treaty? There was nothing she could give him unless it was Riley tied up with a bow on top.

Then he saw the next line where she said she wanted to discuss the possibility of them marrying.

He almost laughed. She wanted to offer her snatch for peace? Maybe if she had a cock to play with, he'd be tempted. But really, no man or woman would ever match up to Riley.

She went on to say that she was willing to discuss terms with him that would allow him to rule the whole realm. She had Riley in her care, and he would be there.

At the bottom, she put the date and time.

Eren scrunched the sheet in one fist as he looked out over the city. Standstills had happened before and needed no notes or negotiation. Both sides would pull back and use the time to fix defenses and such. It was something any kingdom would need. A couple of times the rulers of each side had met because the angels wanted to negotiate and try to end the war. They had offered money and other petty things so that both sides could stop the fighting, keep to themselves, rule their kind, and remain separate.

It had always been denied because the demons didn't want to share their realm with something so disgusting.

No angel lord or queen had ever offered themselves in marriage with the promise of the demon ruler having rule over *both* sides. Nyla's offer was a huge one and completely unheard of. In fact, some of her ancestors would probably roll over in their tombs if they knew.

The angels wouldn't like this too much even though they'd think she was selfless and a heroine for such a sacrifice. Still, they would cringe at the idea of Eren being over them all.

The offer of total rule was beyond tempting. Erebus, Lord of the entire Fallen realm, both angel and demon. There was just one little problem, and it wasn't the fact that he didn't care for Nyla's honeypot. Besides his issue, he'd rather fight and win it by blood and sweat.

The crow could take the response so he grasped it in his hand before he tipped off the roof, glided, and circled the tower to land in his courtyard. The twins stopped making out long enough to wave hello at him. In his office, the crow explored his shelves while he simply wrote that he'd be there on a piece of parchment and signed it. Once he released the crow through his side sitting room window, he returned to his office, and that's when he felt it.

The tug in his chest said he needed to visit Grandfather.

"Fuck," he swore. His heart picked up which was an automatic reaction he always had when he felt the tug and knew what horror lay around the corner.

If he simply went ahead with his life and went to the meeting, the tug would get worse. Grandfather could accept a proper reason if he didn't come right away, but it had to be a damn good one, and anything more than a few days was unacceptable unless he was at the front. It would lead to punishment.

He would have had to go himself anyway. Grandfather would be furious if he wasn't informed of such an offer. Eren wanted to stay in his office, curl up on the couch, cover himself with the blanket, read a book, and pretend nothing else existed.

It was better to get it over with.

The teleportation stone took him to the mouth of the cave. The moving room was a terror as usual. He didn't stop to look at the books but simply went through the doors. The usual dinner wasn't on the table, and he froze. As much as he detested the disgusting parody of kindness and hospitality, he always knew what to expect. Only a glass of wine sat there.

"Come here, boy." Grandfather sat at the head as usual.

Eren approached as his stomach further tightened with nerves. He knelt, kissed the ring, and stood. It took every ounce of will to not back up as far as possible.

"Any news before I tell you mine?"

Eren forced a smile as he noticed how Grandfather seemed stronger. Better-looking wasn't the right word, but he had a feeling one of the things he'd dreaded most was coming.

"Actually, yes. Queen Nyla has offered herself in marriage to me."

Even Grandfather appeared a bit surprised at that. "Tell me everything."

Eren recounted the contents of the letter while he remained standing. Grandfather nodded after he was done.

"She's weak to give up like that. You know Riley needs to be a part of the terms. You get him along with her, otherwise, no deal."

"I'd rather fight for it and not rule the lands through marriage."

"You make me proud with that."

Eren kept his pleasant expression. Like he cared what Grandfather thought. It was probably a lie anyway. Eren's desire to win by war was his own. "She might not agree to give me Riley. I don't know his purpose in coming, but I doubt it's to hand him over on a platter."

"You never know. Perhaps he's just a pet to her, and she cares little for him. Angels aren't much different than demons no matter how much they try to pretend otherwise. No Riley, no marriage. If you get him, you know what to do."

"Of course. I'd bring him straight to you, Grandfather."

"You can keep him as a pet afterward as long as he does his duty. Drink the wine and get in the tomb. I think I can manage it now."

Eren swallowed and reached for the glass. This was exactly what he'd feared. "Grandfather-"

"I don't want to hear complaints."

"It's merely a matter of timing," said Eren. "If I'm in a battle, feeding from me would cause me to die. I'd be easy prey, and it would hold you back. All of your efforts would be wasted."

"I know that well enough," Grandfather snapped while he watched Eren drink. "I can give you a warning tug, and if something is happening where feeding would be a bad idea, you'll be able to push the tug away. Don't abuse that privilege. You'll have time to get to a private spot, and it'll usually be at night. If I require you to come here, you'll feel the tug in your head now. Understand?"

"Yes."

"I likely won't need to take so much. I'm strong enough to where I might be able to have sex now. My helpers will bring someone." Grandfather stood and patted Eren's cheek. "You've done me a great service, boy. Soon, I'll have what I want, and you'll be rewarded. Maybe I'll even give you back your full ability."

Eren downed the last of the wine and managed to arrange his mouth in a smile while the poison worked through his veins. Devil help whoever became Grandfather's sex toy. "It's my pleasure."

"Hurry up. I won't drain you entirely this time."

"Thank you, Grandfather." If only his heart could collapse and kill him right now, but demons couldn't have heart attacks.

Once he was dragged from the tomb, he was dumped on the floor. The wraiths lingered around him while his heart raced. He caught sight of Athena gliding away like she didn't want to watch.

Cold fingers closed around his throat. No. No. No. He wished the wraiths would suck out his life force and end him. More freezing, bony hands pulled him up into a sitting position. He hadn't even noticed the symbols chalked onto the floor.

Grandfather stepped into view and smiled. "Open your mouth, boy."

One of the wraiths grabbed his face, and a dagger gleamed. Eren's heart stuttered as his chest further tightened.

"Open, boy."

There was no other choice. They'd force him, so he opened his mouth and allowed the dagger to slice the top of his tongue. The symbols started to emit a sickly greenish-orange smoke as the room blurred.

Grandfather was suddenly on top of him. The cold hands were gone, but his grip on the back of Eren's head was even worse. Blood trickled from his mouth, and he pressed his lips to Eren's and thrust his tongue in.

His stomach flipped as he tasted the bitter, sour blood, and he heaved when Grandfather's slimy, bloody tongue slicked across his. Savage pain clawed through his chest and stomach as some of the blood trickled down his throat.

There was no way to undo this besides death.

Grandfather clamped a hand over Eren's mouth to prevent him from spitting out the blood. "See? That wasn't so bad. Without you, I'd have waited longer. Your reward will be great. Anything you want, you'll have it."

Eren's eyes rolled into the back of his head as his stomach lurched again, and he swore he tasted bile mixed with the blood, but he couldn't throw up. It felt like spikes were repeatedly stabbing his gut, and sharper pains grew in his chest and skull.

Grandfather pinched his nose shut. "Swallow."

Eren didn't want this. He never had. He tried to remember the feel of Riley's arms around him. The kisses, so willingly given with no disgusting taint of stolen, twisted power, had been the only taste of heaven he knew he'd ever get.

"I've got you."

The only thing that had him was the disgusting beast covering his face. Darkness snatched at Eren as the foul blood trickled down his throat. The savage slashes would consume him. Grandfather's touch was suffocating him. He'd lied. He would kill Eren if it meant gaining back the power he used to wield and the position he'd once held.

"A little of me will always be in you now, boy." Grandfather's words sounded far away, but the hand stroking Eren's face felt too real. "Always."

Eren's head thumped on the stone floor, and frigid air rushed into his burning lungs, but the stabbing in his skull dragged him under.

As soon as he became aware of the hall, he heaved and choked on the vomit as it rushed up. Gagging, he rolled to his side as bloody, acidic puke splattered on the stones and splashed him. The taste only made his stomach rebel even more as it frantically emptied itself. Acid burned his throat he coughed so hard, he thought he'd pass out from lack of air.

He managed to drag in a breath, although it wasn't nearly enough. The bloody vomit swam in his vision, and he knew it meant nothing. The spell was already done, and Grandfather had hooked him further. With his skull thumping, he crawled into the moving room and started to sob in the dark space as his tail wrapped around his leg and squeezed. It wasn't the same.

He was alone. So entirely, truly alone.

As soon as he got out of the cave, Grandfather used the strengthened link as if to remind and show Eren what he was now capable of. Agony lanced through his skull as he collapsed on the ground. It lasted seconds and barely took anything, but it was enough to leave him curled up in the dirt as he shivered.

This was his life now. Grandfather could reach him anywhere now and feed as he pleased. The tomb would be reserved for punishment.

Eren barely remembered teleporting or flying. A few flashes of the sky came to him in ragged fragments, and he found himself standing in his courtyard.

"Lord Erebus sick?"

"Head hurt?"

The blurry forms of the twins standing there wobbled in his vision before the grass rushed up to his face.

He spent three days in bed. When he got up, the twins pretended nothing had happened as usual, like his migraines didn't exist. He appeared normal, and no one would know what had happened, but he still remembered the foul kiss and knew the link between them had solidified.

He wanted to stay in bed and never get up again, but there was nothing to be done except to continue.

A demon teleported him to the Point. The rubble of the wall had been left, but the town itself, once wrecked and destroyed, had been cleaned up and made fit for the soldiers stationed there. Patrols manned the area, but the angels hadn't gone past the town of Fringe.

With two soldiers, Eren headed for the river on foot. This side of the realm had little grey flowers with petals that grew in a spiral. Eren plucked one to look at as he walked, and he let a tendril of black poison crawl from his hand to wilt it before he tossed it away.

The meeting spot was quite far from the flowing water, but he knew what lay beyond his line of sight when he was near the table. The angels had so graciously provided a meal to be polite, not that he gave a shit.

All three of the angels ahead were fliers. He dismissed the first as a common soldier or some lackey of the Queen who was tiny and short. The third drew all of his attention, and his nerves fluttered as they drew closer.

Riley's crimson wings were absolutely fucking gorgeous.

To Eren's surprise, Riley approached the table on his own. If the angels attempted treachery, he was sure he could handle it even though he'd left his two soldiers behind. He doubted they would attempt anything. Damn goody-goodies.

Riley's expression was hard like he was aching to spit in Eren's face and slip a dagger between his ribs. Eren paused behind the chair in the center on his side as he eyed Riley up and down.

He wanted to stroke those red wings, scratch the space between them to hear his pet purr, and bend Riley over the table. Who cared about the food? His cock twitched and threatened to swell at the idea of fucking Riley so hard, he'd scream Eren's name, rumple the pristine tablecloth as he clutched at it, and cum so hard, Eren would have to hold him up afterward.

Directly opposite him, Riley froze as his lips parted slightly. The things Eren wanted to do to that mouth. Riley blushed slightly, and it was surprising he was even capable of it considering the things they'd done together.

He had to be tasting the energy Eren was creating with his filthy thoughts. He treated Riley with an innocent smile. The slightly glazed look that flashed meant it had to be delicious to him.

"Fuck you," Riley spat in a low voice.

"That's how you talk to your Master?"

"You're not my Master. And as I recall, you happily got rid of me."

Eren smirked. "True, but I'm the demon lord, so no matter who bought you, you're still technically mine. You've grown so nicely. The Nevyyn certainly hurried you along, didn't it? I bet those wings feel nice. I'd like to lick that little strip of skin between them while I fuck your ass."

Riley yanked out his chair, sat, and glared at Eren. "Sit."

"As you wish, my little nephalem."

"I'm not yours, and I never will be. Let's get that straight right now. You lost any chance of actually having me the second you decided to toy with me and use your little tricks to wrap me around your finger."

"You're the one that got on your knees for me and asked for it."

"I know what you were doing. Don't try to spin it. We're long past that, and if it wasn't for Nyla, I'd run you through."

Eren regarded Riley's brighter eyes and complexion along with the extra shine to his hair that now included a few reddish strands mixed in with the black. Riley had certainly been good-looking before, but he was better with the glamor gone.

It was a pity his beautiful eyes were so much harder. Eren wanted to see that glazed look that he got when he hit that headspace after a flogging. Or the sleepy satisfaction after a morning when they were both sated in more than one way. For a moment, Eren's stomach twisted, but he forced it away.

"Is this part where you threaten me to watch my mouth around the lovely lady and describe how you'll cut out my tongue if I utter a foul word in her angelic presence?" Eren leaned back in his chair.

"We're here to make negotiations. Both sides must come to an agreement for the marriage, and the contract will be signed in blood to make sure they are followed."

"Obviously." Eren reached for the wine bottle and ripped out the cork.

"If you decide to stick one of us with your scythe, you'll regret it."

"Riley, let me remind you of something." Eren gestured with the wine bottle. "I'm sure you've got a few guards hidden back there somewhere to protect the pretty lady, but let's be real. I may only be a few months older than you, but I have far more experience at fighting than you do. I was top in my age group at Camp and better than a good deal of the older ones. Your petty sword and whatever spells you may have managed to learn so far won't be much of a match. Also, I'm sure I could do some real damage to the other two before your guards haul their asses over."

"Even if you killed me, I'm sure they could fuck you up."

Eren poured some of the green wine into the glass by his plate. "I don't want to kill you, Riley." He lifted the cover on his plate to reveal what looked like roasted mockingbird since the meat was bright yellow. Greens drizzled with sauce filled the rest of the space. "You must enjoy not having to worry about eating anymore."

Riley gave a stiff shrug as Eren took a forkful of the tender meat and stabbed a few greens. He stood and held the fork aimed at Riley's mouth in the way one would feed a small child.

"Have a bite."

"I don't want your food," said Riley.

Eren narrowed his eyes. "Have you got a rare poison in here? Not a lot would affect me, and angels don't usually like low trickery of this sort, but you never know. If you won't eat it, I'll go, and you can kiss the negotiations goodbye."

Riley made to snatch the fork, but Eren held it away. "If you want me to eat, give it to me so we can hurry this up."

"You'll do this my way or I'll go. I imagine Queen Nyla won't be happy if you fuck this up because you feel like being a brat. Be a good boy for me."

If looks could kill. Pure hate burned in Riley's eyes as he leaned forward and allowed Eren to feed him the bite. His teeth were still normal. Eren gave him a wide smile as he sat once more and watched Riley chew the food.

The wine smelled fine, and he sipped it as he watched the halfling. Riley didn't fall over to twitch on the ground or start foaming at the mouth, so Eren finally took a bite.

"Happy?" snarled Riley.

Eren swallowed. "For now. My rules for this are as follows: if you fuck with me, I will not hesitate to kill Queen Nyla, your other little buddy over there, and anyone else I can get my hands on. You'll be taken alive. Understand?"

Riley's gaze burned into him. "Yes, but if you take me alive, you'll regret it."

"Pfft."

Once Riley gestured, the others finally approached and sat.

Chapter Six

The other angel introduced as Giasone could barely even look at the demon lord, and he had a faint expression as if there was a bad smell. Maybe he didn't like lemons. Just to be an ass, Eren scraped his teeth on the tines of his fork when he took another bite, and Giasone twitched at the sound.

Nyla kept her face pleasant as if no rude noise had been created. It was probably the same expression she'd keep plastered on if Eren was in her snatch. He could just imagine her being terribly boring and laying there like a limp fish while he pounded away.

"You look lovely, Queen Nyla," Eren said politely as the others started on their food.

"Thank you. You're looking well, Lord Erebus."

"So you're just dying to marry me and know what my lordly cock feels like?"

Nyla stiffened ever so slightly. "I was hoping we could come to an agreement that would benefit both kingdoms and everyone living in this world. We've been fighting for centuries with neither side winning and ending it. The misery simply continues and passes down to each child. No one knows what it's like to grow up in peace, and I'm sure nearly everyone knows what it's like to lose a loved one at the hands of the other side. You lost your parents. I lost mine, and I never even got a chance to know them since I was grown and hatched after Mother died. Father was already dead long before her. We could stop that for future generations."

Eren arranged his features to appear sympathetic. "Mmhm."

"In return for my people's guaranteed safety, we'd co-rule, and our children would inherit."

"You said I'd be the sole ruler in the letter."

"I would prefer we co-rule."

"I don't."

She cut a piece of the mockingbird meat on her plate. "If you wish to be the sole ruler, that's fine. I'd appreciate it if you accepted my input on certain things regarding my people."

"Maybe."

"I'd require that both sides can mix freely. Anyone can live wherever they please. No one race of angel or demon would be segregated or forced into poor parts of the towns and cities. Jobs would be given based on skill, not what the applicant is."

"Sounds fair."

Riley poured her a glass of wine as she continued. "Our first child would inherit and have the right to marry as they wished. I'd have equal say in their raising and care as they would be *our* children." Eren nodded. "As for me, I only ask that you treat me kindly so that we may grow to love each other."

He wanted to roll his eyes. She'd never love him even if he conquered Earth and laid it at her feet.

"Also, the practice of luring and keeping deviant humans as pets would stop."

"That's a pretty big thing to ask, and the demons won't like it. It's a part of our culture. Pets are something to show off and a source of energy right there in your home."

"We don't keep humans as pets. They could learn to do without. People agree to be bed buddies all of the time, so it's not like I'm asking the demons to give up sex and feeding."

"Exactly," said Riley.

Eren swirled the wine in his glass as Giasone poured himself some. The demons most certainly would balk at giving up their pets. "That'd be the most difficult thing to swing on my side, but let's say yes. Everything else sounds fair to me. We'd eventually have many nephalem."

"I don't think that would be an issue. The more people mix, the more together they'll feel as the centuries pass. Besides, in the distant past, we had nephalem, and no one cared."

"All right. One of my demands would be that you submit to me in every way that I ask whether I tie you up and hang you upside down or take a cane to your ass."

Riley glared at him, and Nyla didn't look too pleased for a moment as the mask slipped.

"I like pain," Eren told her with a slight grin. "Giving, not receiving. You can ask Riley. I can also be ever so kind, and I'd fulfill any dirty fantasies you have. If there's something you absolutely despised, maybe I could give it up."

"All right."

"I would take care of all of your needs such as clothes and whatnot. I would take care of the Lancef for our children too."

"We'd both have a say in our children's raising."

"Yes, you could have a say, but the Lancef is something I would do," Eren said in a firm voice. "Trust me. I would have our children's best issues at heart."

"Fine."

He leaned back in his chair and thought for a moment. A slight ache at the back of his head made him worry, but it quickly went away. He'd had stress headaches when he was younger, so maybe it was that. He felt no tug, so that was good.

"It's a pity you don't have a cock to play with. I'd rather make a child with eggs because snatches don't hold any interest for me. Sex with you would be a huge chore."

She sighed. "We don't have anyone that can do good glamors that last a long time, but we do have a few that can make half-decent ones that last for a little while."

He laughed at the idea of her disguised as a man for a couple of hours. It wasn't the same. "The other demand is that if you're my wife, Riley will be mine. As the lord, I think I should be allowed to keep a pet."

Riley's gaze burned into him, and Nyla hardened her eyes. "No. That's another thing. Riley would be entirely protected and left free. He would be a mediator between both sides to solve disputes and things are too petty to help free up your time. He would only report to you if something was too difficult to resolve without your intervention. Other than that, he would be a free citizen like anyone else."

"I want him," said Eren. "With him, your honey pot could have a break, and you'd also be free to take on lovers if you wish as long as you don't get pregnant by them. I won't have bastards running about my tower."

"No."

"I will never be your pet again." Riley took a sip from his glass.

Eren put on a pouty expression. "I'm sure I could make you feel better, and you'd forgive me for the little scene we had that night."

"Go fuck yourself!"

Nyla grabbed his arm. "Calm yourself. Riley isn't up to take. Also, it would hardly be fair for you to have a pet while no one else is allowed."

"You know this hypothetical, right?" asked Eren. "I really don't want to bond with you. If you were a man, I'd be more tempted."

"This isn't just about sex. It's about the safety and future of angels *and* demons. You could end this war right now. Your children would be safe whether they came from my womb or from an egg. Do you want future members of your line dying in a fruitless war?"

"You're only offering this because we broke through the Point. Otherwise, you'd never consider this. We got further than we ever have before and tipped the scales in our favor. Once we get past Fringe, the Tree of Life will be ours, and we can make many Nevyyns at that point." He leaned forward over the table. "While it's tempting to quickly snatch up everything and have it in my grasp so easily, I'd much prefer to fight for it. We tried to live peacefully in the beginning, but we can't and never will."

"I-"

"Don't try to deny it with your silly lies. Do you think I'm stupid? Little wars will break out, and the same shit will start over once more. If I have to sweat and bleed to have these lands entirely under my command, I will. I'd much rather have you all dead at my feet, and in the end, we will annihilate you and rid the realm of your sins. You can take your marriage proposal and shove it up your ass."

"Then we will go on as before." She pushed away her plate.

"With what? Losing? Be my guest." Eren lifted the cover from a tiny plate near his glass and squinted at the contents.

The Queen stood with a stiff expression and glared at him. Eren looked up and gave her a huge smile as if they were best friends and he was beyond overjoyed at her presence. Two pink spots appeared on her cheeks before she turned and stalked off.

"Waaah." Eren snorted as Giasone made to follow her.

"Riley, come on."

Riley held up a hand. "Give me a minute."

Something had to be up if he was staying.

Giasone gave him a look, but Riley gestured to go. "I'll be fine."

Giasone frowned but went after the Queen.

Eren gazed at Riley's calm face before he poked the square thing on the little plate. It had some sort of shiny stuff on top. "What the fuck is this?"

"It's called cake."

It must have been a human food that he liked, but he hadn't eaten much of his meal, nor even touched his tiny plate.

"It's sweet," added Riley.

"Ahh." Eren took a forkful and figured the slick stuff was honey, although maybe it was mixed with something else. "You do like sweet stuff, don't you? Do you find angel's cum just as good?"

Riley's rigid expression gave nothing away, but Eren had a feeling he hadn't fucked anyone yet. He stood and offered the bite.

"I'm not hungry," said Riley.

"Eat it, or we'll see how fast your friends are," whispered Eren.

Riley's expression suggested that he knew how stupid it was to stay behind alone. He wasn't experienced enough to fight a demon lord. Eren was so tempted to grab him and haul him back. To take him away forever and save him from worse things that could happen. To fuck him and try to cram forever in a few seconds because Eren would never get what he truly wanted.

He'd never had a chance, betrayal or not.

"Eat it," he hissed.

Riley took the bite and some of the honey stuck to his lip. Before he could move away, Eren caught it with his pinky finger. To have those soft lips wrapped around his cock.

Riley flinched back at the direct touch, and the motion sent a stab through Eren's heart. What was left of it anyway. He kept his expression as he sat, locked eyes with the halfling, and stuck the tip of his finger in his mouth to taste the sweetness.

"You smell nice, Riley." Eren watched him chew like it was a task to get through. "Like roses and lavender. It's absolutely divine. I wish I could have made love to you with that smell around you."

"We never made love. You dumped your load in one of my holes and fed off the energy."

How little he knew. Eren took a bite of the cake and found it quite good, but he set down his fork. "You told them to go ahead."

"Don't fly," said Riley. "Walk back."

Eren ran his finger through the honey. "Why?" He received a shrug in response. "I walked here so you wouldn't feel threatened, but I don't see the point when I leave. Have you got some kind of trap waiting for fliers?"

"No. The cake will make you fat. Walk it off." Riley stretched in the chair and flexed his wings with a bored expression.

Eren licked the honey from his finger. Maybe the trap would be sprung if he was on the ground. It was hard to tell, but he had a feeling it would be better to follow Riley's advice. He glanced at the plates and glasses. Riley had barely touched his food. Nyla and Giasone had eaten a little like Eren. Both of the angels hadn't touched their glasses of wine, but Riley had been sipping on his. He wouldn't poison himself.

Either way, if Riley did something for his safety, that meant some part of him still cared.

"Why do you care?"

Riley laughed like that was hilarious. "You've got pebbles for brains." He leaned forward. "You stayed for a few extra minutes because you're sick in the head and obsessed with having and hurting me. Just remember that having an obsession makes you weak, and because I hate you so much, I'll use whatever I can against you to make you suffer."

Eren struggled to keep his composure. It wasn't an obsession. It was love. The line was quite thin in his case, but if he tried to explain that, he'd look even worse. Riley took his wine glass and drained it.

"I am what I am," said Eren.

Riley left the empty glass on the table and stood. "One day, you'll be dead at my feet. That's what you'll be."

"Run along, Riley. I'll find you again one day."

Riley gave him the finger and turned away. Eren watched the gorgeous crimson wings as the only thing he ever truly loved besides his parents walked away.

"Riley," he called. The halfling paused but didn't turn. "There are things I would try to change. For you."

"Fuck off." Riley kept going.

Eren hadn't even meant to say that. He hadn't known what he intended when he called for him. One extra second? But he'd gone and said something stupid.

Anger sparked in his chest to see Riley so hateful toward him. Part of him wanted to keep his promise, and part of him wanted to take that brat over his knee and tan his ass before fucking him.

Eren threw back the last of the wine in his glass before he stood. After one last glance at the red wings moving away, he turned. Unfortunately, Riley would suffer far worse than he had before. Eren just had to get him back, and he would.

He told the two guards that they were walking back too. They probably weren't happy about it, but they simply agreed and followed their lord. Eren didn't see or hear anything suspicious after twenty or so minutes.

The fact that he'd have to go report to Grandfather was a drag, but he quickly forgot about that. The exhaustion slammed into him like a weight.

Arrowak. It had to be that. No wonder Riley hadn't tried to secretly spit out the food. Arrowak took time to kick in, but once it did, it was powerful. The problem was that it often had undesired side effects like vomiting and excessive gas. Nobody wanted to go to sleep and choke on their vomit or be required to have someone watch and keep them on their side.

Overall, it was a pretty useless plant but good enough to make a demon lord fall from the sky and possibly break something. It probably wouldn't kill him, so why would Nyla bother if she suspected he'd refuse her offer? Why had Riley warned him?

"M'lord?"

Eren realized he had stopped walking, and he could barely keep his eyes open. Some bit of Riley cared. The grass blurred, and someone touched his arm. Wait, hadn't Riley had the same wine?

"M'lord? What's wrong?"

"You don't...fuggin' care," Eren slurred before his knees buckled.

The forest looked like the one he lived in as a child when everything was simple, and Riley loved him.

Riley was leaning against a tree.

The last time he had accidentally dragged him into a lucid dream, Eren had manipulated him with the truth. They likely would have grown to be lovers if Eren hadn't been snatched away and forced to return home. Grandfather demanded he get the halfling wrapped around his finger, and he had complied. The dream incident, while not planned by Eren, had worked in his favor.

But this wasn't an accident.

Riley cracked his knuckles. "I learned quickly. One session with a meditator where he touched my forehead, and I was able to control it. He said the third eye is in there. Anyway, as long as I'm asleep, I can lucid dream at will. Nyla graciously paid for it. You wanted to use my ability for something, right? I'm not sure what, but it's not like you'll ever get me back."

Eren curled his lip. "Congratulations. You learned your power."

Riley smirked as the forest started to shift and turn colors. "I prefer the real world and not too much fake shit. Once in a while, it's fun to be more creative."

"Ooh, pretty colors? Is this supposed to scare me or something?"

"No."

The forest changed into a town setting, and he guessed it was somewhere Riley had lived. None of the humans seemed concerned about Eren's appearance, but this was all fake even though the cobblestones felt real under his boots, and someone accidentally brushed by him.

"Are you just bragging?"

Riley stepped closer. "You can feel in a lucid dream."

"Are you going to beat me up? It's not like it'll hurt my actual body. This is still just a dream, so it's not real."

"It's real enough." Riley smiled as the forest returned once more.

"Are you going to cheat and give yourself huge muscles?" Eren stepped closer.

"I don't need to." Riley took another step.

Quick as a flash, Eren grabbed him by the shoulders, pushed him against a tree, and pressed himself against the body he'd missed so much. Their faces hovered inches away, and he swore he caught a taste of energy.

Wait…that shouldn't be possible in a dream, lucid or not.

Riley reacted and shoved him against a brick wall that came from nowhere. He jammed a knee between Eren's legs, forced them apart, and pinned his wrists.

"I haven't seen this side of you," said Eren. "Do we fight and the loser has to bottom?"

Riley suddenly kissed him. The taste of roses and lavender was overwhelming and still not enough. Eren kissed him back, wishing he could keep this moment going for eternity. Riley's knee went a little higher, and the energy, sweet and potent, thickened around them. That shouldn't be possible, but maybe it was fake since this was a dream.

Riley ground his erection against Eren's and made him growl. He didn't know where this was going, but he was sure it wasn't where Riley originally intended.

"I need you," Eren mumbled against his lips as he tried to loosen his wrists. Dream or no, he needed this man in his arms and on his cock.

"Uh-uh." Riley tightened his grip.

"Do you intend to try and shame me by making me bottom for you?"

"I don't think Number One Demon would let a nephalem top him."

"You'd be surprised at what I might allow from you at this point."

Riley's kiss was hard and demanding. The friction as he rubbed on Eren wasn't nearly enough, and Riley spun him around to push him against the stone wall. Pinned, Eren shivered as the nephalem's lips skimmed the back of his neck.

"What if I made it nice and slick?" he murmured. "Would you let me?"

"Fuck," Eren managed to get out as Riley nibbled on his ear. Could he really do it? He hadn't bottomed for anyone since he was young and still exploring what he liked when it came to sex with other demons his age.

Riley's hardness pushed against his ass. Even with their trousers in the way, he could feel the warmth, and he pushed back against it, desperate for any contact with him.

"You're so weak," Riley murmured against his ear. "Like an animal that just follows the instinct to fuck. I said you'd regret it if you snatched me away because you have to sleep sometime."

The sunlight through Eren's eyelids suddenly dimmed. He opened them to see that another stone wall had formed to his left.

"I know what your worst fear is," snarled Riley.

Eren's heart pounded as the room grew smaller. The top closed off, trapping him in darkness.

"Riley! No-"

You fucking used me like a two-bit whore, and you still can't let go!'

"Please-"

"Why should I care about you? You don't care about anything unless it involves death and sticking your dick in something."

Eren tore himself away from Riley, but he simply slammed into a wall inches away. It slid forward and pushed him into Riley. Eren flung his arms around him, desperate for protection even though it was the halfling hurting him.

This was worse than any physical thing he could have done.

"Please, R-Riley. I'm begging you."

"Like I begged you."

"Let me out!"

The room shrank and pushed on Eren. Fuck. He'd die here, trapped in his worst nightmare. The darkness smothered him as he struggled to breathe through lungs stuck in a vise. He tried to latch onto the scent of roses to stay out of the horror in his mind.

Dimly, he realized the small room had been turned on its side, and he gripped Riley.

"I tried not to love you because it hurt so bad," gasped Eren.

"Fuck," Riley muttered as something wet touched Eren's cheek.

He was gone, and the box became so small, Eren was sure it would crush him. He couldn't hit or kick properly. He'd die alone.

It took a second to realize that the screams were his own.

Warm grass was under him, and sunlight pierced his eyelids as he lay and struggled to get air in. The walls were gone, and he was in the open. It was just a trick, and next time, Riley would crush him. He had all the power this time, and Eren deserved it for what he'd done.

Riley sucked in a ragged breath and stared at Eren in horror as a tear dripped down his cheek. "I'm sorry. Fuck. I can't do this. I can't watch that." He bent over and clutched at his head. "Fuuuck."

Eren tried to force his stiff limbs to properly work. Could he run if Riley decided to do it again? Probably not. Where would he go in a dream?

Riley let out a noise like he was in agony. "Stop it! I'm sorry!"

Eren squinted at him. The pain seemed genuine as Riley sank to his knees and held onto his head. "I'm not doing anything. Riley?"

"I'm sorry. Make it stop. Please. I won't do it again."

"I'm not doing it!"

If Grandfather was linked to him, had he been able to sense something? Eren snarled at the thought of Grandfather touching him in any way at all. His chest was still too tight, but the sight of Riley hunching on the ground was too much to bear. He scrambled across the grass and wrapped his arms around the halfling.

"Riley, I-"

"Get off me!" Riley shoved at him.

Blessed blackness and hazy dreams that made no sense but weren't frightening came to Eren before his eyelids fluttered open. The sun was at a different angle now, so he must have been out for some time even after Riley cut the dream.

One of the guards was standing next to him.

"M'lord? Are you all right? You've been asleep. We moved you, but we didn't want to bring you around the others like that."

"That bitch poisoned you," said the other. "Are you sick, or was it just something for sleep?"

"I bet she was hoping he'd fly, fall, and break his neck."

Eren rubbed his face as he rolled onto his back and tried to think of a coherent response.

The tug said he better get to Grandfather.

Chapter Seven

Riley woke up on the grass on the other side of the river outside of Fringe.

"How did it go?" Giasone asked with a tight expression.

Riley wiped his eyes and tried to think. "Fine."

"You threw up, but we moved you away from it, and cleaned your face. Don't worry, no one saw it."

"Lovely." Riley's mouth didn't taste pleasant, and he vowed to never touch arrowak again. Rewek was better.

Nyla came to stand over him. "Why did you get hard in your sleep?" She folded her arms and glared at him like that was a crime.

"Because..." Riley waved a hand. "Guys get hard in their sleep sometimes."

"We can't help it," said Giasone.

"So don't stare at my dick."

"You also cried a little in your sleep," Nyla added.

Fuck. He was supposed to go in, scare the shit out of Eren, and that was it. Making out wasn't a part of the bargain, and he felt like crap because a part of him had done it as a distraction.

The other part of him had wanted it. With the safety of a dream, he wanted to feel that touch again since Eren had no way to hurt or steal him away. He'd even tasted energy which shouldn't have been possible, right?

"What's the problem?" she pressed.

"Uhh." Riley's gut said to not mention the fact that he'd tasted energy in his dream because she'd suspect something odd had happened between them. "It went fine at first. I trapped him in a tiny room on its side. Like a stone coffin. Of course, it terrified him, but he did something to me."

Nyla knelt. "What do you mean?"

"It felt like a knife was in my head. It was so bad, I had to get out. I didn't feel anything when regular dreams took over, but while I was in with him, it was awful."

Worse, he felt drained of what little energy he had to begin with. Eren had somehow sucked it out while hurting him. But then why would he hug Riley and try to comfort him?

Nyla was squinting at him like she didn't believe him, and he knew he better not to mention the bit where the groping and kissing had started making energy. Surely, that wasn't right, and she wouldn't understand why he'd been clashing tongues with the one he hated most.

He hadn't truly needed a distraction. He could have just had a stone room appear around Eren and spent ages torturing him with the tiny space.

She certainly couldn't know about how he'd almost considered fucking Eren so he could taste that delicious energy. She'd think he was insane. Then again, maybe he was.

"Okay." She stood. "If he's got some nasty trick up his sleeve, you better stay away from him in your dreams." She started to head through the trees.

Giasone gave Riley a nasty look. "Are you fucking lying?"

"Excuse me?"

"I can see if your dick decided to perk up. They can pop up at the worst times too, but you also cried a little in your sleep."

"It fucking hurt," stated Riley.

It was true, but he'd cried in the dream because he'd been utterly horrified at himself for what he'd done to Eren. The savage pleasure he'd felt at getting back at the demon had started to weaken with the way Eren had held onto him. It had shattered when he'd heard that terrified scream.

And now he knew what energy from torture tasted like. Like fruits that had a pleasant tang. He'd liked it, and that only horrified him more.

Giasone nodded. "Okay, but you can do this to others in their sleep. I'm sure no one else can make your head hurt."

Nyla had mentioned possibly driving the demon army insane, or at least a portion of it. He hadn't liked that, and now, he knew he couldn't do it.

"I can't," said Riley. "I can't spend night after night torturing people."

"Listen to me. If you do that to multiple demons, and word spreads, even those who haven't been dragged in by you will start to be afraid of sleeping because what if they're next?"

"No!" Riley stood. "I don't have that in me. I can't make someone suffer every single night or think up creative new ways to torment them. I just-I'm not that kind of person! Once was enough."

Giasone came closer. "Look me in the eye and tell me you don't have any feelings for him."

"I don't! What the hell?"

"Why did you stay?"

"I-I told him not to fly."

Giasone tilted his head. "I'd be happy if he busted half of the bones in his body."

"If he died, I wouldn't have been able to do that to him," said Riley. "Also, we didn't think about it beforehand, but if someone is knocked out, I'm not sure if that counts as sleep. I don't think anyone wants to get knocked out so I can experiment on them. I got the chance to make him suffer like he did to me, and that's what I wanted."

He regretted every second of it now. The begging, the grabbing, the scream. Dear God, the scream of a man trapped in his worst nightmare with no way out. He would never do that again.

Giasone held his gaze for a few moments. "So you don't have any feelings left for him?"

"Yeah, sure. I love the guy that had me tied to his bed while he said he was going to sell me, and let me bleed while I tried to get loose. I absolutely love the guy that used me for months." Riley got in his face. "Go fuck yourself."

Giasone backed up a step. "I'm sorry."

"No, I'm sorry. I didn't mean that last bit. You've been nothing but nice, and you could have stuck me on the street and walked away."

Giasone rubbed his face. "I'm sorry too. I thought maybe you still had feelings for him in some way because you cried. Even when that guy that cheated on me left, I still kinda loved him for a while afterward even though it hurt. I knew he wouldn't change, but I wished he would."

"What Eren did was worse than cheating. I just don't have it in me to torture someone anyway. It seems like something a demon would do for fun, and I'm not like them even if I am part demon."

Giasone seemed to believe him. As they headed through the little copse of trees and toward Fringe, Riley tried not to think of the kiss or any bit of that horrid stint. Part of him did hate Eren, but he'd never do that again.

The other half of him did have feelings. Not like before, but the kiss and the touching had felt so damn good. He could still almost taste and smell the demon.

Why would it hurt so bad to love Riley? That hadn't made sense.

He couldn't explain the pain either unless Eren had some secret ability for protection. Maybe he'd regretted it too, hence the hug. It was better to keep away from him and not risk that again.

This didn't change anything in the long run. Eren would never be different. He'd keep this war going even if it killed him. He was obsessive, bent on destruction, death, and what he couldn't have.

It was better if he died. His child would just keep it all going if this war wasn't settled once and for all, but at least it wouldn't be *Eren*.

With the demon lord dead, Riley could try to leave that part of his history where it belonged: in the past. He'd never heal with the obsessive lord constantly lusting after him.

Now, he just had to think of a way to explain his other new ability. He wanted to use his power to its full potential, and he had a feeling there was a lot he could do.

Giasone teleported them back. At home that night, Riley slipped into a lucid dream. The meditator had said that he needed to simply want it when he went to sleep at night, and he'd touched a spot on Riley's forehead because apparently there was a spot deep in the brain that controlled sleep and also magic to an extent. The third eye. Riley didn't fully get that, but whatever the meditator did made it easy to lucid dream.

He preferred the forest scenery, but he added a nice blanket and made his clothes disappear. Picking someone was harder.

He almost thought about James, but he quickly shook his head. No way. He couldn't start spending his nights with a dead man. Leaving would become agony, and it felt wrong.

He could always use Eren, just not the real one.

Dream Eren didn't say nasty shit and felt so damn good against him. Giasone and Nyla would think he was utterly insane, but he didn't care. He let dream Eren pound him from behind as he watched the green smoke form. It was working. He didn't have to fuck anybody in real life if he didn't want to.

He could be his own power source. The thought was almost more exciting than the feel of his orgasm nearing.

Riley came when dream Eren did who vanished as soon as he was done. Riley didn't need fake hugs and kisses from that bastard. He was done with him. He rolled over and peered at the green pearl above him.

"Bloody fucking hell. I did it."

The sweet pearl was crunchy, and he felt his magic increase.

"Holy shit!" he yelled when he woke up. Buddy jumped up from the foot of the bed to slobber on him. "Calm down, boy."

A creak came from the sitting room. "Riley? Are you all right?"

Riley shoved on a pair of sleep pants. He hadn't cum in his sleep, but his dick was as hard as a rock, and he'd likely leaked pre-cum on his drawers. At least he could fuck in his lucid dreams and not randomly blow all over himself.

"I made a pearl!" he said as he hurried into the sitting room.

"Oh." Giasone tried to look around him and into the bedroom. "If you're going to bring someone home, can you at least mention it?"

"No, I did it by myself!" said Riley. "In a lucid dream. I fucked some random guy and made a pearl!"

Giasone rubbed his eyes. "That was a normal dream. Nobody can make energy or pearls in their sleep even if they dream about the most gorgeous angel available."

"I just made one," said Riley. "I thought up someone, let him pound me, watched the smoke form, and made a green pearl. I know what a lucid dream is."

"Uhhh..." The angel blinked at him as Buddy ambled in and wagged. "Very funny."

"I'm not kidding!"

"You can't be your own energy source. That's not how it works."

"We make energy by masturbation or lusty thoughts."

"That's different. It's only a little, and a pearl needs two."

"I just did it with a guy who wasn't actually there, sooo...somehow it worked."

"Who you'd think of?"

“Who fucking cares?” Riley instantly regretted his defensive tone.

Giasone looked at him, probably thinking it was Eren.

“Sorry, I thought maybe you thought it was my husband, but I forgot that I never said I was married once."

“Wait, you have a husband?”

“He died a while back.” Riley folded his arms. “I wasn’t thinking about him because it’d be weird to sleep with a dead guy.”

“It’s just a dream.”

“Yeah, but still. I made up a guy based on someone I fucked ages ago.”

Just a dream? If Riley had said Eren, Giasone would have made a big deal out of it.

“I’m sorry about your husband, but if you’re able to make energy on your own…” Giasone started pacing back and forth. “You promise you’re not yanking my leg?”

“I swear.”

“Do you have any idea how fucking unbelievable that is? Do you think you could feed another in a lucid dream?”

“Maybe, but I don’t feel like trying right now.” Riley hesitated. “Can you not tell Nyla about this?”

“Why not? That’s an amazing ability!”

“I don’t mind doing stuff for you guys, but everybody’s going to keep looking at me more and more like a spectacle or a traveling fair.” Riley scratched his arm. “I’m already different.”

Giasone paused. “Different isn’t bad.”

“It might be seen as bad if I dream and feed myself,” said Riley. “That’s pretty abnormal.”

“All right, we can keep it quiet for now.”

“Also, it’s late, and I think I’d prefer to simply sleep now.”

Riley had used rewek to get to sleep earlier. After the arrowak, he hadn’t been tired, but he didn’t want to mess up his typical sleep schedule. Rewek was also easier to wake up with if needed. As he held the bottle while sitting on the edge of his bed, a new thought occurred to him.

The rewek was bitter, and he added a few drops to a spoon and chased it with water from a cup on his bedside to get rid of the taste. Once he was standing in the forest again, he took a deep breath and tried to focus.

When he opened his eyes, a young teenage boy with black hair and blue eyes stood there in his sleep clothes with a faintly confused expression.

"Prince Jack?" he asked.

"Hm? Yeah?" The teenager glanced around.

"You're really Prince Jack?"

Prince Jack nodded. "Er, yes."

"What's your favorite food?" Riley expected him to mention a savory dish since royalty could afford anything.

"Cake is my favorite food," Prince Jack said without hesitation. "Are you an angel?"

"Not the kind you're probably thinking. You can go."

He made Prince Jack disappear, and his heart rate increased a little. He'd had an idea of what the teenage Crown Prince of Camaday looked like since most people at least had some vague clue, but he'd never seen the Royal Family or even a portrait. But now he knew for a fact he could summon anyone as long as he knew of their existence.

Prince Jack would probably think he'd had the strangest dream when he woke up. He'd likely forget about it pretty soon and go about his life, not knowing that he'd spoken to a genuine nephalem.

Closing his eyes, Riley focused again. When he opened them, he gasped.

Father stood in front of him. He had green eyes, black hair, and a pair of midnight blue wings folded against his back. They were about the same height and build, although Father had more muscle and the look of someone who did a lot of physical activity.

"Father?"

Father's eyes definitely locked onto him for a moment.

"Where are you?" asked Riley. "Why did you-"

"Don't call on me again."

Father vanished without Riley doing anything. Shame filled him as he wondered if Father hated him and regretted creating a child. Would Mother be the same way?

He closed his eyes and focused on bringing her. When he opened them, nobody was there. He tried again and struggled to focus on bringing *his Mother* to stand there before him, but no one came.

If Father came, and Mother didn't, he had a feeling that meant one was alive, and one was dead. Something had happened to her either in birth or perhaps in war, but there was no way to know.

He considered dragging Father back and demanding answers, but he would likely vanish again. Riley didn't want to look at the one who created him and regretted it.

Was there anything else he could do? Could he make his soul travel somewhere for real? He figured that's what he was doing. If he could drag others in, that must have meant their soul was in his dream. Either way, it would be nice to go somewhere and actually see real stuff that was happening.

He made his surroundings change to look like the Great Hall of the Royal Family, although it was just what he imagined. If there was a way, how could he do it? On a random whim, he switched to his bedroom and found himself standing in the darkened room. He tried to make it daytime so he could see while he thought more on this, but it didn't work.

Why couldn't he change that?

Turning, he noticed his bed, but it wasn't him in it, it was Giasone, and he was weeping. Just enough moonlight came through the window for him to make out the angel's blue wings.

"Giasone? What's wrong?"

The angel didn't answer or seem to realize he was being watched. Riley squinted and tried to make the door open, but that didn't work either. What the fuck was going on? He moved for it and found his hand went through it which made him jerk it back. Something wasn't right, and he realized he had no clue what he was doing now.

After passing through the door, he noticed the sitting room was a little different. A faded green rug was in front of the couch, there was a mismatched armchair to one side of it, and a cracked blue vase sat on the mantelpiece. Giasone's current room was empty.

Giasone seemed to have fallen asleep when Riley returned to his room. Weirded out by this, he squeezed his eyes shut and woke up in his bed.

It was too soon after the rewek, and he felt out of it. Rolling over, he managed to fall asleep again, too tired to care about what he'd just done.

In the morning, Giasone was drinking some smelly tea that he seemed to enjoy even though he didn't need it. Riley had his spellbook, but he could barely concentrate as he thought about the previous night. He finally decided to ask.

"Did you used to have a blue vase with a crack up on the mantelpiece?"

Giasone looked up from his own book across the table and narrowed his eyes. "How do you know that?"

Riley explained what happened, although he left out the part with Father. Giasone sat back and folded his arms with an amazed yet sour expression.

"You're just full of surprises, aren't you?"

"Erm, I guess."

"That sounds like you invaded a memory." Giasone pointed at Riley's closed bedroom door. "That used to be my room back when I was with Asshole."

"Oh, the guy who cheated?"

"Yeah. Not too long after I told Asshole to get lost, I decided to switch rooms, and I changed a few things around here. I wanted something different, sort of like a fresh start, I guess." Giasone frowned. "That's why you couldn't touch stuff. It was a memory."

"Oh. I'm sorry. I didn't mean to pry. I just tried to be in my room because I was playing around with manipulating things just for something to do. I wanted to know if I could go somewhere for real, and I guess I did in a way, although I didn't intend to go back in time."

"Don't tell anyone you saw me crying."

"I won't!"

Giasone leaned forward. "Do you know how amazing you are?"

"I'd rather be normal."

The angel snorted. "What's that here?"

"I'd rather be regular ole' Riley on Earth."

"Regular ole' Riley who'd live a looonng time." Giasone smiled. "Don't be ashamed to be amazing. The fact that you can enter memories is unheard of. We have to experiment with it!"

"Like what?"

"Can you enter anyone's memories? In fact, take a little rewek and see if you can enter Eren's."

"Why? I don't want to see his memories."

"Maybe you can find one of him speaking with others about plans to attack or something."

"Oh. Your memory was kind of random. What if I end up with boring stuff about him being a toddler?"

He was probably already a little shit at that age.

"Hmmm." Giasone squinted. "Just try to pick up anything. Let instinct guide you, and don't overthink it. That's how we all figure out our abilities. Lay on the couch and try."

"Right now?"

"Hell, yes! If I had your ability, I would."

"Fine."

Riley lay on the couch and let the rewek work.

He figured he'd try that morning since it was simple, and he could easily picture it. But when he opened his eyes, the cracked blue vase was there, the fire was bright, and Giasone was arguing with some other angel who had a cat-like tail. It was swishing with agitation as they yelled. Riley caught some choice insults and realized this must have been when Giasone found out that Asshole was cheating.

He quickly imagined the woods and was there so he could have a second to regroup his thoughts. Maybe he'd "forget" to mention seeing that to Giasone. There was experimenting with his abilities, and then there was prying and being horribly nosy.

Eren. He figured he'd start with a memory that he was in since it was easier. The one of them in the office seemed good.

When he opened his eyes, he was there, but Eren wasn't doing anything except sitting at his desk.

"Hi," said Riley.

"Hi," dream Eren said because it was expected.

"Damn it." Riley went to the door to find it solid.

"What are you doing?"

"Be quiet for a moment."

Eren shut up, and Riley stood there, trying to focus on making it a memory. When he looked around again, it was the same. Damn it. How had he entered Giasone's memory so easily?

Both of his had been sad or angry times, so maybe that was it. Maybe the memory had to have more emotion, so Riley tried to think of his first day at Eren's when the twins put him in the bedroom. He'd been frightened, so that should work. He found himself naked in Eren's room with the lead, but he was able to change the wall colors.

"Shit."

He wondered if he could push himself further back in time, and he focused on that so he didn't have to see the angel arguing with Asshole. Picturing himself back in Giasone's house, he found them fucking on the couch while orange smoke formed a pearl.

"Oh, God, no!"

He appeared in the woods, his safe spot, while he tried to scrub that image from his brain. Giasone was right in some way. Instinct seemed to work, and he'd simply gone further back like he wanted. As he sat, he tried to think of why he could access Giasone's memories so easily, but nothing else.

Maybe it wasn't something to do with the angel, but the location itself. All of those memories were full of emotion in some way, so perhaps it left a way for him in, not that Riley could explain how. The only way to find out was to go to a different location and see if he could access what was there.

He scrunched his eyes shut and woke up on the couch.

"How did it go?" Giasone gave him an eager look.

"Take me next door to Nyla's," mumbled Riley.

"Why?"

"Just do it. I'll tell you in a bit." He grabbed the bottle of rewek.

A few angels that walked by in the street probably thought Riley was drunk. His eyes felt heavy even though he started to wake up a bit as they entered Nyla's Hall. He took another drop of rewek and simply lay on the floor as Giasone closed the doors.

"You're sleeping on the floor?"

"Shh." Riley closed his eyes.

It was easy. The hall was full of angels that Riley could go through, and they all were looking at someone seated and speaking on the dais.

"The spell has kicked in, so we can't deny it. The Queen…is dead."

Some of the angels had watery eyes, and one looked like he was trying to hold back so much emotion, it made him appear constipated. Riley approached the dais as he stared at the man in the chair. He had faintly pinkish skin, but another image seemed to be overlaid with him. It was an angel Lancef, and the image was of a woman with red hair. The combination of two bodies, one male and one female with differing clothes would surely give anyone a headache after a while if they looked at it long enough. It was hard to focus on either. The expressions matched, and any movement was too.

The Lancef bit his lip, making the image of the Queen do the same. "We'll create an heir with her eggs, and you'll swear allegiance to the new ruler when he's old enough."

He. Of course, they'd expected a boy since females were rare. Riley closed his eyes and tried to picture Nyla herself in this hall.

He found himself upstairs in her private quarters. A couple of dolls lay on the floor, and the Lancef was sitting on the couch with Nyla who was a little girl. Smaller and delicate, she leaned on the man's arm while he read her a story.

With no parents, this memory must have been a treasure to her. Riley tried to go backward before the Queen's death, opened his eyes, and found a red-haired woman standing at the window and weeping. She was too tall to be Nyla.

Coming around, he saw that she had a belly under her dress. She was beautiful with her red hair and blue eyes. Her tan skin was a little too perfect and clear which seemed unnatural to him, but it didn't look bad at all.

If this was the last Queen, who he didn't know the name of, she must have lost the baby since Nyla was the only child. Perhaps angels and demons could suffer complications, and she knew something was wrong. Or maybe her husband had died, and she had just learned of it.

Whatever happened, the little life in her stomach must not have made it.

Riley didn't want to be here anymore. Some memories were better left in the past.

He woke up to find Nyla and Giasone watching him as they sat on the edge of the dais.

"What did you see?" Nyla had a pinched expression.

"Your Mother was beautiful." Riley wiped his eyes as he rolled onto his side.

"I told her," said Giasone. "She came down to find you asleep on her floor."

Great. Nyla looked at him like he belonged in a cage at a traveling fair to be stared at by peasants.

"You saw my Mother?" asked Nyla. "Lilith?"

"Yeah." He sat up. "She was beautiful."

Nyla stared at her knees and picked at the seam on a ruffle. "What was she doing?"

"Erm..." He paused, thinking he should leave out the pregnant part. It might be too touchy.

"Tell me!"

"She was pregnant and crying by a window upstairs. I don't know what was wrong, but you don't have siblings, right?"

Nyla shook her head. "No. Nobody ever mentioned a miscarriage or a stillbirth either."

"Maybe she wanted that to be forgotten." Giasone patted her on the back. "It must have been hard."

"I still wish someone would have told me!" She stood and hurried to get on her knees by Riley. "You'd do something for me, right? I'm your Queen."

"Yeah, sure."

"Would you go into the Wraithlands and try to find a memory of her?"

"Wait, what?"

Giasone jumped up. "You can't send him there!"

"Not alone. You could go with him."

"I'm not going there. That place is terrible."

"I heard that place is gloomy and-" Riley started.

"Yes, it is, but people used to live there ages ago, in the beginning," she said. "There are some ruins, and the place is held in by a sort of fence to keep the wraiths in."

"The what?" asked Riley.

"Why do you think it's called the Wraithlands?" asked Giasone. "It's certainly not filled with unicorns and dancing elves."

"What's a wraith?" asked Riley.

"It's like...a dead thing," said Nyla. "Honestly, we're not entirely sure what they are."

"I'm not going in there! I'm not fucking with dead things."

"Riley, please! My Mother vanished, and they never found a body, but nobody thoroughly searched there because it's too big and too dangerous. I have a Lancef which is-"

"I know what a Lancef is and how that works."

"Once mine took on her image, he knew she was dead. Since we could never find a body anywhere else in our realm, she might have gone there. We're sure demons didn't kill her because they would have gloated about it."

"Why would she go there?"

"I don't know, but if she did, I want to know what happened to her! It's the only option we have. Maybe…maybe wraiths did something with her body, and that's why nobody found it there, but you could check for a memory."

"If she's died, we might never find a body or-"

"I just want a memory of her!" Nyla grabbed his hands. "Please! I'm begging you. I want to know what happened to my Mother. If it was yours, and I could do this for you, I would!"

He bit his lip as he considered it.

Chapter Eight

Dear God, what had Riley agreed to?

The border to the Wraithlands was a clear but shimmering wall that went up as high as he could see and stretched out on either side. As they stood on the grass, the sun shone down, and the air was cool, but beyond the border, the Wraithlands were dark, dank, and desolate. Clouds covered the sky, and the ground was mostly dirt, rocks, and stubby, brown grass.

"These will keep those things away?" he asked, gesturing at the blue orbs they each held on thick leather cords. Giasone and Nyla had educated him a little, and he knew the Wraithlands sapped energy from light orbs pretty fast.

Giasone nodded. "Yeah. Some of them have gone scavenging for stuff, but nobody has ever mapped the whole area. There's nothing really worth mapping anyway as far as we know so far."

Nyla had said that nobody knew why this area was like that or where wraiths came from. She assumed they were dead souls from a long time ago, magic that had gone wrong and twisted angels or demons, or some form of being that existed since the beginning of time but didn't fit in with either side. After all, other realms and fairies existed too. Some said wraiths were a subspecies of demons that came from Hell where the Devil resided, but even he didn't want them.

The front door to the nearby shack opened and made Riley jump. An old angel with streaks of grey in his rust-colored hair stepped out and glared at them.

"This ain't a place to be playing," he squawked.

"We're not playing," called Giasone. "We're on an errand."

The angel grumbled, headed back in, and slammed the door so hard, a shingle fell from the roof.

"Don't mind him. He was born grumpy."

"He stays here to watch this?" asked Riley.

"Yeah. The border has never broken or anything like that, but it's better if someone sticks around just in case. We have a few other angels that live by it. If anything ever happened, they'd set off a light circle."

"A what?"

"It goes up and blows outward."

There was nothing to do but go forward. Anybody could walk through the border, but it kept wraiths in. It felt like cold water except Riley didn't get wet from it. The angels had a magical barrier up to protect Fringe and keep demons out, but when he'd gone through it, it had given him a ticklish feeling.

In the past week, he'd been fucking dream Eren to make pearls and give himself energy. Sometimes, it made him cum in his sleep which was a great annoyance, but at least he had more power now although he'd only set one weak spell.

The grey lands were a little colder than the rest of the mild realm, although Riley felt fine. The temperature didn't seem to affect him that much now, and he didn't start sweating under his shirt and coat. The blue orbs swung slightly as they walked. Riley couldn't see anything beyond except for more dirt and stubby brown grass. The odd quiet gave him the creeps even though nothing was around.

"What's there to scavenge?" he asked.

"Some have brought back pottery and bits of clothing. Useless stuff like that. Deserters have left through here too. War can really fuck up some angels."

"What's to stop the demons from bringing Lucia the Light Maker through here and having her lead the whole army into angel territory?" asked Riley. "She can charge orbs."

Giasone side-eyed him. "Bringing huge groups in here is also a bad idea. It makes the lightning strike whoever is on the ground, not just fliers. The whole demon army wouldn't get very far."

Riley couldn't believe that lightning was somehow attracted to anyone that attempted flight here. Giasone had told him that earlier. The whole place was cursed and felt like a death trap.

They fell silent as they walked. After a couple of hours, Riley thought he spotted a flicker of movement to one side, and Giasone noticed it too since he grabbed Riley's arm.

"It won't touch us. We've got the light."

He sounded like he was trying to convince himself. A shiver ran down Riley's back as a black shape drifted closer. The hooded wraith was completely covered in its cloak, and it seemed to glide instead of walk. The edges of the fabric were tattered, and he couldn't see a face under the hood, just darkness.

He could feel it looking at him, and his wings twitched with the urge to hurry up and fly away from that thing even though that was the worst idea ever.

The wraith didn't get closer, and after several seconds, it turned to glide away. Riley and Giasone remained frozen as they watched its rippling cloak soon vanish in the faint mist that was creeping in.

"Are you sure we can't fly and make this faster?" asked Riley.

"No!"

"What if we stayed low or used your shield-"

Giasone frantically shook his head as he released his death grip. "It always attracts lightning, and some have tried shields, but it keeps getting stronger. If you get shocked, it'll break the light too, and the wraiths will sense where you're at. They'll come. They *always* know if something living is around with no light."

That made Riley feel like he was being watched by a wraith that was hoping for the light to go out so it could pounce. Or more like glide over and suck out his energy and life. They could only be killed with fire, and Riley hadn't even set the spark spell yet. Sparks from his fingertips would be pretty useless against wraiths.

"Come on." Giasone tugged on his sleeve.

After a good twenty minutes, they found an area that had square stones. Some were half-buried in the ground. Bits of rotted wood lay scattered around, and Giasone said it was assumed this place used to be a village, and the stones were hearths. People used to have their hearth in the center of their homes, and they'd make a fire on it. Riley found a few pieces of blackened, twisted metal. That might have been something to hold up pots over a fire, although he couldn't tell for sure.

"Let me try this place," he said.

"All right."

Riley had no choice but to lie on the ground. After the rewek made him sleep, he found a memory but not of a happy village.

It was hazy, and he had trouble making out a lot of finer details, but he could tell what was happening. Half of the village was on fire. People dressed in strange clothing ran about shrieking. A woman with a baby darted by Riley, but an arrow hit her back in a blaze of yellow light. She fell, and the baby wailed as it hit the ground. An angel with hair that looked to be made of pure gold came forward around a hut. Riley assumed it meant to save the baby as it approached the woman, but it brought its boot down on the child's skull.

Riley gasped as the bones cracked, and the angel ground its boot like it was squashing a stubborn bug. It looked up at him, and his eyes widened. It shouldn't be able to see him.

He ran through a few screaming people and turned to see it marching toward a man with a spear. It hadn't been looking at him, but at the human foolishly ready to fight.

Blood splattered moments later as the angel tore the man limb from limb like a rag doll. Riley turned to see a demon hurl a spear at him, and he shouted, but it passed through. Someone behind him screamed.

Riley flew above the mass so he could stop being freaked out that someone was ready to attack him. Angels and demons both slaughtered the inhabitants with weapons and magic. Behind the burning wreckage of a home, a woman screamed as an angel raped her and made crimson smoke. Riley turned away in disgust.

No one was spared. A young man was dragged away into the smoking wheat fields by a yellow and silver demon with a forked tongue hanging from its mouth, and he had a feeling it would meet the same fate as the woman.

He forced himself to wake up, unable to bear the brutality and slaughter.

"What?" Giasone asked when Riley blearily sat up with a disgusted sound.

He described what he saw. Giasone said it sounded like something from the beginning of this realm's time.

"It wasn't always pure hate between us," he said. "There are almost no records of that time, but we do know that they brought humans here, and they weren't intended to be pets like the way demons use humans now."

"Then why bring people?"

"Something to rule over? Perhaps this village did something wrong."

"And they had to kill the children too?!"

Giasone made a face. "We wouldn't do that now, of course, but who knows what some of those early demons and angels were like or what demands they made?"

"Hmm. I guess."

"Come on, we should get going if that's it."

"I don't think anything has happened here since that war." Riley stood, hating the drugged feeling that the rewek gave him if he woke up so soon. No wonder Eren had seemed drunk that night. "That was the first thing I saw."

This whole errand was a bit ridiculous. Lilith could have died *anywhere* in this place, and it would take ages to dream search it. Riley wasn't even sure how far his radius went considering that he was outside. If Nyla wasn't the Queen, he probably would have said no, but he could understand her urgency.

They walked fast. Thanks to what little they knew from others who had been in here, there were a couple of houses which made no sense to Riley. If no one had lived here in ages, how could there be any homes?

Eventually, they saw a shape in the fog. Riley was pretty sure he saw something else far more sinister in the fog to his left, but they had the light, and the wraith didn't seem interested in checking them out.

"Let me guess? Magic keeps the house intact?"

"I think so," said Giasone. "I have no idea who made it or why. It's also quite hard to make them last."

"But not to shoot energy from your fingers?"

Giasone snorted. "Believe it or not, yes. Being able to preserve inanimate things for ages is a rare ability."

The stone house was dark and old. There were scratches on the door which Riley didn't like. It made him think of wraith dogs pawing at it to get in, not that such a thing existed.

"There are no wraith dogs, right?" he asked.

Giasone paused. "Er, no."

"Okay, good. Just checking."

The door had no lock, and it squeaked open when Giasone pushed it. No wraiths came flying out at them, so they entered. Noticing a hook in the ceiling, Giasone reached up to hang his orb from it, and he closed the door.

The house was one room. An old bed that was covered in dust took up one corner, and Riley set his orb down by the foot. The fireplace was cold and bare, and a shelf held a few small items such as cups, a pot, and a couple of other random things. The floorboards creaked, and Riley could smell the dust as they walked around.

"This place needs a good sweeping." Giasone spotted a rickety broom in the corner that looked ready to fall apart.

"The bedding doesn't look that old, so I guess someone stayed here?"

"Yeah, I'm sure a few have."

Giasone swept out the place the best he could, and Riley shook out the bedding. It still smelled musty, but it would have to do.

He remade the bed, and Giasone dug through his pack. With an almost reverent expression, he pulled out a twig.

Riley had learned about their Tree of Life. It had a few uses, never died, and there were a couple of specialty spells that could be done with it. Most magic required energy and certain pearls, but a few advanced rituals needed items.

Having a piece of it brought good luck, and Riley had taken a little splinter from it earlier before they left. It was in his pocket, but he had no idea if it would actually make him lucky.

Giasone licked the tip of the twig, and a blue fire appeared.

"That'll last for quite a while," he said.

He put the orbs out, and they sat on the bed with the twig standing upright in a cup. It wasn't much better than a single candle, but it was enough to keep wraiths away. Even though this house had no windows, they'd somehow know.

"What's the other house like? Is it small like this?"

"I'm not sure," said Giasone.

"If there are two houses here, why doesn't someone set up a big expedition? You could bring twigs and orbs and really map out this whole area. If you kept the groups small, you could have one or two run orbs and stuff in, right?"

Giasone frowned. "It's not that easy. Some say this place makes people go mad."

Riley raised an eyebrow. "They become insane?"

Giasone shrugged. "Yeah."

"Yeah? We just came into a place that might make us insane? You didn't tell me that before!"

"It's supposed to take a while. We don't know if it's true or not, but who wants to find out? As far as we know, the longest anyone has ever stayed is a week. They weren't crazy when they came back, but what if that's pushing it? What if it takes one week and one day? Or two? Maybe two weeks here is safe." He threw up his hands. "Ask someone to take the risk to see how long they'll last."

"Erm, no, thanks."

"See? It's not so easy."

"Sorry."

"Besides, it's probably just more barren land and ruins." Giasone sighed. "It sucks that we lost so many records. The book that mentions people possibly going insane references another that we don't have at all."

"What happened to that stuff?"

"Time. Fire. We used to have a huge library centuries ago. It was much bigger than what we have now. I can only imagine the secrets that thing held, but it supposedly caught on fire somehow. A few things were salvaged, but far more was lost. It was after the women stopped being born for the most part." Giasone's eyes lit up. "I bet you could go to it in a dream memory, and memorize things! We know the location, so you could sleep there, and we could write it down.

"I don't know how long I have in a memory," said Riley, thinking of something he hadn't considered. "I doubt I could spend days there."

"True."

"And memorizing stuff is a lot of work. Whole books worth of information?" Riley cocked his head. "You flatter me with such faith. And I can't touch stuff, remember?"

"Oh. I didn't think of that...You could read over someone's shoulder!"

"Let's be realistic. Besides, it's a library, so I doubt much emotional stuff happened besides the fire unless angels were crying while reading sappy romances in there."

"It was just a thought. Are you ready to sleep and see if anything happened here?"

"Yeah."

Giasone sat on the floor and let Riley have the bed. More rewek helped him to drop off.

The house looked much nicer, and Lilith was standing in front of the fire with her back to Riley as she hummed a tune that sounded rather like a lullaby. This must have been the last memory to make an impact here, and Nyla was right. She had been here.

Lilith turned, and she held a little baby with a tuft of black hair sticking up. Her face looked drawn and lit up at the same time as if she'd just been through a great strain and joy at once. The baby couldn't have been more than three days old.

She continued humming as the baby slept in her arms. Riley wondered if it was sickly, and he jumped when someone knocked on the door. Dear God, did a wraith kill her and the baby? Then he remembered the light would keep them away, and he was pretty sure wraiths didn't knock to come in.

Whoever it was, they hurried in before she could speak, and she didn't seem alarmed at all. Riley stared at the black-haired, green-eyed man as several things fell into place. There was no way. He glanced at the baby with its little tuft of black hair, his Father, and Queen Lilith holding her son.

Nyla was Riley's half-sister. The missing Queen was his Mother, and for some reason, he had been placed on a human's doorstep while he was only a few days old.

Chapter Nine

Eren stiffly stood in front of Grandfather and tried to not let the piercing gaze make him break his composure.

"Why didn't you attack him in the dream?"

Eren tilted his head. "Attacking him there wouldn't do anything. It's not his physical body."

Grandfather pursed his dry lips. The rest of him was looking a little better. His horns didn't even seem so dull anymore. His skin still had a grey tint and was dry, and he was a far cry from what he must have looked like before. Unfortunately, the white in his hair was also receding.

"Even in a dream, fear is a useful tool as he just proved to you. The mind feels it. It sounds like you had the chance to hurt him, but you didn't, and you allowed him to get the upper hand. He did that to fuck with you."

The words were like a knife to Eren. Of course, Riley had stuffed him in a small space to terrify him. And he'd regretted it.

"You're lucky I could sense something and intervene. Your fear came through."

"How could you protect me in a dream?" Eren wished he hadn't. The idea of the foul thing before him touching his pet made him want to choke the bastard.

Grandfather smirked. "Our link allowed it, and you're lucky for it." The smirk dropped. "I wish I could tell what you're doing all of the time and have the ability to protect you."

Use. Not protect.

"You took too long to get here."

"I have war preparations," Eren said smoothly. "Things must be done to take Fringe and press forward. The sooner we get farther in, the sooner Riley can be found so I can bring him to you."

"Hmm."

Eren tried not to look at the corpse on the floor within the edge of the light or wonder how the wraiths had managed to acquire the demon for their lord's pleasure. Grandfather had often required sacrifices before.

Thankfully, the wraiths were too loyal to him, so they wouldn't wander off and wreak havoc in the realm.

Grandfather tapped his fingers on the table. “Do you see my sacrifice?”

“Yes.” Eren kept his face arranged as though he didn’t care about the demon’s fate.

“The poor little forager's life was made great by his short service to me.”

Those who knew him probably wept as they searched and wondered what had happened to him.

Grandfather smiled as he lifted his chin and regarded Eren. “His energy was good. Unfortunately, Bellim's links with the others are pitiful. They can’t communicate much with him anymore. That barrier around the Wraithlands is too strong for them.” He shook his head. “One day, we’ll take it down, but his consort has a stronger link with him now, so that’s an improvement.”

Eren glanced at the demon. To be made to lay under such an abomination…

Grandfather continued as he too looked at the body, and Bellim drifted closer. “They don’t communicate with each other in a way like you or I do, and amongst themselves, they aren’t much better than ants, but Bellim tells me now that she saw two angels in the Wraithlands, and one has red wings and black hair.”

Eren paused. “You think that’s Riley?”

“Considering you just told me what he looks like…Are red wings common now?”

“No, but they’re not completely impossible, and I don’t see why Riley would go to such a place unless he's suddenly decided to become an explorer. It’s likely deserters. If they come out near the demon side, our patrols will get them.” Eren tacked on a smile. “More fuel for another Nevyyn. Banna can’t wait to make another, and with the Tree of Life, we’ll have plenty.”

“I want you to go check,” said Grandfather. “Bellim’s consort can’t follow them and tell him more at the same time, so you have to.”

“Why can’t she follow and tell him more?”

“Because the blocking magic of that place is still strong. She has to be closer to the edge. If Riley is there, you need to get him. We can’t control the others and tell them not to kill him, and I want him alive. No accidents.” He leaned forward. “If it’s him, bring him to me immediately. You have my permission to kill any wraiths if needed. They won't listen to anything you say, and I can't stop them from trying to harm you. Do you understand me? I can't lose you to them."

To anyone that heard those last two sentences, Grandfather would sound like he truly cared about his grandson's well-being. He only cared about his favorite source being lost to him forever.

Eren nodded. "Very well."

"If you find him already dead, then bring his corpse back. If it's two other angels, kill them or bring them alive to Banna. I don't care what you do with them."

"You don't want them?"

"Bellim will bring me another demon. My own must serve me now. I can have an angel later."

Eren didn't dare ask what he would do with it. "As you wish."

"I'd like to feed from you, but you'll need your strength. Go." Grandfather held out his hand so Eren could kneel and kiss the ring.

No time in the tomb. Eren wanted to run once he stood, but he forced himself to walk out at a normal pace. Appearing eager to get away wasn't a good idea. As he stood in the room while it moved up, his heart pounded in his tight chest, and he tried to imagine having time with Riley again, but his pet hated him. It wasn't the same, and Eren would have to bring him here.

He would get him back later as a reward. Except...The future threatened to choke him as the dark space continued to smother him. If the room stopped and kept him trapped…

He got out as always.

Grandfather's cave was near the edge of the demon side of the Fallen realm in the west. Some form of magic blocked those who had never been there before, so no random demon could find it on their own. Eren figured that was some old forgotten magic from the beginning.

There was an outpost that wasn't too far if he flew high and fast. If Riley was in the Wraithlands, Eren couldn't dally too much.

The Commander looked at him like he was crazy when he learned the demon lord was going into the Wraithlands.

"What for? I thought the main army was going after Fringe, and nothing has happened here lately."

"They are taking Fringe."

"Without you?"

"They'll go when I say," snapped Eren. "Now get what I need, and hurry up."

Once he had what he needed, he flew toward the Wraithlands although he landed before entering so he didn't get hit by lightning. He made a face at the wet feeling as he passed through the barrier. This would be so much faster if he could fly. The orb swung lightly as he walked fast.

If Riley was here, Eren had no way of knowing where he was, and he wondered why the halfling would come here. Light exploration had shown there was little use to anything, although some liked old bits of history.

He was several hours in and heading toward the angel's side when a wraith approached, although it didn't dare come near the light. It tilted its head, and the skeletal hands twitched as it hovered.

"Are you Bellim's consort?" he asked.

The wraith took a few seconds to incline its head. This far, its link was probably already weakened, and if he went much farther, it would lose it and want to kill him. The only thing it would remember was its urge to destroy living things with no light, and the bond of its once lover. It obviously somehow knew to seek that out and could speak to Bellim when it was close enough, but he wondered how much it remembered.

Enough to know to report something to its past lover. That meant Eren had better be careful.

"Carry on," he said. "Don't let me bother you."

The wraith started to move ahead. It paused to look at him, and he followed it. Content, it kept drifting along with its cloak rippling. Even Eren didn't understand what these things were entirely, but he had a feeling. They probably used to be followers of Grandfather. Bellim must have been important at one time. Hell, he might even have sacrificed several children to gain more favor and magic which was why he was one of the few that stayed with Grandfather. All three of those at Grandfather's place must have been especially loyal at one time.

Everyone else had been lesser, and now, they couldn't be controlled.

After a while, the wraith seemed to forget what it was doing since it stopped leading. Afraid of the light, it hovered, and Eren could feel its gaze boring into him.

"Have you forgotten me?" he asked. "Run along. Go seek Bellim. You probably don't even really remember him now, do you? You just mindlessly follow the link. Fool."

Since it couldn't have him, it started to drift off. Eren watched it as it changed course to head back to where he had come from, probably seeking the source of its link. It sped up until it disappeared quite quickly.

Eren paused as his eyes widened. Wraiths didn't typically move that fast. Could Bellim's magic boost have done that? There was no point in standing there and wondering, so he continued striding along. It would probably say it had seen a demon with horns and black wings, not knowing who Eren truly was. Either way, it would seek to find Eren again to help before forgetting after a bit once more.

He almost felt sorry for it.

He started jogging to speed things up. Several others drifted by in a group, hungering for him but unable to get too close. They lost interest and left. Eren continued in the direction that the first wraith had been leading him.

When he reached a house, he circled it. He'd heard of a few places that seemed to have been preserved, although had no idea how or why they seemed more modern. The house seemed abandoned, and he finally tried the door and entered. The smell, so sweet and tempting, was tinged with a coppery one that made his stomach twist.

Cups littered the floor. A splatter of blood marred the dusty surface, and Eren's heart thumped as he breathed in the odor of roses, lavender, and something else. The other's odor was like an insult.

He searched the small house, hoping for some clue as to what happened. A few remaining items were old, but not old enough to have been here for centuries. It was almost like someone had lived here some decades ago, which wasn't right. Why risk the possible madness?

Riley's purpose here had to have been particularly important, especially since he came so soon after changing and acquiring powers. The bed looked like it had been slept on too.

If he came here with a supposed friend, where were they, and why was Riley's blood on the floor?

Chapter Ten

"Orpheus, you have a son." Lilith smiled at her lover as Riley watched.

Orpheus set his light orb on the floor as he looked at the baby. Some of the hardness about his face melted away for a moment. "Can I hold him?"

"Yes."

He took baby Riley like he was a priceless relic and cradled him. The baby opened his eyes and stretched out his tiny arms. Riley hurried closer to see even though most babies had blue eyes when they were born. Apparently, that wasn't the same for demon babies, and nephalem were the same. One eye was blue and the other was green.

Among the black hair, Riley saw a few red strands.

"He's beautiful," Orpheus said as baby Riley made tiny fists and closed his eyes. He handed the baby back to Lilith. "You know what must be done now."

"I've decided something else-"

"You can't expect the people to accept him. He's a nephalem, and they'll know what we've done."

"They will because I'm going to betroth him. Since Athena is pregnant, I'm going to offer that Riley and her son marry when they're old enough."

Orpheus stared at her. "You can't be serious. She'll never accept that."

"They're babies," said Athena. "Or they will be. Erebus isn't born yet, but they'll only be a few months apart, and they can grow up knowing each other. Even if it ends up being a girl, and they have to pick a different name, same thing."

Riley gaped at her. She'd planned to betroth him to Eren before the demon lord was even born?

Orpheus looked away for a few seconds. "Lilith-"

"No, you listen to me," she said. "Do you want us to give up our son to humans and have him live in a world where he'll never be accepted?"

"I can put a glamor on him," said Orpheus. "Mine are excellent, and it'll last forever on Earth. I know a man there, and he would take care of the child."

"A stranger to me!" she hissed. "I don't know this person, and my son won't be raised by some mystery man."

"I know him. He'd never harm Riley."

"And what about when he's old enough to marry?" she said. "He'll grow slower, and they might brush that off as an odd condition, but it'll become noticeable that he doesn't age the same. What will people say when his wife starts to grow old, and he looks young?"

He ducked his head. "I don't want that life for him either, but I'm sure he'll figure something about him isn't normal. He'll learn to hide and move around. Overall, he can have a good life."

She pursed her lips. "No. I'll ask for a meeting with Athena. As a woman, she'll understand the future her son is being born into. One where he might die in war at any time. With both sides bonded through their marriage, Erebus and Riley will live. They'll keep each other safe and save countless future lives and babies."

He slowly shook his head. "You know this won't work. Do you think it's solely her choice? Her husband will never agree to betroth his son to a nephalem. He'd rather see you all dead. Do you know what he'd do to me if he found out that I've been meeting with the Queen of the angels?"

"You proved that a demon can love an angel," she argued. "They could-"

"And I wish I hadn't because now we'll both lose something, and that hurts far worse," he said.

"I think one Mother to another will make this work."

"Dade won't agree to it," he retorted. "He's different now too. In the past few years, he's changed. Some of the spark is dead."

She squinted at him. "What do you mean?"

"I don't know. Maybe the war is cracking him. He wants Banna to create some kind of weapon, and she's trying, but nothing is really working. I don't even think it's her failures doing this to him."

"You know we're trying too. We fail the same, and the war goes on. Countless lives are lost. You said Athena is a bit kinder, and I will write to her soon."

"And you're just going to bring the baby home in the meantime?"

"I can keep him hidden. I'll manage since it'll just be for a while."

"You're insane."

"I'm offering something else that they won't be able to resist."

"What?"

"The Pisces Rings."

He drew closer. "What the hell did you just say?"

She raised her chin. "Our children can have the Pisces Rings."

"That's a myth. It's nearly a forgotten one, and utter bullshit-"

"They're not. I know where they're at, and with those, our two boys can have one more empire at their disposal. One last, short war, and everything between heaven and hell is theirs."

Orpheus stepped back with an expression of disgust. "Those are fake, and even demons care little for-"

She laughed. "Only because it would be such a pain to be so weak. With the rings, it won't be a problem. How do you think they managed in the beginning?"

Riley had no idea what the hell they were talking about. Lilith seemed to think these rings were great, but Orpheus was looking at her like she had suggested eating kittens for breakfast."

"They won't be happy if you're lying."

"I'm not lying," she said. "I'm the only one that knows where they are, and I'll only reveal the location if the terms are met. My son will marry Athena's, both sides will have saf-"

"You're mad! You'd best not ever speak of this again. Give me Riley."

"I will not give him to you. Our son and Athena's will rule a great empire. Riley is a Picses, and Eren is sure to be a Scorpio. They'll be the perfect match and can wield the rings. Imagine seeing your own son in such a position of power and happy with his husband."

"I don't want that for him. It'll make him hard, cruel, and he'll-"

"You can go." Athena went to sit on the bed. "I won't say a word about who his Father is if that's what you want, but I've made my decision. I'm done with fighting and never getting anywhere."

Orpheus's face grew harder as he drew closer. "Give him to me. I will not have our child used in some plot-"

"It's not just some plot. It's fitting for our boys."

"Is this why you slept with me? Did you plan this out too so we'd have a baby in February? Huh? If those rings are real, and you truly know where they are, then that means you used me, and I was foolish to think you were better than the rest of the angels!"

She bit her lip. "I do love you. I'd rather you be at my side in the future."

His face darkened. "You don't deny it, so you used me. I won't be at your side if the future entails this. Riley is my child too, and he's not a tool."

"It's our best chance to end this war."

"And start a new one!"

"A short one."

"Lilith, please." He sat next to her although she turned her head away. "You know I've seen things. I've been around for a long time. Power can make people cruel. I don't want that for him."

Something glinted by his sleeve.

"Leave," she hissed. "I know you love me too, so leave me and our son alone."

"Lilith!" shouted Riley, seeing the glint grow longer.

Of course, she couldn't hear him, and in her foolish love for a demon, she never expected the worst betrayal. Her gasp proved it when the dagger entered between her ribs.

Orpheus was already snatching baby Riley before her grip could slacken and loosen. Baby Riley, who had slept through the arguing, awoke at the sudden movement and started to fuss as Orpheus stood and hastily backed away with him.

"You can't-" She clutched at the dagger, but the damage was already done. "You wouldn't..."

Orpheus's cheek twitched. "I will if it keeps you from turning our son into a monster and breeding more."

"They're just humans-"

"They're not. They're so much more. I thought you were too, but I guess it was a mistake for either of us to trust the other."

Blood ran from Lilith's mouth as she stared at him.

"I'm sorry." His face crumpled into tears. "I didn't want this. I thought..."

Beyond help, she slumped on the bed. Orpheus sobbed as he held baby Riley who waved his fists and wailed. Riley watched the blossom of blood grow on his Mother's dress while a red thread from her mouth traveled down her chin and neck. Her sightless eyes seemed to stare at him.

"What the fuck?" Riley screamed at his Father.

The demon didn't answer as he turned away with the baby. His shoulders shook as he rocked him.

How was Riley supposed to tell Nyla that his Father had killed their Mother?

"It'll be alright. I'll put you somewhere safe. A place where you won't be used, and you can experience some normal life." Baby Riley seemed to calm down at the sound of Father's whispers. Riley moved around to see as Orpheus adjusted the baby's blanket a little. "They can be foul, but there are many good ones too."

He went to the lit twig in the fireplace, blew it out, and carefully placed it in his pocket. Holding Riley, he took his light orb and left the house.

Afraid the memory would end, Riley hurried to follow, but maybe boundaries didn't matter once he was in it. Orpheus took his son across the Wraithlands and walked as if he'd never grow tired. Riley followed and occasionally saw other shapes in the dark. Father stopped once to place Riley down and tie the chain of the orb to his belt.

Orpheus continued even when it grew light. Or what was considered light in this dank place. The mist was heavy, and Riley followed closely even though nothing could touch him here. A couple of times, Orpheus's face tightened like he wanted to cry again. Baby Riley fussed and grizzled a few times, and Riley was about to say he needed to be changed and fed, not that he'd be heard. Then he remembered that demon and angel babies must not need to worry about being fed either, and that meant they wouldn't make a mess in their nappies.

Orpheus must have been tired, especially when it grew dark again, but Riley felt no fatigue as he followed. Orpheus kept striding along as if he had one goal and wouldn't stop until he'd reached it. The occasional wraith glided by and watched.

One started following and didn't lose interest. Orpheus hadn't seemed to care about the others, but when he noticed one wasn't giving up, he paused.

"Go away or I'll kill you," he snarled.

The wraith floated above the ground as it watched. Father started toward it with the orb, and it backed away before hastily gliding off.

Orpheus squinted as he stared after it with a suspicious expression. Seemingly satisfied that it was gone, he kept going.

The border where he exited on the demon side must have been far from any patrols or civilization. Safe from wraiths, he put out the orb and took flight. Riley followed him, and they went higher than he'd dared to go just yet. Still not tired, he took advantage of the safety as he kept up with Father. The forest seemed endless as Orpheus flapped and occasionally glided on the wind. Baby Riley slept for that portion, protected by his blankets and Father's arms.

Riley detected a shimmer ahead, and Father flew right into it. After about two minutes, the shimmer stopped, and the forest suddenly appeared white. Snowflakes drifted down, and Riley assumed they had passed into the human world. Father must have said the spell in his head.

After a few more minutes, Orpheus flew down and landed in a tree. Riley hovered next to him as Father held baby Riley and was silent for a while. A light appeared in the distance to signal the coming dawn.

Riley knew what was coming, although he wouldn't fully believe it until he saw it with his own eyes.

"I guess those rings are bad," he said. "I don't know what they mean or signify, but I can tell you, Eren and I are not a good match. He's a selfish bastard, although if I grew up there, maybe I would be too. I guess Mother thought Eren and I would take over the petty humans, right?"

Whatever those rings were, they must have held some sort of great power that could only be wielded by a Scorpio and a Pisces, although that made little sense to him. He'd never put much stock in people of different signs getting along well because it all sounded like nonsense. Besides, taking over would still be a pain since demons lost their magic over time on Earth. Perhaps they'd have to go in shifts unless the rings somehow prevented it.

"I didn't think an angel could be bad," Riley muttered. "Especially my own Mother…The angels seem so decent. They don't even torture souls on their way to hell. But what made Mother like that? Why would she want me to marry Eren and rule everything? The angels don't even keep pets. Did she simply want to be the Mother of a powerful King?"

Orpheus lifted his head to stare at the sky as it slowly grew brighter while his lips moved in silence. He licked his thumb and gently pressed it to baby Riley's forehead. After a faint popping sound, Riley's red strands vanished, and his complexion dimmed ever so slightly, although he still looked like a healthy baby.

"You'll be like a human now," Father whispered. "You'll experience so much here. I'd rather watch you grow up, but I have to do this. No one can know of you, and you'll always be safe as long as you learn to hide your age. I know that'll bring hardship, but it's better than being Lilith's tool. You don't need to own the world to find happiness in it."

In the distance to one side, Riley could make out faint shapes. A town. Everything looked different since he was high up, but he knew this area. It was where it all started and ended for him on Earth.

Orpheus flew out. The wooden house looked the same to Riley except for a board on the porch floor that needed to be replaced since the corner was warped. He expected Father to place baby Riley by the door, knock, and hurry away.

Instead, he stood in front of the door and knocked.

"Uhhh..." Riley waited to see if Orpheus would at least disguise himself with a glamor, but he merely tucked his wings close to his body.

There was no way.

"Who's there?" called Grevin.

"I saved you forty years ago when you nearly drowned in the river as a child," called the demon. "I'm sure you remember the name, Orpheus."

Grevin opened the door in his night clothes. For a moment, he stared at his visitor with shock etched on his face.

"Can I come in?" asked Orpheus.

Grevin's eyes flicked down to the baby. "Of course. I wouldn't be here today if it wasn't for you."

Riley gaped at his Uncle as he entered. "You lied to me. You said you found me on your doorstep one night, and I'd simply been left there."

He'd known about other *things* and never once said a word to Riley. He never mentioned nearly drowning as a child and being saved. He could have said a man pulled him out or something, but he'd kept that completely hidden.

“Do you want tea or something?” asked Grevin. “I just got the fire going, but I haven’t made anything yet.”

Orpheus’s lips twitched. “I don’t need tea or food, but thanks.”

“Erm, do you eat?”

“I can, but it’s rather useless.”

Grevin blinked and went to the table by the fire. “Have a seat. Er, you have a kid?”

“He’s my son. I didn’t steal him.” It was partly the truth. Orpheus sat and shifted Riley who stretched his arms and made a noise, seemingly content with himself. “I’ve come to check on you a few times. You haven't moved that far.”

Grevin’s eyes widened. “You have?”

“Yes. I just wanted to make sure you’re alright. I like your kind and find them rather interesting overall. I guess you don’t care to marry or have children.”

Grevin scratched his messy hair. “You probably think I’m wasting my life after you saved it, but I’ve never been the marrying sort. I wanted kids, but I never wanted anyone in that manner. To marry and have them with, I mean.”

“Do you like men?”

“No. I don’t care for either. I’ve had male and female friends and never wanted more. I’m content on my own, and I’ve enjoyed my life even without a wife.”

Orpheus nodded. “Then your life is not wasted. You don’t need to be bound to another to enjoy it.”

Grevin hesitated. “Why did you save me back then?”

Orpheus adjusted baby Riley’s blanket. “It would be a pity for a fresh, innocent soul to die so young. Since I saved yours, and you wanted children, would you take my son in and raise him? It’s not safe back at my home.”

Grevin’s mouth opened slightly as he looked at baby Riley who appeared quite normal even before the glamor. “You want me to take a demon child?”

“He’s a nephalem. Demon and angel. See his eyes? That’s a condition among humans, but in my world, blue and green mean half and half.”

“Ah. Where’s his Mother?”

“The labor was difficult,” Orpheus said shortly. “Magic can’t fix everything.”

"Oh. I'm sorry. But wouldn't he be safer back home with you? I'm just a human."

"Nobody will know he's here," said Orpheus. "He's under a spell, so when he grows older, he'll still appear human. Living here will drain out any magic, and he'll be normal except for his growth. It'll be slow, and people will likely think he's stunted or something. I can't do anything about that, but I think it's manageable."

Grevin slowly nodded. "So he can't do anything unnatural or strange?" He glanced at the baby as if he expected him to flick a finger and make the house explode.

"No. Being in the human world for too long makes my kind lose their magic. If he has an inherent ability, it won't emerge if he doesn't go through normal puberty. He won't think he's anything but human. Magic would take a bit too long to explain, and I must return soon, but I want you to raise him like any other child. My world is stuck in a war, and I want him to live like a little human boy. No wars, no fighting, just the things that you humans enjoy and treasure so much. Teach him some fighting so he can defend himself if need be, but let him have the peace he won't have in my world. I don't want him to know about his kind. Let him be as human as possible."

"All right. I can do that."

Orpheus kissed baby Riley's forehead before he stood, and his face tightened as he held out his son to the man who kept so much from Riley but gave him so much at the same time. Grevin took baby Riley, and Orpheus pulled a coin purse from his pocket.

"To help with his expenses." He placed it on the table. "The faces are of dead Kings, but I don't think the humans will mind."

Grevin shook his head. "A penny's weight matters more. I guess you live a long time if you have money like that."

Orpheus paused. "You could say that. I've seen far more Kings than most demons. After a while, Riley will need to eat and drink as humans do."

"I'll get a goat for the milk."

"Thank you for this."

"Thanks for pulling me from the river."

"Some of my kind think humans are worthless, but it's ones like you that prove them all wrong."

Riley followed Father into the yard. Orpheus glanced up at the brightening sky as his face threatened to crumple again. Without a backward glance, he spread his dark wings and took off. Riley watched him fly low over the trees and vanish in the distance before he turned to the house. Grevin stood at the doorway with baby Riley.

"I guess it's you and me now, little guy."

Riley's throat tightened as the sight started to blur. Grevin had done what Orpheus asked. Despite his difficulty in making friends and thinking he was a dwarf for a while, Grevin's lie to explain his growth, Riley had felt loved by his Uncle. He'd thought he was a human, played, and enjoyed many of the things humans did just like Orpheus wanted.

Until that day with the cart.

Chapter Eleven

Riley woke up on the bed to find tears on his face, and he realized this was the same bed that Mother had died on. Orpheus must have returned and dealt with her body, but Riley didn't want to look for it. It was probably buried outside somewhere, but it didn't matter anymore.

He started to sob, and Giasone got up from the floor. "Riley, it's fine. I'm here."

"No, it's not!"

"Look at me."

"No! It's my fault!"

Giasone touched his face. "Whatever you saw, it's the past. It's done. It's not your fault. Was it another war, or-"

"No," whispered Riley. "Lilith was here. She was my Mother."

"What?"

If Riley hadn't been conceived, Nyla would have her Mother. Orpheus wouldn't have had to kill her, right? Nyla would hate her half-brother.

"Riley?" Giasone pulled on his arm to make him sit up and gave a nervous laugh. "Lilith can't be your Mother."

Riley wiped his face. "She was. She hid the pregnancy with a glamor because I guess she only needed something to hide her stomach, and she must have faked being fine so nobody would suspect. Fuck! Nyla's going to hate me. I wasn't supposed to be born!"

"Hey!" Giasone took his shoulders. "Calm down. Nyla isn't going to hate you. She's not like that. Tell me what happened."

Riley told him everything he saw. Both were quiet for a long moment afterward. It had felt rather good to unload it all, although the shock lingered.

"I don't think Nyla is expecting all that, but she'll be glad to know," said Giasone. "Not knowing what happened to someone you loved is harder. This way, she can find closure and make peace with the facts. It's not your fault, Riley. You didn't ask to be conceived. It just happened, and all the events before and after were out of your control."

"I guess Father's name doesn't ring a bell? He wasn't some famed demon feared on the battlefield or anything?"

Giasone shook his head. "No. Not that I know of. I'm sorry. He might be dead now too."

"What are these Pisces Rings?"

Giasone rolled his eyes. "What a pack of lies."

"You know about them?"

Giasone drew his feet up on the bed and wrapped his arms around his knees. "They might have been real at one point. They're mentioned in a few works. When the demons and angels were first on Earth, they didn't have to worry about losing their magic. Both sides took human women as wives and had children with them, although angels did that more. After quite some time, it was noticed that some started losing their magic."

"So what happened?"

"That part is a bit vague," said Giasone. "To be honest, I'm not sure how this world was created except that our Fathers did it. A couple of books speak as though one should have already read something else, but that work must be long lost. It says the Fathers knew they needed a new home, and with Noah building the ark, they had to go soon because God wanted to erase most of creation and start over."

"So some of you are nephilim," Riley said suddenly, trying to remember what he'd read in the Bible, although it had been a while. "Human and angel."

Giasone flushed. "We're angels."

"Why the look?"

"Any human blood among our side was bred out after a time," said Giasone. "We're just angels."

"Oh, that makes sense. Is nephilim an insult? Or was it?"

"Well…sort of. It's like being called a polluter or filth. We were hated by God for creating new races. Demons and angels mixing wasn't so bad, but if we had bred humans away, that meant Jesus never would have been born. He had to come from a human woman. I don't think the first *wanted* to breed away humans. They just wanted the women because they were beautiful. Demons later mated with them too because no females had fallen. God only created male angels. Women from both sides came later. But any human blood on the demon's side is bred out too by now."

"So they just wanted to fuck?"

"Yeah, and have kids. We regretted falling, and that's why we're different from demons, who didn't give a fuck but still didn't want to join Lucifer. We wanted to go back, the demons didn't, and then Lucifer had his own demons who were happy to follow him."

"Oh."

"Anyway, I don't know where the rings came from, but a demon and an angel supposedly mated and figured out how to halt the loss of magic. I don't get that part, and the book doesn't explain it. Somehow, this realm was created afterward, and most of our ancestors flocked here. Humans were brought to rule over, and we tried to live in peace. Of course, you see how well that worked out.

"Not well." Riley, propped up on his elbow, shifted on his side a bit. "You said most came here?"

"I think some wanted to stay on Earth. Maybe they thought God would spare them, but He didn't. He only wanted humans on Earth. It needed to happen so Jesus could be later born to a human woman."

"And God didn't mind you all living here even though you technically have access to Earth? You can create halflings if you want."

"I think the part with us losing our magic is the price paid. Halflings of the human variety don't have any magic now, remember? You're a *nephalem*, so that's different. If you were part human, the most you could hope for is a few basic things like turning on a light or some pretty tricks. Human blood now dilutes demon or angel blood. It's very rare for humans to have abilities of any sort, and those that do like seeing the future most likely aren't halflings. And no, I don't know why some humans have abilities like that."

"So you don't know anything else about the rings?"

"No. I guess they make it so others don't lose their magic or something like that. I thought maybe they were destroyed or lost, but if Lilith was offering their location as a way to get Athena to agree to her deal..." He trailed off. "I have no idea where they'd be or how she would know."

“Maybe she found a secret book or...” Riley was at a loss for ways as to how she obtained some information.

“I don’t see how,” said Giasone. "Why wouldn't anyone else know?"

“Maybe she was lying.”

“I wouldn’t lie to a demon Queen about something like that, but that sounds likely. Maybe if she got Athena to agree, and they betrothed their sons, and then it turned out Lilith was lying…” Giasone shook his head.

“She was desperate.” Riley flopped on his back. “Dear God, she must have imagined me and Eren ruling over Earth. Every human would be a pet.”

Giasone made a face. “That’s stupid too because angels don’t do that.”

“But demons do.”

“The angels wouldn’t have agreed. What if that started a war right there?”

Riley could imagine the angels revolting and breaking the new peace over such a thing. “She wanted to change things, but the overall outcome would’ve been the same. No peace. I guess I would have been happy to be with Eren because this is all I would have known. We both would have been a pair of sadistic bastards happily shedding angel blood.”

“Erebus,” Giasone said with a cold note in his voice.

Riley felt a pinch of shame. “It’s just a habit.”

“A habit that you could break.”

“Erebus.”

Giasone’s smile seemed slightly stiff. “Anyway, you wouldn’t be sadistic.”

“Growing up with him, I would.”

“Lilith would have raised you,” said Giasone. “Maybe she wanted to be the Mother of a King, but she wouldn’t have allowed you to be cruel. She was a good Queen.”

“My Father didn’t seem to think so.”

“He was probably only looking at it from his point of view since he was a demon.”

Riley closed his eyes. When Lucia had been performing on the blood moon, she’d created two gold rings that overlapped in the center. Eren had said it was the symbol of Pisces which was

Riley's birth sign. Apparently, that was important for the rings, and he needed to be bonded with a Scorpio like Eren.

"Why would our signs be important?" he asked.

"Some are supposed to get along better than others. It's not a guarantee."

None of that made much sense to him, and it didn't matter. The secret of the Rings died with Lilith. Whatever she knew was lost again, and Riley certainly wasn't going to be with that damn bastard.

Who wanted a husband that betrayed them for magic? He'd rather be with James any day of the week.

Riley rolled over. "I want to sleep."

"You've spent a lot of time sleeping."

"I know, but this was a lot to think about. My parents-I want to blank it all out for a bit. Then we can go back, all right? Besides, aren't you tired by now?"

"Yeah."

Riley shifted over. "The bed's big enough to share. Just don't kick me."

"Pfft. If you snore like that again, I'll smother you."

"I don't snore!"

"Yeah, you do. Every wraith probably heard you."

Riley took a decent dose of rewek and was out pretty fast. He'd said he'd simply sleep, but he ended up lucid dreaming. In the woods, he thought again about sleeping naturally. Or he could call Father, but Orpheus had said to never do that again. If he appeared, he had to be alive, right? But maybe he'd be furious at Riley being on the angel's side now.

He summoned dream Eren. Why not fuck and feed? He could think about other shit later and enjoy something for a bit.

As dream Eren kissed him, Riley wished more than ever he could have the old version. If only it hadn't been fake.

He'd eaten the pearl when he awoke to Giasone hugging him from behind. Riley's cock was as stiff as a board, but luckily, he hadn't cum in his sleep. Something hard was pressing against the crack of his ass, and he realized the angel had something in mind.

"What are you doing?" he asked.

"You taste delicious," Giasone murmured. "You must have been having quite the filthy dream."

"Uhhh. Yeah. I can feed like that, so why not?"

"Who did you picture?"

"Just some guy that I fucked once years ago."

Giasone touched his hip. "I'm sure it's great in a dream, but the real thing is much better."

"It seems the same to me."

"You haven't done it with anyone real since you changed, have you?"

"No."

"In real life, I wouldn't go away afterward," said Giasone. "I brought oil because I was hoping we could do something."

"Out in the Wraithlands?"

Fuck. He liked Giasone, but he didn't want to get into something with someone else.

"I figured we'd stop to rest at some point. We can feed anywhere. We've been living together for a while, and..."

Riley squeezed his eyes shut. "I'm sorry, but I'm not looking to get into a new relationship, okay? It's not you."

"I understand that, but we could still fuck. Two men getting release isn't wrong. Angels fuck all the time, and it doesn't mean they have to bond and go live happily ever after. I'm sure your dreams are realistic and nice, but I don't see how it could be better than the real thing."

Giasone's energy tasted pretty good, not like Eren's, but he'd enjoy it. He was hard, so why waste it and get achy balls?

"We could..."

Giasone's hand immediately moved to grasp him through his trousers. "Turn over."

He got on top to kiss Riley who responded and tried to ignore the guilt in his stomach. He could do this. Maybe a new dick in his ass would help him forget the old one. Or he could fuck Giasone. He hadn't topped anyone in ages, and without kinky stuff, he enjoyed doing that once in a while.

Giasone started fumbling with his belt. The regret churned worse as it loosened. All he could think about was Eren on top of him, hands groping, the tail stroking him. The insane rush of being pinned and fucked while those two different-colored eyes gave him that predatory look he loved so much. The glint of fangs while Eren ordered him to take it. The way Eren had sometimes rubbed small circles on his back when they cuddled afterward in the dark bedroom.

The hand grasping his cock was wrong. The other sliding up his shirt was wrong too, and the look he was getting would never match. The guilt coiled hard and tight, and he knew he couldn't do it.

"Get off me." Riley pushed Giasone's hand away. "I can't."

Giasone froze for a split second before he got off. "What the fuck is your problem?"

"What's with the attitude?"

Giasone stood at the side of the bed with his erection clearly visible through his trousers in the blue light from the twig. "Attitude? I'm thinking I'm about to get laid, and you can't fucking bear to do it?"

"It's not you! I just-even for an orgasm, I can't do it! For fuck's sake." Riley started trying to stuff himself back in his trousers.

"Why not?"

"What the fuck do you mean? Shit still hurts, okay? Excuse me for needing more time to get over it."

"To get over him?!"

"It's not just him!" shouted Riley, scrambling to think of something else. "What the fuck is wrong is with you? Do you think he's the only one I ever had real feelings for?"

"It's because I'm not Erebus, isn't it?"

"Did it ever occur to you that maybe I thought of my husband? You know? My dead husband that I only got to spend a year with after we married. If I think about him sometimes-I...I try not to remember, but it still fucking hurts."

Giasone pressed his lips together. "Okay. I could see that, but I think you're lying."

"I think you can go fuck yourself."

Damn Eren always invaded Riley's thoughts and turned everything all wrong. It was that fucking, sadistic son of a bitch Eren who had such a hold on him even after all this time to the point where Riley only wanted to fuck him in his lucid dreams.

Giasone pointed at him. "I would believe it, but you were making energy that day you got Erebus into your dreams. Torture can make it, but it tasted too sweet. Nyla and I knew you must have been doing something with him. Something you shouldn't have been doing with the man you supposedly hate!"

Riley's mouth dropped. They had known he'd been able to make energy in his sleep even before he really realized it, and they hadn't said shit about it. He hadn't even thought about them being able to taste it while he was asleep. Nyla had only mentioned him getting an erection.

"You think-are you insane?"

"If you hate him, why would you-"

"I kissed him a little to get him to put his guard down," said Riley. "I didn't feel like fighting with him even in a dream."

"You could have just made a room form around him. Do you think I'm stupid? You control it all in a lucid dream. He was completely at your mercy. You were doing stuff in there that you didn't need to, and you were enjoying it. I bet when you fuck in your lucid dreams, you probably conjure him up. Hell, maybe you actually drag the real Erebus in, and you two fuck."

"I don't!"

"You're so resistant to fucking anyone."

"Did you want to fuck right after your last guy cheated on you?"

Giasone leaned over and put his hands on the edge of the bed. "I was a miserable sack of shit for a week. By week two, I started to feel better. I went out and got laid the third week, and it helped me to get over that loser. It's been a lot longer for you, Riley. You're a liar."

"Screw you!"

"How do I know if you're not? Maybe you're telling *Eren* things about us."

"You better take that back."

Giasone jerked back as Riley moved as if to punch him. "Don't even try it. I might be a healer, but I can also beat your ass ten ways to Sunday."

"I'll zap your ass if you do."

"Yeah, with the energy you get from fucking Erebus."

"I fuck James in my dreams, okay?" The lie slid out before he could stop it. He shouldn't be lying to his friend, but he had to fix this so they didn't go back home while stewing in hate. Or worse, Giasone would tell Nyla he was a traitor. "I miss him. It's fake, but I barely got any time with him-"

"If it wasn't for the energy that day you went after Erebus, I'd likely believe you." Giasone snatched the twig and went for the orbs as he snapped his fingers. "You're a liar, Riley, and it's a pity because I thought you might be really something. Maybe this was all a plan concocted by you both to get a spy in here."

"How fucking dare you!"

Giasone had both orbs on, and he blew out the twig before tucking it in his pocket. He marched toward their packs and grabbed his. Riley realized what he intended, and he jumped off of the bed.

"Don't you fucking dare!"

Giasone had his pack shouldered, and his dagger flashed. Riley didn't move fast enough, and he felt the tip slice through the flesh in his side.

"Fuck!"

Green energy flashed from Riley's hand. Giasone put up his shield, and it absorbed it without effort.

"Not strong enough." Giasone started backing toward the door as the Tree of Life glinted in the light of the orbs. "I know you don't have anything to get through my shields."

He was right. Riley wouldn't last long in a real battle.

"Please, Giasone. I'm not a spy."

"I think you are, and that's what I'll tell Nyla. She's suspicious of you too. I'd kill you myself, but I think death by wraiths is more fitting for a spy."

"Giasone! I swear I'm not! Don't leave me here!"

The angel slammed the door and plunged Riley into darkness as his side throbbed.

Chapter Twelve

Riley tried not to panic as the darkness seemed to press on him. He almost expected a wraith to kick open the door right then and lunge for him. Gingerly, he reached under his shirt to feel the cut, and he sucked in a breath as he tried to probe it.

It wasn't deep enough to have cut his organs or anything important, and he'd probably make it on his own. It'd take a little more than that to kill him. He took a deep breath and reminded himself that his body was sturdier now.

Still, he needed to wrap it. Wincing, he managed to get off his coat and shirt. Using the sleeves of the coat which were thicker and denser than his shirt, he knotted the ends together and tied his makeshift bandage around his waist. It wasn't a very good one, but it would have to do.

"Fuck!" he shouted as he tightened the knot which sent a shock of pain through the wound. It probably would've been far more painful if he was a human, but it was enough to make him want to punch someone. Preferably, Giasone.

He was going to beat that bastard to a pulp. Magic or not. He'd do it the old-fashioned way with his fists and make that fucker wish he'd never left Riley behind.

Except he would never get out of the Wraithlands alive. With no light, the wraiths would be upon him before he got halfway back to the barrier. If he tried to fly, lightning would knock him out of the sky. Then wraiths would be upon him. Or they might get him in the sky. Nyla had mentioned they could fly, although they seemed to prefer being on the ground for the most part.

After he put on his shirt, he suddenly remembered something and reached into his pocket. What if it fell out? What if it was too small?

He licked the splinter, and a tiny blue flame blossomed on the end, although it was hardly enough to do anything by. Still, it was a light, and his heart stopped pounding so hard.

It picked right back up as something scratched on the door outside.

"I have light! Fuck off, you disgusting bastards! Go waft off and fall in a ditch!"

The wraith scratched again.

Maybe it wasn't strong enough to keep them away from the house. Riley had to get close to the foot of the bed to properly see where he'd dumped his pack. He could just make out his own blood on the floor too, and it looked black in the barely-there light.

He shouldered his pack and thought about his sword. Fire was needed to kill wraiths, but he still buckled it on, fumbling with the belt one-handed. He had to lie on the bed to do it. Keeping the tiny bit of wood pinched between his fingers, he stood, grabbed his pack, and squared his shoulders.

He just had to get past the barrier, and he was free of this place.

His wound burned as he opened the door and marched out. Three wraiths hissed at him as they noticed the light.

"Not so tough, now, huh?" He shouldered his pack. "A little light gets you all scared. Bitches. Go fall in a ditch."

He started walking. Even if he had a hundred light orbs, he'd still hate the sight of those things. He heard a noise behind him and noticed the three wraiths hadn't left to go fall into a ditch as requested. They were following him.

"Fuck off or I'll put down my trousers and blind you with my arse."

He started walking again. It was misty, and he couldn't see very far ahead. It also wasn't very light out, but if he kept going straight, he'd reach the barrier.

Out of the mist, another wraith came, and it lunged. Riley shouted and jerked the light at it. It pulled back and swiped at its face as if the light had hurt it, and Riley started running.

"Shit, shit, shit."

Maybe the light was too small to properly protect him. It probably made them leery but with four after him...He glanced behind him and realized all four were following about six feet away.

Riley turned and started walking backward as held out the splinter. "Go. Fuck. Yourselves."

One wraith made as if to lunge which made Riley jump again, but the bastard didn't attack. They were fucking with him. The rotten bastards were toying with him, and that showed they had some brains beyond killing.

One let out a sound like a raspy laugh. Riley shivered, and his wound ached. If he pulled his sword and used it, it wouldn't kill them. Nyla said it was like cutting smoke except with these guys, they reformed. A sword with magic fire could work, but that was too advanced for him.

He shot green energy at one, but it went through it. The wraith hissed as a hole formed in its midsection and started to refill. Two others lunged at him.

Riley screamed as he took off running to the side to avoid them. His side burned as his feet pounded on the ground and his pack bounced. Nobody ever said he needed a certain amount of light! Giasone hadn't "forgotten" the bit he had, and if he did, it didn't fucking matter because these things would get him anyway.

The blue fire flickered as the wraiths all let out their strange laughs and followed. Riley tried to think of what was in his arsenal of magic. It wasn't set yet, but he could make a shitty shield. It would only block physical attacks. Wraiths would probably blow right through it and laugh while they did so.

He had nothing useful.

Riley was sure he had managed to go for about a mile, but the wraiths followed like a hunter hoping to wear out his prey. Something swiped at his shoulders, and he almost tripped. He was sure it had just taken a pinch of his energy. Another wraith came from the mist to his side, and he swerved to avoid it.

One from behind shoved him down. Riley almost dropped the twig, and he frantically thrust it out at the nearest one. The light made it hiss, but another grabbed his head.

"FUCK!" he screamed.

Just the touch was draining his strength from him. One snatched his leg, and his arm trembled from the effort as he tried to swipe at the one holding his head. It let out a rattling breath.

He was going to die out here just like Giasone wanted. Drained of energy, strength, and life. His cut throbbed and felt wet under the cloth covering it. He tried to kick at the one holding onto his leg, but another took its chances with the light to jump on his chest. He shoved the burning splinter into the black gap it had for a face.

The wraith screamed but stayed on him. Riley would take one out with him if he could. He caught a glimpse of its terrifying face. Taunt, grey skin, blank, grey eyes, and a face like a skeleton. No flesh padded its bones, and its black teeth were bared at him. His arm was grabbed and yanked. The splinter fell away from his weak grasp, and the light went out. All he could see was mist and smokey cloaks as the wraiths pinned him to the ground. His pack dug into his back as his struggles weakened.

This was it. He was dying. At least no one would miss him.

A wraith screamed as something silver and fiery swung. Its cloaked head flew. Black wings flashed in the faint light as the scythe swung again.

Riley was suddenly released in a flurry of hisses, swirling cloaks, and silver glints. The sensation of his strength being sucked away stopped, but he lay stunned for a moment, still weakened. Eren stood over him with his scythe ready as eight wraiths faced off with him.

"Who's next?" he snarled. "I'll cut off your fucking head, and we'll see if you can fix that."

The wraiths eyed him, clearly judging him to be more of a threat. The fire on the scythe probably scared them too.

Eren nudged Riley's arm with his boot. "This would be a really good time to get the hell up."

"I'm working on it." He managed to get to his knees and tried to feel for the splinter in the dark.

"Riley! Up!"

"I need the splinter!"

"Fuck your splinter!"

Eren grabbed Riley by the back of his neck and dragged him up. The wraiths all lunged at that moment. One came from the mist and jumped on Eren's back. His scythe cut one, but the bastard on his back made him stumble.

Without thinking, Riley grabbed it. Bony fingers immediately wrapped around his throat as it decided he was an easier target. Another screamed as it must have been hit by the scythe.

The one trying to choke Riley was ripped off and cut in half.

Eren grabbed Riley's arm and pulled him into a run. "I don't have enough left for many swings, so you better run fast."

Riley chanced a glance. The light was growing so poor, even his eyes were having difficulty, but he was pretty sure the number of wraiths had increased to about twenty. They gave chase as Eren pulled Riley along. Weren't they scared of the flame? Didn't they realize that Eren could kill them?

"Eren!" he shouted as one came from his left.

Eren snarled and swung as its bony fingers came within inches of Riley. As soon as the head came off, the fire disappeared from the blade.

"Fuck." Eren pushed Riley in the back. "Just keep going."

Wraiths hissed behind him. Riley ran as fast as his weakened legs would allow. A huge flash of light came from behind him, and he glanced to see Eren face them all as a pentagram shot lightning from its five points and blasted holes through the wraiths. One was so twisted, Riley could barely tell where its head was.

They started merging back together. Eren swung at one to cut it, but that only slowed it. The pentagram flashed again, but the light it emitted didn't seem to be scaring them enough.

Riley slowed. "Eren, come on!"

Eren cleaved another in half. The dark mass had grown even bigger, and it writhed as lightning flashed through them. Screams rang out, but the injured wraiths started attempting to heal. Eren made a shoving motion at the pentagram. It moved into the group as he turned to run. A second later, lightning shot out again.

Riley reached for Eren's arm to pull him along, but the mass was already trying to approach.

"There!" Eren pointed at something, although Riley couldn't see. The demon lord's night vision must have been much better, but after a few seconds, he made out a shape. It turned out to be a huge house, and Eren threw open the thankfully unlocked door. He shoved Riley into the gaping black space and slammed the door closed.

Riley scrambled backward on his ass as Eren started drawing a shape in the air. His fingers left purple, glowing streaks, and the lines started to solidify into a glowing Flower of Life. It started to spin as he pressed his palms against the center.

The door handle rattled. The Flower spun so fast, the lines couldn't be told apart anymore. A strip of grey light appeared as the door cracked open, and Riley hastily stood as he dropped his pack, ready to run again. He had no idea where to go in here, but he'd drag Eren with him.

The purple blur slammed into it and made it close. A wraith screamed. For a moment, the glow lit up the walls so brightly, Riley could see everything, but it faded.

Eren breathed heavily as the wraiths scratched at the door and rattled the handle. “They’re getting smarter. One attacked me and knocked me right down. My damn light orb broke. I could recharge it if I had one. Fucking bastards.” His weapon disappeared in a faint whirl of silver. “It probably wanted my case.”

He turned, and for a moment, Riley was utterly enthralled with the sight of his glowing eyes even though he’d nearly been made into wraith food.

Then he remembered that the last time they met, Riley had done something absolutely awful to him. Eren probably despised him, and saving him didn’t mean shit. He turned to run even though he couldn’t make out much. Eren’s boots pounded behind him, and a second later, his weight tackled Riley’s back. Eren’s arms locked around his chest and pulled him back.

“Stop running around like an idiot! This house is locked up tighter than a King’s treasury for the next twelve hours, and you're not going anywhere.”

“Fuck off!”

Eren wrestled Riley back and to the floor. The bastard was still stronger than him.

"Get off!"

“Stop!” snarled Eren. “I can smell the blood, and I know you're wounded. You’ll aggravate it.”

“Then let go of me!”

Eren’s eyes came quite close. “Then stop moving, and let me heal it.”

“You hate me.”

“I just saved you. I found *and* saved you. I keep my promises, but I doubt you kept yours.”

“I didn’t promise you anything.”

“Yes, you did. Now hold still so I can heal it instead of having you bleed all over the place.” He must have been able to see the blood on Riley’s shirt, and he lifted it. “What is that?”

“My coat. I used the sleeves.” Riley sucked in a breath as Eren started undoing the knot. It seemed like he was trying to be gentle, but the fabric rubbed on the cut. All of the running and being knocked down by wraiths certainly hadn’t helped it either.

"How come I can't see as well as you?"

"Because you need more time. Night vision usually takes longer. I was born with mine." Eren finally removed the makeshift bandage. "That's not pretty."

With Riley's eyes further adjusting to the darkness, he could make out the faint shape of the demon lord. Eren must have cut his forearm because after a few rustles, something wet hit him, and the pain started to fade as the cut was sealed.

"Done," said Eren. "Drink."

Riley didn't have time to think or complain. Eren's forearm was pressed to his lips, and he tasted the sweetness. Instinctively, he tried to jerk his head away at the thought of swallowing someone's blood even though he'd done it before.

Eren didn't let him. "Wraiths touched you so just do it."

Riley felt a bit better afterward, although it didn't replenish his magic. Eren wiped up his torso the best he could with the coat and lowered his shirt.

"Are you going to tell me how you were wounded? That's not how wraiths work."

"No, and thanks." Riley sat up. The last thing Eren needed to know was how Giasone thought he was a damn traitor. Scratching continued on the door. "Are you sure those things can't get in?"

"The lock spell I did will keep everything out for twelve hours." Eren paused. "You came here with someone, so why did they attack you?"

"And just how would you know if someone came with me?"

"Are you stupid enough to go on an excursion in the Wraithlands by yourself?"

"No!"

"Then you came in with someone, and since you're cut, something happened. They attacked, left you, and you were out wandering alone. I saw your blood in the house and smelled it. You're lucky I was so close. I was attacked as soon as I left the house, but I killed that sneaky bastard. I heard you scream and followed. So what happened?"

"The details don't matter."

"Suit yourself."

Eren stood, and Riley remained on the floor to think about his options. There weren't many, so it didn't take long. They could leave once the lock spell wore off. Or maybe Eren could undo it earlier. Either way, Riley would be a sitting duck on his own. He could try to fly for as long as possible, although he'd be struck by lightning before he got far. Wraiths would kill him, and that was a bad way to go.

Or he could stick with Eren who might have some trick up his sleeve to get them out of here and away from the monsters outside. That meant he'd take Riley back, and whatever happened then wouldn't be good.

A greyish square behind him must have been a window, and Eren's dark form stood by it. "There must be forty out there. Fuck. There are a couple that are too fast."

"Huh?"

"Two are floating around, but they're fast. Wraiths shouldn't be that fast."

The ones that had chased Riley had been able to float at roughly the pace he could run. "They're also supposed to be scared of light. I had a splinter from the Tree of Life."

Eren snorted. "You need a bigger light. Something so small might not seem risky enough to them. I wouldn't call them brainy, but anything living is tasty to drain. You were like a walking dinner plate."

"No ever mentioned needing a bigger light."

"Because most people don't walk around with splinters."

"Do you have a light?"

"No, not a spell for one. I can make a shield that emits a little and recharge a light orb, but such things are useless against them. If one attacked me when I had a light orb, then that means they must have gotten smarter. Even if we both had one right now, I think they'd risk it if we stepped out."

"Why?"

Eren's hesitation was barely perceptible. "I don't know."

Riley narrowed his eyes at the demon's shape. "So why were you wandering about the Wraithlands? Did you get bored with killing angels and decide you needed a little vacation?"

"I have my own reasons."

How would he know that Riley was here? He must have. "Nice idea to have a spy on our side."

Eren chuckled. "I wish."

"Like you'd tell me anyway." Riley rolled his eyes.

Eren's boots clomped closer. "I give you my word. I don't have a spy on the angel's side."

"Your word means shit."

The boots stopped about a foot behind Riley who thought of his sword. Eren, with years of fighting under his belt, could turn him into a pile of meat with his scythe in about three seconds. Damn it.

"When I've made a promise to you, I meant it. I can't protect you from every single thing especially since you ran off, but I have found you and saved you twice now before certain death. Just like I promised when we were children."

"And then, you turn around and do things to hurt me. You're a fucking, selfish prick who used me for betrayal magic and dumped me when you were done. Anyone could have bought me."

"I knew Nez would buy you and where his shift would be that day. I didn't mean that when I said I'd come back only to fuck you."

"You also want my ability."

"I barely need it unless you can also sleep and snap your fingers to make the angels croak. I'd rather kill them all with my bare hands. I wanted you to go to someone who would treat you nicely, and I had his watch changed to the jail. I told him to buy you."

"Wait-what? No, you didn't!"

"Nez doesn't wish to have sex, and I didn't want you in the hands of some cruel bastard even for a second. I'll take you back now."

Riley slowly turned his head. "You expect me to be your fancy pet again?"

"I would have taken you back after a bit anyway. Nez knew this and was commanded to say nothing. You've changed now, so that-"

Riley could hardly believe his ears. The bastard thought he could take him back and pretend like nothing happened?

"Did you suspect I was a nephalem? Why go through with selling me *after* you had the pearl?"

Eren was silent for a moment. "The fact that you can lucid dream made me suspicious."

"So I did pull you in before?" asked Riley.

"Yes."

Just like Riley thought. "Guess what? You can go fuck yourself up the arse with a splintery wooden pole. I'm not your fancy pet to use for an ability. That makes you even worse because you'd only take me back when I'm more useful."

"It's not just that." Eren hesitated. "I *need* you, Riley."

"You need a hole in the head. You're fucked up to get me so wrapped around your finger and pull that shit. You think you can just toy with people's feelings, sell them, take them back, and keep using them? Do you really think I'd ever trust you again like I did before? What in God's name is wrong with you? Are you fucking mad?" Riley stood to face him. "You're a sick, twisted, demon who only cares for himself and what he can get. You need to fall in a fucking hole and die."

Eren's eyes didn't blink for several seconds. "I care about my people and those children you saw."

"I think that's secondary, otherwise you wouldn't be trying to manipulate me again. That's all you do. The act you pulled when you had a migraine for one. Those might be fake-"

Eren drew closer. "My migraines are not an act, and don't pretend you fucking know me inside and out. You don't know shit about my life or what I've been through! I didn't want to leave you when we were children, and while you were on Earth and living in peace, I was learning how to kill and knowing that someone might gut me one day on the field. I've known since I was a child that I might not even live to middle age. I could lose *everything* if I lose this war, including you, my home, my life, and everything my line has worked to protect."

"You betrayed me!"

"I couldn't rape you, but I still needed magic, nephalem or not. That's why I pretended not to know you, and why I lied about not remembering us. I didn't even want to do that, but I must win this war. If the Nevyyn failed…"

"So just what special spell did you do with the pearl you got from me?" snarled Riley.

"Betrayal fuels everything. My strikes were stronger. I was faster. My shields were stronger, and the blast radius from the Nevyyn should have hurt me since I got too close, but it didn't. I didn't even feel the transference of the agony of the angels and prisoners in it. It's powerful."

"With a price," said Riley. "You won't make friends if you keep doing that."

"It seemed worth it to get past the Point. If you were born into this, you'd do whatever you can to win and end it. I don't want children because I don't want to bring something into this world. I'd rather my line end if I can't win instead of putting this weight on another who might also fail. We're all just fodder at this point, and I need to win so new generations can know what it's like to live in peace."

"You had a chance to end it." Riley folded his arms. "You refused and said you'd rather see us all dead at your feet."

Eren rolled his eyes. "Even if I did like women, I'd never let an angel snake into my bed. She'd stab me in the back the first chance she got. Angels are worse than demons any day of the week."

Of course. It was us versus *them*, and *them* was always worse. Riley had learned enough about general history to know that. "At least we don't keep humans as pets."

Eren made a scoffing noise. "There are worse things than having a man on a leash."

"Worse than pets who get repeatedly raped?"

"You know so little of this world."

"Like what?"

Eren drew closer and hovered his lips over Riley's cheek. He could feel the little puffs of air on his face. "I would say what, but the trouble is that my only bright spot wouldn't even believe me now. You'd say I'm a liar."

Riley remained wooden and unyielding as the demon's lips brushed his cheek. Lemon and sunshine filled his every breath. To his shame, his cock twitched in interest at the proximity. Too soon, the feathery touch was gone, and Eren's eyes vanished as he turned away. His boots clomped on the floor, and a door slammed.

A second later, he heard a thump, and Eren swore like he'd tripped on something.

Riley stood there as a wraith scratched on the door in a fruitless attempt to get in. He knew this war had to be brutal for everyone because they knew nothing else. Of course, Eren would want to end it, but Riley wouldn't do what he'd done.

Then again, would he go to great lengths if he'd been raised here? Beyond keeping his secret of loving an angel, Orpheus also didn't want Riley to be used and grow up here.

He had a demon within twenty feet of him. A demon that he could ask about the rings. His kind had lost a lot of works too, but they might know something different. Riley wasn't sure if he should mention his parents or the fact that Lilith had been considering betrothing her son to Eren before he was even born.

Another thing that bothered him was that Eren had mentioned that Riley didn't know what he'd been through. He still had no idea why Eren had been in the woods or why he had disappeared.

Or why small spaces were his worst fear.

He made a frustrated noise, not wanting to go pester Eren. If the demon lord had gone to pout by himself, he might lash out in anger, and they'd simply have another argument.

Also, his cock needed to calm down. Damn that bastard for having such a hold on him to where he couldn't fuck others for fun and energy.

He started walking with his arms out, and his foot hit his pack, so he shouldered it. What little he could make out was pretty much useless. After going left and feeling about, he found a railing, and his boot hit something. Stairs. The last thing he needed was to fall down and hurt himself, so he made his way up while holding onto the railing which he could barely make out.

In the hallway, he couldn't even discern shapes. It was darker than a tomb up here. Along the wall, he found a door and opened it. It was empty when he walked around it, using the faint square of grey from the window to keep his bearings.

When he peered through the grimy glass, he was sure he could see movement from the wraiths. Damn things. Riley sighed and slumped against the wall.

Chapter Thirteen

Eren sat in the dark room for a couple of hours, knowing that if he got him and Riley out, he'd have to take his beloved pet to Grandfather. The knowledge burned like utter fire.

Grandfather had known of Riley's existence, although how was a mystery. Somehow, he'd even known where Riley was. Eren figured it was the same wraith, Bellim, who had pretended to be Mother had something to do with that, although he couldn't quite figure out how.

Refusal to bring Riley to the realm wouldn't have gone well for Eren. He'd had someone set the spell near where he lived to lure him. How he wished he could have told Grandfather to go fuck himself, but he'd never had a choice in this. Even if he killed himself to cut off Grandfather's power for a bit, he'd use Eren's heir. How could he doom a child to such a fate even if he'd never meet it?

He thumped his head against the wall in anger. Once Grandfather was done using Riley's power to defeat all opposition, Eren could have him back, but his pet would probably be broken by that point. The only thing Eren loved would be a shell.

He'd heard creaks and knew Riley was upstairs somewhere. It'd be kinder to kill him and end it, but Eren didn't see how he was supposed to bring his scythe down on him. It was unthinkable. There was nowhere they could go. Nowhere to escape. Just a burden that would be passed down if Eren didn't win this war and do what Grandfather ordered.

Even if Riley died, Grandfather would soon get what he wanted. It would just take longer.

A couple of hours passed, and he figured he'd go try to talk to Riley. Maybe if he groveled for forgiveness, Riley would give it in part, but the idea turned his stomach. Demon lords didn't grovel. What he really wanted to do was lay Riley down and make him gasp with pleasure.

The pain came without warning. The stabbing was just as bad as if he was in the tomb. He bit his tongue hard enough to taste blood and still couldn't stop himself from screaming. He couldn't do this now. What if the walls closed in on him? He'd never get out.

"RILEY!"

Eren dug his fingers into the floor, wishing for a way out. He was always trapped. His Father had signed him over for this. His own son. Hands grabbed him, and he screamed again, thinking the wraiths were going to drain him. They'd go after Riley next, and Eren couldn't save him.

"It's just me!"

Riley's arms encased him as a particularly savage burst of pain made Eren arch his back. As swiftly as it came, it was all gone, and he went limp in the halfling's embrace. Riley said nothing for several moments as Eren heavily breathed against his chest, afraid it would come again. Grandfather never did such a short feeding.

"Does your head hurt?"

"Dream," Eren managed to get out. Riley had him, but he couldn't protect him. Not really. Still, he fisted the halfling's shirt, desperate for the solid warmth to keep him grounded.

"You sounded like you were in pain," Riley said in a low voice.

"I thought I was in a box." The lie easily slid out. It must have been a warning, although Eren wasn't sure why.

Riley paused, and he probably didn't believe it, but he didn't push it. "Sit up. You're not in a box, okay? You're in a room, and there's plenty of space."

Eren sat up, but he snaked his arms around him, needing the touch. Riley stiffened a little even though he didn't pull away. The action still hurt Eren. It was his fault that his pet didn't want his touch anymore.

"I should have stayed in the Abyss," he muttered without thinking.

"The what?"

"Nothing."

"No, tell me."

Eren sighed against his shoulder. "It's just a story."

"You could tell me and try to take your mind off the dream."

Eren breathed in his rose and lavender smell. "When we die, we can't go to Heaven or Hell. We're not welcome in either place, so our souls go to the Abyss. There, we can be reborn. It might be years or centuries before we get a new life, and we won't remember the old one. It's like being made new."

"Hm."

"It's not real."

"And how would you know if you don't remember?"

"Riley, our population now is bigger than before. Granted, many die on both sides, but we still have more now, and we turn prisoners into demons to nudge up the birthrate. Where would the extra souls come from?"

"Erm…I don't know. So what would happen when you die?"

"We probably become nothing."

"But how do you know if it's just a story?" pressed Riley. "Souls must go on somehow, right?"

"Because it was in a book from the 2nd century that literally said, 'Reubenow's Stories' on the front."

Riley was quiet for a moment. "Becoming nothing sounds like a waste. I don't see how a soul would become nothing."

"You grew up hearing Priests talk about going to Heaven."

"Pastors. I'm not Catholic. But what if it was real? Just pretend for a moment. What if you could live more than once?"

Eren nuzzled his neck. "Sounds like torture to me. Do you think I'd want to be reborn over and over again just to keep fighting and never getting anywhere?"

Riley pulled away a little at the nuzzling. Eren's heart dropped, but he thought of something that he knew Riley would like. "I can give you something."

"Like what?"

"I'm sure you've been fucking angels left and right-"

"Excuse me?" Riley's glowing blue and green eyes narrowed. "What the fuck did you just say to me?"

Eren squinted. "You're practically like a demon tasting energy for the first time, except you're older and don't have to wait to fuck." The idea of him kneeling for some angel made him beyond furious, and he had to make an effort to keep his voice flippant.

"That doesn't mean I've been a whore."

"If you're an angel or a demon, it doesn't mean you're a whore because it's rather like feeding for us. Do you call a human a glutton for eating three times a day to fulfill that need?"

"I haven't fucked anybody."

Eren laughed. The idea of an angel or demon tasting energy and not screwing at least once was unfathomable unless they were a nosexual. Eren had broken the rules against sex as soon as possible with another demon of the same age who could barely wait to bend over and experience it with him at Camp.

"Sure, Riley. Why wouldn't you fuck someone? Did your dick fall off? Is that some nephalem problem that I wasn't aware of?"

"My dick works just fine," snapped Riley. "I've been feeding from myself."

"You must have the strongest right hand in the world and no refractory period."

"I don't want to fuck anybody. I don't just bend over for anyone that wants to put their cock in me."

Eren leaned in toward him. "So you did keep your promise to me? The one you made about not fucking anyone."

"Not because you mean anything to me. I just needed a break."

Eren held another laugh back. A break? Like he believed that. He reached into his coat, pulled out the leather case, and undid the ties. "Here. The wraith that attacked me didn't get this, and I'm sure you must be hungry. Drink up, but maybe not the blue, okay? Blue always tastes particularly gross." He took one vial and pushed the case over to Riley. The vials glowed in different colors. "I wish these could fuel the fire on my scythe. Unfortunately, that isn't inherent to me. There wasn't any orange."

"How do you have so many of these?"

"I'm a demon lord. I can have whatever I want."

Riley picked one up and made a disgusted sound a moment later. "Ew!"

"Bottled magic tastes stale. Suck it up and drink." Eren downed his. "You haven't had any yet if you're not fucking?"

"No." Riley drank most of the vials and pushed the case over. "Here."

A couple of yellow ones and the blue one remained. Riley had told Eren to fuck himself with a splintery wooden pole earlier, and yet here he was, making sure Eren had some energy. His hate wasn't complete.

Riley scooted over to sit next to him. "Tell me a story. It's not like there's much else to do here."

Eren could think of a couple of things to do. Both involved Riley naked and on his knees where he belonged like a good little pet. "Like what?"

Riley must have tasted the little spark of energy, but he said nothing about it. "What are the Pisces Rings?"

"Where the hell did you hear about that?"

"In a book."

"Another myth. Or they're long gone somewhere and will never be found. It kept demons from losing their magic on Earth back in the beginning. I don't know much else about them."

"Hmm. Do you know anyone named Orpheus?"

"No. Why?"

"Nothing."

What a weak excuse. Riley was fishing for something although Eren couldn't imagine what. He truly didn't know anyone named Orpheus, so he couldn't help Riley with that. Maybe it was his demon parent, but how would he learn that?

"Let's see. I remember something." Eren shifted a little against the wall and earned himself the feeling of Riley's arm against his. He didn't pull away, and Eren smirked for a second. Riley would move away if he fully hated him and didn't have an ounce of trust left. "Back in the old days, people used to worship a god named Baal. Or they thought he was a god. They would have built idols and temples for a kitty if someone important said to do so."

Riley snorted.

"What they didn't know was that Baal used to be real before the Flood. He was one of the Fallen, and some took positions as gods because they liked humans worshiping them. They thought it fitting. They demanded offerings to keep little groups under their thumbs. Sometimes, orgies and ritualistic sex were used to keep the 'gods' happy because they liked the energy. Sometimes, the demons or angels even shared certain magic with people who had a talent for it. There used to be more humans like that back then."

"Why?"

"I don't know," said Eren. "Maybe it was because God hadn't decided to tighten things up just yet. Baal was considered to be the god of life and fertility. The humans thought that he fought against Mot, the god of death and sterility. If Baal won, they would have seven years of fertility. If not, famine and drought would last for seven years. It was easy to let humans believe things and not correct them. A demon or angel could even slide into the role of some already made-up deity, and the humans accepted it. Baal liked the offerings and the worship, but he grew greedy. He wanted sacrifices for the energy, magic, and the control it would bring him, and he usually demanded first-born children, which were given."

Riley gasped. "They gave up their own children for him?"

Eren shrugged. "Some did. They thought that saying no would result in years of famine. Why not kill one child to save your others? What if they all died of hunger? It's wrong and disgusting, but he demanded it. The other Fallen didn't like him for this, but he said he could ask what he wanted of his people. Baal also wanted his own sister, Anat, to be his consort, but she didn't want to mate with her brother."

"This guy sounds really fucked up," said Riley.

"He was. God declared that He would flood the earth to kill all of the Fallen and their offspring. Noah and his family were permitted to live. Since my kind and the angels weren't allowed on the arc he was building, they had to find a new place to live. The Norse gods of Asgard didn't want us-"

"Wait, those are real?!"`

"They're real," said Eren. "They didn't like us, so we couldn't go there. I guess our powers scared them. We had to make a new land, so our Fathers from both sides figured out a way to create a new world that was on Earth but technically separate so the flood wouldn't touch us. They took humans with them, and I guess God decided we could do as we pleased in this realm since He didn't intervene. He flooded the Earth, and all died except for Noah, his family, and the animals he brought on the ark. Everyone here lived through it, and for a time, angels and demons worked together.

"Baal still demanded sacrifices from the people, and the others told him to stop. Anat still wouldn't be his consort, and in a rage, he killed her one day. Two demons decided to take him down, and they killed him. The details on that are fuzzy. After that, no one was permitted to worship him among the humans, and they killed any who dared to.

"On Earth, there were no more Fallen, but writings on stone tablets survived, and Baal was worshiped once more for a time because the new people that came after the Flood didn't know he was dead. New gods were invented in various cultures, old ones were made into something new or twisted around, and humans continued believing in silly things. Eventually, the peace that the Fallen had was broken, and here we are, still embroiled in war."

"You don't know who killed Baal?" asked Riley.

"No. Not exactly. Another thing that was lost."

"Have you read the Bible?"

"Yeah. We have a couple of those brought back by visitors to Earth. It left out an awful lot."

"So you know about Elijah and how he had the prophets of Baal killed?"

Eren nodded even though Riley wouldn't be able to see it. "Yeah."

"I noticed it never said Baal was an idol. Other gods were mentioned as idols or statues, but not him. He wasn't God, but he was...something that existed."

"Because he was a real being at one time. Perhaps God told Moses that when he wrote the First Testament."

"What was Mot like?"

"I'm not sure if a demon by that name really existed, but if Mot was real, I'm sure he wasn't fighting with Baal."

"Where do the Pisces Rings fit in that?" asked Riley.

"I don't know. If you figure out how to go back in time to record everything, let me know."

Riley went quiet for a moment. "Are you sure nobody ever remembers a past life?"

"If they did, they kept their mouths shut about it," replied Eren. "That would be an interesting ability, but I think so many lives would make a person go insane."

"What are we going to do here?" asked Riley, who seemed to have had enough of old stories. "We don't need to eat or drink, but we can't just stay behind a locked door forever. This dark house will make us go insane, and if it's true we'll go mad from being here, we'll be at each other's throats."

"We have time, and I'd rather not test the theory. The problem is that I don't have any more fire, and my scythe only pauses them for a bit. I know I probably seem like a great god at fighting to you, but several dozen wraiths would certainly bring me down. A rot spell wouldn't even work against them." Eren fell silent as he thought. "There might be a way out, but we'll have to make a pearl."

"Nice try."

"Or we can get jolted by lightning. I mean, you like that, but you might find it to be worse than the gag. Dying like that probably isn't fun. Devil below, this place is a fucking death trap."

"You're just trying to get me to bend over."

"I'm trying to save your life," snapped Eren. "Do you want to get out of here and have a chance at living?"

"How do I know if you're not lying to me again?"

Here they went again. Fighting. Riley started to say something else, but Eren, more than done with the arguing, grabbed him by the collar of his shirt and yanked him closer to find his lips in the dark. Riley made a surprised noise as he attempted to jerk away, but Eren grabbed the back of his head.

The kiss turned messy as Riley fisted Eren's shirt instead of trying to get away. "You can't fuck me," he mumbled against Eren's lips.

"You're practically climbing into my lap."

Riley managed to pull his head away as he straddled Eren. "We don't have oil, but you can always get on your knees and suck me off. How about that?"

Eren swiftly grabbed Riley's wrists and pushed him backward on the floor. "Does that answer your question?"

Riley's pathetic attempts to roll them were laughable against Eren's strength. He allowed it and chuckled when the halfling got on top of him. "I'm not letting you have control of me this time. Suck me off, and we'll get out of here in one piece."

Eren flipped them and solidly pinned Riley's wrists. "No. If we have sex, I dominate."

"You were about to let me top you last time."

"That was temporary madness," Eren said in a lofty voice. "I've recovered my senses."

"You're still mad."

"And you still want me in control."

"That doesn't change the fact that we don't have oil, and-hey!" Riley struggled as Eren started to turn him over. "You're not fucking me dry!"

Eren got him on his stomach and leaned down. "I would never do that to you. But there's something else to pretend that won't hurt you. On your knees, pet." Riley obeyed and started undoing his belt. "You must hate me since you're so eager."

“Shut up. I just want to get out of here.”

That’s why the energy was so strong and his cock was harder than a rock when Eren grasped him and rubbed a thumb over his slit to spread the pre-cum around. Sure. Eren managed to reach the case and slide it over. It was a waste of stored energy, and it wasn’t the same as oil, but something wet would help.

“Whatever, you’re doing, hurry up before I blow on the floor,” said Riley.

Eren smeared the yellow liquid from one vial on his cock and Riley’s inner thighs. “Have you done intercrural?”

“Interwhat?”

Eren slipped his cock between Riley’s thighs. “Like this.”

“No.”

“Keep your thighs together. Nice and tight.”

It wasn’t the same as his pet’s ass, but he could get off like this. He growled as he started to thrust. There was nothing like the feel of Riley’s body against his.

"Fuck," he mumbled against the nephalem's shoulder.

“Nice to see that you’re enjoying yourself,” grunted Riley. "I’m not going to get off by having my thighs fucked. Are you just going to leave me hanging?"

Eren reached around to stroke him. “Is that better, my sweet little pet?”

“Y-yes.”

“Yes, what?” Riley said nothing, so Eren stopped stroking. “Say it, or I’ll deny you.”

“Yes, Master,” grumbled Riley.

“A little louder.” Eren gave him a few gentle strokes.

“Yes, Master!”

“Good pets get rewarded.”

Eren jerked the halfling and continued fucking his thighs. Orange smoke swirled around them as it drifted upward. Riley moaned as he accepted his place which was under Eren.

He could already feel his balls tightening. A copy was nothing compared to this even if he couldn’t be inside of his pet. No one could match up to the nephalem, and he wished he could stay right there with Riley forever. No war. No Grandfather. No duties. Just the one he loved more than anything and couldn’t truly have. The pleasure peaked as he frantically stroked his pet’s cock.

Riley groaned as he spurted and bucked his hips, desperately fucking the demon's grip. Eren shuddered as he gave a last thrust and bowed his head to kiss Riley's back as the pleasure ebbed while he kept his cock buried.

The good stuff never lasted forever. It was always too quick and fleeting.

He pulled away, and Riley turned around to kiss him. Eren held his face as his tongue teased past Riley's lips. For a moment, his heart squeezed because if Riley hated him, he wouldn't be offering the kiss since the pearl was already made.

If only they could both go away somewhere forever.

Too soon, Riley broke off the kiss, and he started laughing. "Your cock!"

Even demons don't like to have their dicks laughed at, but Eren knew why when he looked down at his softening cock.

Riley snorted. "Maybe you should run outside like that. All the wraiths would run away in terror from your glowing dick."

Eren chuckled. "The insides of your thighs are glowing too."

Eren cut off a corner of his coat so they could wipe themselves up. He ate the pearl, and they lay on the floor. Riley scooted to be against him so they could kiss.

Nothing could match up to that either.

"Why can't you always be like this?" Riley asked once he rested his head on Eren's shoulder.

Eren said nothing to that. He could if Grandfather wasn't growing stronger and stronger by leeching from his grandson. Riley would know nothing but happiness with the demon lord if things were different. He wrapped an arm around the nephalem, determined to get what he could before it was all gone and ruined.

Chapter Fourteen

Riley didn't sleep for ages since he'd had quite a lot lately. He lay awake and listened to Eren's even breathing. His tail was coiled around Riley's leg, possessive as always.

If the demon lord could always be like this, it would work. Since Riley came to join him here, he hadn't been plotting someone's demise unless wraiths counted, killed anyone, made threats, or manipulated Riley. This temporary truce wouldn't last, but it was nice for now.

Everyone was temporary for Riley.

He thought about checking for the history of the house, but he didn't want to know. He'd learned enough and barely had time to process it so far. When he finally fell asleep, he let it take its course.

Eren appeared miserable when he woke Riley. "It's morning. Or what passes for the morning here."

The only window in the room was boarded up. A collapsed crate lay near the door. They walked around the house and found almost nothing except for some rotted wood bits that might have been furniture once.

"I wonder who lived here," Eren said as they came back downstairs. "The Wraithlands have been around since...I'll assume a century or so after the Flood."

"This seems too modern for an ancient place. It's old, but it's still something I would expect back home. How would they have a type of home with architecture from the fifteenth or sixteenth century?" Riley eyed the nearest wall as he stood by a window, and he was pretty sure no one knew what crown or base molding was back then. "Who would build this out here?"

Eren shrugged. "I don't know. The wraiths certainly won't tell us."

The wraiths hadn't given up. They milled around outside, and one shot up to the window that Riley was peering through, which made him jump back. None of the others had been that fast when he'd been chased.

"You said they're learning?"

"They must if one attacked me and broke my damn orb. Plus, they don't usually move *that* fast."

"Why now?"

"I don't know, but I have a plan to get out. Let's go to the attic hatch."

They'd seen the attic hatch earlier, and Eren led him up the stairs.

"Wait, I needed to ask something," said Riley.

"Save it for later."

"I want to know why you were in the woods, and what happened when you vanished."

"Not now."

"Eren, I'm serious-"

"The spell will wear off soon. I can tell you later when we don't have a pack of wraiths drooling over us." Eren didn't even glance behind him as they hurried up.

He was right, and that was the only reason why Riley shut up, but he had a feeling Eren didn't want to tell him. Later wasn't going to happen.

As soon as they got out, he'd either have to run and fly like hell and hope for the best, or...He didn't have a decent plan to get away from Eren.

Another door in the dark attic led to the roof. It was slanted, but not so badly that they couldn't stand. The mist wasn't as heavy today, and Eren looked toward where the barrier would be, not that they could see it from there. The closest way to get out would mean they'd both be on the angel's side.

"Um...how do you plan to get out of angel territory?" Riley wasn't planning on going back with him, not if he could help it, but he'd worry about that if they got out of the Wraithlands alive.

"Fly. How else?"

"The mountainous barriers will have traps," said Riley.

"That's to get in," said Eren. "If I took a bunch of fliers and simply tried to come in that way, traps would be a huge issue, and patrols would be alerted. Getting out is different. They don't expect a demon to be *leaving*."

"Oh."

"Enough about that. I know you don't trust me fully, and you probably never will, but can you trust me enough for this?"

It wasn't like Riley had much of a choice. "Yes."

"We're going to fly high, and we're going to go fast. I'm pretty sure I'm swifter than you since I've had more practice, so don't let go of my hand. Don't let your wings hit mine. I have two ideas."

"The lightning-"

"If we're faster, we have a chance at dodging. Now listen."

Once Eren finished, Riley glanced down. He couldn't see the ground, but a wraith was floating up as if it suspected they might be up there.

"Fuck!"

Eren grabbed Riley's hand. "Let's go."

Eren was a lot faster as he flapped, and they went up at an angle. He'd be faster if he wasn't holding onto Riley who stayed out as far as he could go and was careful to make sure his wings didn't hit Eren's. He wasn't sure if this was madness and would result in their deaths or what, but what other choice did they have?

The dark clouds shifted, and Eren suddenly jerked them to the left. A bolt of lightning flew by Riley who tried not to shout. Even though it hadn't hit, it came too close for comfort. Below, the wraiths followed with three swift ones at the head of the pack.

Eren didn't look down and remained focused on his goal of them going as high as possible. The air grew colder, and Riley's eyes watered. Moments later, they were in the clouds. The thick, grey fog surrounded them, and his wings grew heavy with moisture. How high did the clouds go? It felt like forever as lightning crackled somewhere.

A moment later, they emerged above. It was like looking at a land entirely covered in a grey fog, but even the sunlight was off and strange up here. It was also bitterly cold, and the air was thinner.

Eren kept straight as he flapped, but he shot a grin at Riley. He'd been betting that the lightning would go down, not up, and after a minute, it seemed that he was right. Flashes lit up the clouds a couple of times, but nothing happened. Riley hoped the wraiths got jolted a few times.

After several minutes, the swift wraiths came up to follow. They were the ones that Eren might have to worry most about, but he was still outpacing them.

Lightning erupted from a cloud to the side, almost got Eren's wing, and forced him to spin once and tug Riley along. He flapped wildly as he struggled to get his bearings in that one terrifying second. Considering their speed and height, he hoped the barrier wasn't far because if the lightning could go up, Eren only had one other weapon up his sleeve.

"Tuck!" shouted Eren.

Riley tucked his wings in and was completely reliant on Eren now. His life or death was in the demon lord's hands. Eren pulled him to his chest, tucked his own wings, and headed straight down like an arrow shot from a bow.

The speed grew terrifying as Riley held onto him. Eren tilted them left and barely avoided another strike. All Riley could see was Eren's shirt and grey in his peripheral.

He tipped his head back to look down as they left the clouds and plummeted to the ground. Below, wraiths waited like a pack of predators. Eren swooped and managed to get them going straight again, and his arms tensed with the strain as he held Riley.

He only slowed enough so Riley could fly again and hold onto his hand like before. The delay cost them since the wraiths were gaining. The swift ones were closer.

Eren slowed again so Riley could keep up and made his scythe appear. The wraiths probably thought he was tired. The clouds heaved, ready to throw another bolt out.

Eren flipped so he was facing the clouds and swept a hand out. A glowing shield with a pentagram appeared at an angle just before a bolt of lightning hit it. Eren struck it with his flaming scythe.

Riley only caught a glimpse, but it was enough. Eren's plan to slow the fastest wraiths had worked, but they had emerged from the clouds farther back. The lightning reflected off the angled shield and blasted toward them as fire wrapped around the hot, jagged light and was carried along.

The swift wraiths screamed as they were hit, and Riley and Eren were already flying.

The rest of the pack tried to follow, but they couldn't keep up with the pair. The faster ones were probably fixing themselves somewhere in the back, or maybe they had fallen to the ground. Either way, they'd have a hell of a time catching up.

Eren jerked them a few times and barely avoided more strikes. Ahead, the barrier shimmered, promising freedom. They were almost out, and for a second, relief washed through Riley until another flash came. Eren didn't move fast enough.

"Fuck!"

The shock passed through Eren to Riley. Although it must have been dulled for him, every muscle in his body tensed as his wings tried to lock up at the pain. The ground rushed toward them as Eren somehow managed to draw him to his chest. All Riley could see was feathers, the ground in the wrong direction, the right way, wrong again, and blurry grey before they passed through the barrier.

Eren tightened his arms and took the brunt as they slammed into the ground and skidded. Everything came to a complete stop. For a moment, Riley lay against his chest, utterly stunned and limp. A twitch ran through his left wing as it spasmed and went still again.

It took several seconds for him to realize that the demon had barely managed to turn them so he'd suffer the impact instead of Riley.

"Eren." He lifted his head.

For a horrifying moment, he thought Eren was dead from the lightning and the crash, but his chest was moving. Riley reached for his neck, felt his pulse was strong, and listened to his heart. The beats were steady and seemed normal to him.

Such a fall would have likely killed a human or at least broken several important things. Eren had just been knocked out, and he'd probably have some scrapes under his clothes. Riley stiffly rolled off, winced, and looked at the barrier. Wraiths were coming, but they were slowing as if knowing it was hopeless now.

"Fuck you!" Riley got to his knees, flipped them off, and turned. The tip of Eren's right wing was scorched. "Bloody hell, that could've been worse."

Riley checked around Eren's head, but he didn't seem to have busted his skull as far as he could tell. He'd live and wake up in a while, although he'd probably be as sore as hell for at least a bit.

Riley spotted his pack a few feet away with the straps broken. He got to his feet and had to smooth some feathers that were cockeyed. He'd trusted Eren, lived because of it, and now…

He hated the sight of Eren passed out on the ground because he'd done his best to make sure Riley wasn't hurt. He didn't have to do that, but he had.

Riley still had to go now. Once Eren woke up and could tell up from down, he'd haul him off to be his pet again.

The trust didn't go that far. What they'd had before was ruined, and nothing would truly fix it. For a moment, he wanted to scream because the bits of Eren that sometimes showed weren't enough, and it didn't matter that Riley still loved him. Eren's goals and wants would always overshadow his good parts.

But what did Riley have to go back to with the angels? Giasone would have already told Nyla that their new halfling resident was a traitor. He looked into the distance and tried to think if he could salvage this. Maybe he could talk to Nyla and make her see reason.

After all, they were siblings too. If he couldn't convince her, he'd be in deep shit, and it might cost his life. If he went with the demon lord, he was sure Eren wouldn't kill him, but he'd never have freedom either, and his ability was probably too valuable to forget about.

Nyla or Eren.

He tied one of the pack's straps together so he could hang it from his shoulder. He picked up Eren, tried to keep his wings from dragging, failed, and carried him away from the barrier so he didn't wake up later to find wraiths gawking at him. Once he came to a copse of trees, he laid the demon in the grass, and sank to his knees by his side.

"Goodbye, Eren."

He planted a kiss on the demon's lips, inhaled the scent of lemon, sunshine, and woodsmoke, and stood. Maybe Nyla would put him to death. If Riley couldn't escape and his end loomed, at least he'd had a little time with Eren.

He started to walk away when he heard a moan.

"Riley…where are you?"

He turned to find Eren struggling to his knees, and he backed up. "I'm going."

"Wait…" Eren blinked and seemed to be having trouble focusing his eyes. The wing with the burned tip sagged. "You can't go back there."

Riley turned and started walking again.

"You can't trust them!" Eren shouted after him. "You think I'm bad? The Queen-"

Riley spun around. "Thank you for saving me, and for what you did back there. All of it. Even the sex. I enjoyed it, and there is a little good in you, but it's not enough. You can't fix *us*. That's gone. I can never trust you again like I did before, and you can't fix that. I don't want to be a pet or a slave. I want to be free."

Eren seemed to be struggling to stay up on his knees. "You could be my pet in the bedroom and have all the freedoms you'd ever want outside it. You're not a human or a cambion. We...we could own each other."

For a moment, that was beyond tempting. In fact, it almost sounded like a marriage. But Riley's heart couldn't take another battering if Eren went back on his word.

"Promise me," he said, still not entirely sure that he could even say yes to it because the possibility of more betrayal still loomed.

Eren opened his mouth and paused.

Riley shook his head. It was stupid to even think for a second that such a thing could happen after the first betrayal. "That's my answer."

"I-"

"No!"

"Riley. Riley! I *need* you!"

Riley didn't turn around that time, and he took to the air. Eren shouted something else, but Riley was already too far.

Eren was probably too weak to follow, and even once he felt better, going deeper into angel territory on his own was a bad idea. Riley damn near flew into exhaustion as he went, desperate to put space between them just in case. The demon's last words rang in his head. If he needed Riley so badly, why wouldn't he make a promise?

He found an outpost town that was mostly filled with training soldiers. They stared at him, clearly knowing who he was. He was the only one with red wings he'd seen so far, and that news must have traveled fast. He found a shitty-looking inn and wondered if he could barter for a room to sleep in with something in his pack.

"What the hell happened to you?" The innkeeper blinked his entirely black eyes at Riley who suddenly remembered all of the dark blue blood on his shirt. Apparently, his blood wasn't red anymore.

"I had, erm, an accident, but I'm fine." Riley internally cringed at the lame excuse. "I'm still kinda new at flying."

“God save you. Be careful! Do you want a place to stay? I’d be honored if I could say the only nephalem stayed at my inn.”

“Will you sign my breast?” A woman tugged down the front of her dress to reveal the aforementioned breast.

“I’d like a room. I’d rather not sign body parts.”

“But I could tell everyone that Riley the nephalem touched my tit!”

“Uhm, I’m good.”

What the hell?

He took the room, had a bath, and washed the blood from his clothes. It was strange how some angels were so awed by him like he was some kind of god.

He’d put on his spare clothes when he heard a knock on the door. Opening it revealed the woman from downstairs.

She fluttered her pink eyelashes. “Do you want a freebie? I think we’d make a lovely pearl together.”

He could already taste her energy. “Sorry, I’m not into ladies.”

“Oh.” She touched the gold disk hanging on a cord around her neck. In a split second, Riley found himself looking at a man, and not a bad-looking one either. He leaned on the doorway. “How about now?”

“Uh…I’m tired too. More like utterly exhausted.”

The man snorted. “Ah, I tried.”

“That’s a type of glamor?” Riley pointed to the necklace.

“Yeah. There aren’t many women, and many haven’t been with one, so they’re curious.” The man shrugged. “Sex as a woman is pretty good. The glamor only lasts for an hour, but this thing has plenty of charges in it. It changes *everything*.” He raised an eyebrow at Riley. “Even if I take it off, the magic sticks for the whole hour. I know a guy. I play sex slave for a week for him, and he gives me one for free. It’s not the best glamor, but it works for me.”

“Would you trade for it?”

The man bit his lip. “Like what?”

“I have a sword.” Riley had a feeling that wouldn’t be enough.

The man rubbed his chin. “Let me see it. I have another.”

Riley had to sign her breast as well once she changed back. She pranced off with her tit still hanging out to go show off downstairs. Riley chuckled and closed his door. Maybe being a tavern prostitute wasn’t a way to wealth, but the sword had been pretty well made, so she could sell it for a good bit. She could also keep it and tell everyone that she had the sword of Riley the nephalem.

He put on the necklace, stood in front of the cracked looking glass on the wall, and pushed his finger on the center of the gold disc. A strange tingle shot through his body.

“Bloody hell.”

Riley’s wings, eyes, and height stayed the same, but he found himself in a woman's body for the first time, and his hair turned blonde. It was surprisingly itchy. Most people probably wouldn’t be happy with this glamor, and the prostitute had left out that side effect, although maybe he didn’t get it.

Riley checked in his trousers and wondered what would happen if he shifted back during sex while a guy was in his snatch. Something horrible, no doubt. Some things were better left unknown. He laughed as he imagined Eren’s reaction if he saw this. He’d probably curl his lip and ask how long he’d be forced to look at Riley in this state.

His plan had been that if he had to run, he could change his looks, but his wings and eyes marked him. Damn it. He hadn't thought about that, and now, he’d lost a good sword for a cheap trick that lasted for an hour. He flopped on his bed, scratched himself, pushed the disc to change, and reached for the bottle of rewek. At least he could get his sleep schedule back on track for now.

The next morning, he left after thanking the innkeeper. The prostitute winked at him and pulled up his shirt to show Riley’s name scrawled on his pec.

“My friends are so jealous! I told them I slept with you and that you have a massive dick!”

“Uh, thanks, I guess? Can anyone teleport here?”

"The Commander can."

"Thanks."

Thankfully, teleporting wasn't so bad since he was used to it. His heart pounded as he rushed to fly to Nyla’s tower. She must have had some kind of magical thing upstairs that told her when someone entered because she came rushing down the stairs before he got halfway up.

“You’re back!” Her eyes lit up, something he hadn’t been expecting, but she tilted her head as she seemed to notice his pack. “Giasone didn’t come to see me too?”

“No…”

“I thought he’d say hi first before heading home.”

“You haven’t seen him?”

“No. How would I if you just returned?”

“Wait a minute.” He started to head back down.

“What-”

“Hang on a minute!”

He ignored whatever she shouted and raced out. Next door, Giasone wasn’t home, and the place felt empty. His teacup was in its usual place to dry in the kitchen. The spoon he used to scoop the herbs from the tin was still carelessly tossed next to it as usual, the fire was embers, and nothing looked different.

He’d had plenty of time to get back which meant that something had happened to him on the way out. If the wraiths attacked Eren, they could have done the same to Giasone. If they ganged up on him like they had with Riley and Eren, they could have taken him out, magic or not.

Riley had been saved at the cost of someone else.

He dumped his pack in his room and returned. Nyla was waiting in the Hall with her hands on her hips.

“Where is Giasone?” she demanded.

“I-I don’t know.” A tiny prick of pain and tension started in the back of his skull. Great. He was probably about to get a headache from stress.

“What do you mean you don’t know?!”

She had suspected his loyalties lay elsewhere, and now, this was his chance to spin things in his favor. It was scummy, but if Giasone was dead, which he most assuredly was, Riley needed the Queen to believe him.

He sat on the edge of the dais and avoided her eyes. “Fuck, Nyla. I hoped he'd change his mind.”

She marched up to him. “Where is he? I swear, if you don’t tell me in five seconds-”

“He betrayed us both.”

“You have one minute to explain yourself.” She stood directly in front of him with such a stiff, queenly look, he almost wanted to shrivel despite her slightness.

"We got to this little house, and I checked the memories, and then, erm, we fucked a couple of times," he said. Nyla made a motion to keep talking, more concerned with the recent disappearance than the old one of her Mother. "Giasone asked me to go with him. He wanted to leave, but I said no."

She shook her head. "Leave? To go where?"

"Earth," Riley said in a low voice. "He said he was tired of this."

"He would never do that. He wouldn't leave me!"

"That's what he told me! I said no and asked what you would think if he disappeared like that, but he said it was too much, and he wanted to risk Earth. I said my eyes glow, and he gave me a bunch of shit about never going out at night, and that we'd manage somehow since I can magic away my wings now, and that ability doesn't go away even if we lose our energy. He-he got so fucking mad at me, but I thought that after we slept, he'd get over it and come to his senses. When I woke up, he took the light orbs and fucking left me in the dark. All I had was a little splinter in my pocket from the twig. I took it for luck. I'm sorry. Even though he left me and didn't want me to tell what he said, I still thought maybe he'd come back anyway…to you."

He felt like shit as he watched her face crumple. Even if they had both suspected him, Nyla and Giasone had been friends for a long time.

"He wouldn't do that!" she shouted at him. "He wouldn't just leave like that! And why the hell would he abandon you in the dark?"

"Because I refused to go. I-I might have told him to go fuck himself and that he wasn't really your friend…I'm sorry. I didn't really think he would go, but he must not have wanted me to tell you either. That's partly why I thought he'd be here when I returned because maybe he'd left me there so I wouldn't tell you. If he was planning to desert, and I wouldn't, I was a loose end at that point. But if he's not here, he left me behind like that so he'd have a good head start and-"

She sobbed and ran for the door to go upstairs. Fuck. He hadn't wanted to see her cry, but she seemed to believe his hastily made-up story, and it wasn't like she could ask Giasone now. He let her have a few minutes before he went upstairs. Buddy's barks at his approach warmed his heart for a moment, but the sight of Nyla on the floor in her sitting room ruined it.

Buddy seemed torn between attacking Riley with slobbery kisses and comforting Nyla who was sobbing. Riley knelt by her as he tried to pet Buddy and fend off his tongue.

"I'm sorry." He put an arm around her as Buddy flopped on the floor, gave her a desperate look, and showed his belly as if that would make her feel better. "I begged him not to go, but I think the war is just too hard for some."

"I tried to end it. I really tried, but Lord Erebus wouldn't take it-"

"I know, and Giasone didn't want you to marry that scumbag, but I don't think he wants to fight anymore either. The Nevyyn was likely the last straw or nearly so. I guess he thought I'd come since I know Earth, and we'd be together. I didn't think he felt *that* strongly about me."

She gave him a quick glance, and he knew she was probing despite her grief. "You lived together. You didn't feel anything like that for him?"

"We started fucking before we left," lied Riley. "I think in time I would have grown more genuine feelings for him, but jeez, I didn't even marry my husband that fast."

"You had a husband?"

"Yeah." Riley took a deep breath, shoved those thoughts back into their box, and focused on the matter at hand. "I liked him, but not enough to *abandon* you when the demons are practically banging on our front doors."

She sniffled. "You stayed for me?"

"Yeah. I'm not much of a fighter, and I'd probably piss myself in a battle, but I'm not going anywhere."

She flung her arms around him. "I'll send soldiers to look for him just in case."

"I don't think there's much of a chance of that."

"Still...I have to try. They can look around a little on Earth. Energy doesn't vanish immediately. We've been friends since childhood, and I know this war is hard for everyone, but I can't just let him go like that."

"Listen to me. Do you imprison deserters?"

"Of course. The angel's lives are on the line."

"Don't be too hard on him," he said. "If he was willing to leave you, he must be struggling in his head. He was probably hiding it so he wouldn't worry you, but don't punish him for that. I know he must still care about you, but he couldn't take it. Don't punish him for cracking under the strain. Not everyone can go on forever like it's nothing."

She wiped her eyes. "I can't believe he left us."

"There's another thing, and it's partly why I couldn't leave you…I found out what happened to your Mother."

Chapter Fifteen

"You lost him!"

The slap snapped Eren's head to the side, and the crack was particularly loud in the cavernous space. Rage boiled up in him, but he quickly tamped it down knowing that if he showed an ounce of it, Grandfather's fury would only increase.

The slap showed that Grandfather's strength was increasing.

"The landing knocked me out cold," said Eren. "It all happened so fast, and I took the worst of it."

He'd do it again if it meant keeping Riley safe. That had been his only thought in those few seconds as the world spun, and he knew he had lost control. The shock had cramped his wings so badly, he knew they'd have a rough landing.

Grandfather's silver and red eyes flicked to Eren's wingtip where the feathers still showed scorch marks.

"It might be better this way," Eren dared to say.

"And just why is that?"

Eren stood straight and ignored the faint stinging in his cheek. "Things would actually be easier if he comes back to me on his own. The angels probably seem good to him, but I doubt it'll be long before something happens. I know how Riley is. If he willingly comes back and with the hope that we're better, a bit of trust-"

"I don't care about betrayal magic," said Grandfather. "I need *him.* That pearl you got from him was good enough to get you through the battle at The Point and feed me as well."

"Not betrayal magic," said Eren. "If he trusted me enough, and I could break things gently to him, he might be more willing to help you. You'd have to change the blood contract so I can be honest with-"

Grandfather came closer and stared at Eren. "Is this some plot to stab me in the back? Telling him about this would make him run. If he wouldn't approve of what the angels do, he won't approve of this. He grew up with humans."

Eren kept his eyes locked on Grandfather. "I could twist things a bit too. The angels can be stopped. Every single one could be slaughtered, and I'd dance on their graves, and Earth…that's happening no matter what anyone says, and no one can stop you or me. Even if every single human army is united, they couldn't stand up to us, and there is certainly nothing that a halfling can do besides accept it. Whether he refuses or agrees is irrelevant in the long run, and I think he's smart enough to realize that."

"So? What's your point?"

"It would be easier for you and me if he's willing. It's a small chance, but it's there. If he runs from the angels, where can he go but me? If he runs from both sides, where will he live? There are only two sides to this realm, and he can't live among humans. He'll see me as his only option. Besides, since his lucid dreaming is more powerful than I anticipated, he doesn't necessarily need to torment people of power into agreement or possible insanity. The more stubborn ones will likely need that, but kindness can also be used to sway those in control. Since he grew up with humans, I think he could use that to sway others."

Grandfather laughed. "Kindness? They're cattle."

"I needed kindness to make Riley trust me. It can have its uses."

"Because you were weak and couldn't rape him."

"It's not my thing. It's just brutality with no finesse."

Grandfather snorted. "Continue, my dear boy."

"We'll have more pets overall if the people can be convinced to kneel. The entire process will be faster, and Earth would be brought to heel with fewer casualties. If Asgard intervenes, and they undoubtedly will since Odin still offers a slight measure of protection to humans, Riley could also work on their leaders and gods. If some could be brought to our side, it would be interesting to see how Asgardian magic and abilities could be mixed with ours. They'll be tough to crack, so if not, they could be annihilated if need be. Either way, Riley's willingness would be a great asset, and it would save you the time and effort of forcing him to submit. Besides, when I get my pet back, I'd rather he not be broken and worthless. If I wanted a doll to fuck, I can have that at a whorehouse."

Grandfather nodded. "Those are good points. Your way would make everything smooth, quick, and efficient. This is why you're a good ruler. You think in terms like that, and the demons thrive under you, but you're forgetting something. These won't be demons that you're ruling. They'll be like sheep. Save your smarts for the demons. Humans are merely a thing to use. Their lives are shorter, and they lack our abilities and strength."

"Of course, but animals respond to kindness too. A horse will pull a load all day for a stall with clean hay, food, water, a sugar cube, and some encouragement."

"But you forget something else too. I want them to suffer. I want them to mourn when they see they're loved ones being raped, tortured, and killed. I want the living ones to know that any disobedience will be met with agony and brutality so that they will stay in their place. You forget that they may think of rebellion in the future, and I will not have it."

Grandfather leaned forward as he spoke, and Eren kept his expression neutral as he listened.

"It will be their eternal punishment for practically forgetting me and treating me as a footnote in their Bible. I want them to slaughter their own children on altars for a sliver of my favor even as those children beg for mercy. I want them to see their babies as food when I take away their sustenance. I want to see Fathers, husbands, and brothers offer the women in their families to the demons to fuck and use as they see fit. And then I want them to present themselves for the same treatment."

Grandfather chuckled as he went to sit at his table. Athena hovered by the tomb, and wraiths fluttered in the shadows. He leaned back in his chair and folded his hands on his stomach which wasn't so concave anymore.

"Torture is a joy, correct?"

"It's delicious," agreed Eren.

"I know you and others enjoy the services the prison offers. The agony is a feast, and with the magic and the skill of the torturers, it's an art. But no one seems to have the real art down, and that's to make others torture their own loved ones and friends out of pure fear. A man must feel anguish and like he is being ripped to pieces as he puts his own child on an altar to die, but he must be afraid enough to follow through with the act. He'll torment his own child and himself in his terror, and that, my dear boy, is the most exquisite thing you will ever taste. My power will be unparalleled, and you will rule the cattle with me over you and everyone else. You won't even care about Riley when you have your pick of humans from all races and walks of life."

Eren would never stop caring for Riley.

"Maybe you could even have an Asgardian pet. You could have a whole collection of pets that suit your tastes to use in any way that you please. Safety would be of no concern anymore since you could get a new one whenever you want. Besides, I want my tool to suffer as well. His fear will show the cattle that if a nephalem can't stand up to me, they have no hope either. It will also show the Asgardians that they can't hope to win."

"As you wish, Grandfather."

No other answer would work.

"I should punish you for losing him with a week in the tomb, but perhaps it's best if he finds out about the angels. I'm sure he will soon, and if he's on his own, it'll be easier to snatch him, and he'll know they can't help him either. I'm surprised that cunt hasn't gotten her claws into him yet. He can mention what they're like just in case the humans ever have hope of help from them too. I'm sure a few angels will escape to Earth, although they won't be able to hide forever. I'd rather they receive no help from them. Let them feel alone like I did while I spent centuries barely clinging on with only a few loyal to keep me from completely dying."

Grandfather snapped his fingers, and Bellim wafted forward.

"Do you want to know something interesting?"

"What?" asked Eren.

"Bellim's time with that demon has proven interesting. Since his consort has grown a little smarter and a little more powerful, this has helped the other wraiths." He grinned at Bellim who remained in place. "I might have helped that along now that I can fuck again. Bellim has helped me to create energy."

Eren wanted to recoil at the nasty thought. The idea of him sticking his cock in such a thing almost made him want to vomit.

"She's made them a little smarter. That's why one attacked you. It wasn't planned, and they're not smart enough to learn who to stay away from yet."

Eren swallowed. "Oh."

"He's not happy that you hurt and killed some of his fellows, but I said it was required to keep Riley safe because he's no use to me if he's dead. The others are still too eager to feed and are animalistic in that regard. Perhaps that will change, but we'll see. His consort may be able to teach them more as their bond grows a little. That pain you felt was a warning to hurry up and not let your feelings get in the way. You're asking me to be kind also makes me think you care more for him than me."

"I don't, Grandfather. He's merely a tool."

Grandfather leaned forward. "You tried to kill me once."

"And your punishments showed that was wrong. I was young and foolish, but you corrected me."

"Your dislike of rape also shows weakness."

"Plenty of demons don't engage in that simple brutality."

Grandfather narrowed his eyes. "To serve me, you need to be willing to do anything even if you find it distasteful. If it wasn't for my mercy, you wouldn't be alive."

"He means nothing. Of course, I enjoyed the friendship as a kid because I had no one else and knew nothing, but I know my place and what I am now."

"You better. Get in the tomb."

Eren's heart started pounding. He'd hoped to escape that.

"I need a good feed."

"Grandfather-"

"Five days instead of four. You know you're not to argue."

When Eren was dragged from the tomb five days later and left to collapse on the floor, he had a feeling this would never end. Even with Earth under Grandfather's heel, he'd probably still enjoy torturing Eren. The demon lord was also merely a tool in his eyes just like Riley.

Death was better than this.

It took three days for the migraine to go away. The army at the Point was waiting. He had to replenish his magic and go fight. He had to continue because there was no other way. Wash and dressed on the day he planned to be teleported there, he sat on the edge of his bed and flopped back.

He could end himself since he wasn't invincible. The thought was tempting after so many years. He'd told himself repeatedly that he could handle what Grandfather wanted even though he had no desire to rule Earth. He could handle warping future generations that would have endless humans to pick from to torture and rape. He could handle his line growing darker and worse once he was dead and gone.

"I can't," he whispered.

Of course, no one answered. The only one he loved was far away and not coming back of his own accord. Eren would get him and do what Grandfather asked because he had no choice. If he ended himself, Grandfather would merely wait until a child of Eren's seed was born.

Eren's Lacenf would do the same job for the new future ruler. Calan was possibly the only demon in centuries that could erase small portions of memories without turning the other into a dithering wreck and cracking them beyond repair. Dade had known his secret, forced him to sign the blood contract, and allowed him in on the secret of Grandfather.

Calan had been trapped at that point. He probably cursed the day he ever dared to confide in Dade.

Once his parents died in the war, Calan erased young Eren's memories. Bellim placed him on Earth with the books and left him there. Somehow, Grandfather had known of Riley and his location. He knew two children would become friends and wouldn't care about their differences because the world hadn't warped either to hate "others."

Eren hadn't had a choice about what he put the contract for his own future heir. Grandfather had watched Eren write it out and sign it with his blood. Calan had signed too and was bound to keep his mouth shut. The poor demon never had a choice.

Eren didn't want to place a burden on his future child. How could he pass down years of torture to a new source for Grandfather so he could collect whatever power he still needed? The new heir would have to go get Riley, and even if something happened to Riley, Grandfather could still manage.

He just wanted the tool because Riley was a new way to torment people: even in their sleep, a person could be manipulated or tormented.

But without Riley, Grandfather would still take over.

No, Eren wouldn't dare put anything on a future child, and he couldn't quite bear the thought of leaving Riley behind even though he'd be forced to do a terrible thing.

He dragged himself up so he could keep going.

Chapter Sixteen

Riley begged Nyla to not announce that he was the heir if something happened to her. Technically, she said he should be the lord of the angels because he had been born before her, something he hadn't even considered. The horror on his face at the prospect of ruling must have also helped shake the suspicions she had of him.

He didn't want to be the lord of anything, and he didn't even want to be second in line to her. For someone that grew up playing barefoot in the woods and scrubbing his own drawers when he and Uncle Grevin did laundry, the idea of being boosted up to such a high position was jarring.

She said she had to tell a few close people so they would know if something happened to her. Riley agreed to that since it was logical, but he didn't want people generally knowing. They'd either be more awed by him, which he didn't want, or they'd hate him even more, which he also didn't want. Not everyone appreciated his demon side, and even if someone didn't mind him, that thinking might change if someone with demon blood was over them.

Riley sat in Giasone's house a couple of days later. Or his house now. Nyla said he could stay there and not worry about rent. He looked around the sitting room as conflicting feelings buzzed in his mind. Giasone had left him there to die an awful death, but at the same time, Riley felt the angel hadn't deserved to die from wraiths. If Giasone had only been able to see that Riley wasn't secretly working with Eren, he wouldn't have done that.

The angel truly believed that Riley was a danger to the angels and Nyla, his best friend. He'd filled her ear with things, and they'd both sensed his energy when Riley lucid-dreamed and put Eren in a box.

It was too late to ever make him believe otherwise, and Riley was safe now partly because of his death.

And Eren.

He glanced at Buddy who was laying on the floor with his massive head between his paws. One eye was still half blue and green, and the other was half silver and purple. The river and the barrier were the last line of real defense against the demons, although that wouldn't last for long. If they took Fringe, they'd come farther. The fact that they won the Point meant they had a real chance of ending things in their favor.

The only other option was that the angels would repel them and kill so many, the demons would have no choice but to retreat. If enough of their soldiers had been lost, the angels could chase, cut down even more, and start to take back land.

If Eren won, he'd take Riley back. There was no doubt about that. He'd never let his "pet" go.

"I should, but I don't regret the sex," said Riley. "The bastards still got a hold on me even though I hate him too."

Buddy flicked his eyes over and whined as Riley thought of how Eren had taken the worst of the fall to protect him. He'd hurt himself and must have known that if possible, the halfling would run. He'd still done it.

"I guess you bonded with him because of the good bits, and I guess you're special too. Not bad for a runt, huh? You're definitely not small now."

Buddy stood to come over and rest his head on Riley's leg.

"I'm still not going back, and that means we can't let the demons go farther."

The demons would soon have a weapon if they took Fringe.

"I would slap you right across the face if you weren't my half-brother," Nyla hissed at him as they paused in the street. Riley had managed to catch her as she was leaving her tower so he could tell her what he thought they should do. "Didn't Giasone tell you anything about the Tree of Life?"

"Um…you can light the sticks, and the twigs can bring you good luck."

She huffed as they started walking. "You didn't grow up here, and you don't fully get the importance, so I shouldn't be so mad. The Tree has been here since the beginning."

"It didn't look that grand to me. Shouldn't it be bigger if it's that old?"

She cut her eyes at him. "Bigger isn't always better, and in the beginning, it was planted here. There's some magic that can be done with it, but it's more like a symbol. An angel planted it at the start."

"The angels will be done for if Eren and his army get a hold of it," said Riley. "They'll make a hundred Nevyyns because they certainly won't care about how precious the Tree is to you."

"We're not burning it down!"

"Will something drastic happen if we do? Will this part of the world break off and go up in flames or something? Will we all instantly collapse and die?"

"No, but-"

"I can tell you, if that Banna bitch makes a bunch of Nevyyns, everything you know will be blown to bits. I *saw* that thing, and I *felt* it. I wouldn't be here if Giasone hadn't come down and shielded me. This time he won't be around to protect me, you, or anyone in the case of Nevyyns. With a bunch of them, no one will be able to protect us for long."

Her face tightened at the mention of Giasone. "To cut it down- some shields bear the symbols of the Tree of Life and the Flower of Life."

"Is there a Flower somewhere?"

"No, that's more symbolic. Maybe there was a Flower a long time ago, but there isn't one now. Cutting down the Tree of Life would be like burning a Bible in the human world."

He nodded. "Yes, that would be unthinkable, but I'd rather burn it if someone found a way to turn the Bible into a lethal weapon that causes insane agony and kills everyone that's too close. If we lose Fringe, we're basically handing over a weapon to the demons. You might as well have the entire army kill themselves! Is that what you want? Do you want everything that you've worked to protect to be destroyed by your own Tree of Life? Do you think our Mother would want that? Or the rest of the line before us?"

She bit her lip. "No. Then again, I don't know what Mother wanted considering she fucked a demon, and he ended up killing her. I guess he felt sorry for you being a baby, but he clearly didn't give a fuck about her in the end. I can't believe she snuck off to be with him. Why would she do that? What the fuck had she been thinking?"

"I don't know," said Riley. Because Orpheus had somehow shown her that demons were quite all rabid dogs that wanted to spill every angel's blood. She had shown him that angels weren't like that either. Because maybe they would have made a good couple if the two sides to this world weren't at each other's throats. "Maybe he used a love spell."

"There's no such thing."

"Well…demons are a sneaky bunch of fuckers. I would know."

She looked up at him. "Haven't you tried to summon your Father? He has to sleep sometime."

"I did, but nothing happened. I tried to summon Mother too, but…" He waved a hand. "It seems I can't bring dead people to my dreams. I tried to summon my husband too. Same thing. Once they're gone, that's it. I can make a fake version of them, but that's like creating a doll. It's not them."

"You must have really loved your husband."

"Yeah. About the Tree."

Anger flashed on her face. "Fine. We'll burn it down so the demons don't get a hold of it. You know, you really need to let go of your husband."

"Excuse me?" he snapped.

"It's for your own well-being."

Riley had to make a real effort to keep his voice down so others passing by didn't hear and stare. "Oh, what? Are you pissed that your nephalem brother married a mortal?"

"That's not what I meant," she huffed. "It's not that you married a human. People have to move forward, and you won't even talk about him."

"You could have moved forward, but you sent me into the Wraithlands to find out what happened to your Mother."

"I thank you for that because I have closure now, and I gained a brother for it. I'm assuming you know what happened to James, and nothing will be gained by letting his death hold you back. If I bring him up, you immediately change the subject."

"It hurts. We barely got any time."

"Do you fuck him in your dreams?"

No. It was Eren. Always damn Eren. "Yeah. I know it's not really him, but…"

If Nyla thought about the sexual energy they picked up from him when he was supposed to torment Eren, she said nothing. "That's not healthy. I know it's just a fantasy made real for you, but you have sexual freedom here and should use it. You can be with angels who are alive. You said you were fucking Giasone, and maybe he wouldn't care since nothing was super serious yet, but I think after a while, no one would want to play second to your dreams."

"Why the hell are you lecturing me about this? I only got a year with James after we married."

"If we win this war or at least keep them from getting farther, we'll have decades ahead," said Nyla. "I just want you to be happy. You don't even have to get married to do it. Just enjoy being with others and don't let the dead hold you back. What if you get close to someone, but you're still seeing and fucking James in your dreams? That's not fair to the living. Besides, you're lucky that you get full energy every time."

"Huh?"

"I don't get as much as others," she said.

He squinted at her. "Why not?"

She blew out a breath. "It's a rare problem. Pearls don't give me the same strength. It made it hard when I was practicing spells because I can't replenish at the rate of everyone else. Since you have to cast a lot to set it, I'd run out faster, and that slowed me down. It's so annoying."

He frowned. "Sorry."

"It's all right."

"Don't you guys collect energy here?"

"Yes."

"Erm, how do you do that if you don't have a prison like the demons?"

"There's a place northwest of here. The employee's job is to fuck all day."

"That sounds exhausting."

She snorted. "Okay, not all day, but they do it a lot, and they collect energy." She made a face. "We still haven't found a way to make it taste fresh and not stale."

Nyla wouldn't go to battle, but she said she had sent a letter to Fringe. Riley would go to make sure the Tree was burned down and see it with his own eyes. He was also in charge of making sure no angels had twigs or sticks from it. Banna didn't need much to create a Nevyyn, and if any bit of the Tree was found on an angel corpse, assuming Fringe was overrun, she could make it.

It was clear how she made the first. Orpheus had taken Lilith's twig and handed it over. It must have taken a while to figure out what to do with the twig, but sure enough, Banna turned it into something destructive.

Riley didn't enjoy the look the Commander gave him while he stood in the main guardhouse at Fringe with Buddy at his side.

"I read the note she sent, but still-" The Commander's dark purple eyes seemed ready to bulge out of his head. Even the crow perched on the windowsill gave Riley a dirty look. "This is unthinkable."

"If we keep it and lose this place, they'll use it against us. Do you want that?"

The Commander seemed to deflate. "No. I was there at the Point. I don't want to see that again. Some of the angels that were too close and went mad are still insane."

Riley shuddered and remembered the horrible agony he'd felt until Giasone protected him. He still didn't like to think about it, and he could see why some angels had gone insane.

"What happened to them?"

The Commander sighed. "They'll be taken care of, but some things can't be fixed."

"That will happen to a lot more if we don't burn it down."

"I've already sent guards around to make sure no one is trying to hide a piece of it. Let's go. There's no point in delaying it."

Other angels came to watch. Some were grumbling, and Riley received a couple of glares as if this was his fault. It sort of was, but surely, someone would have thought of it if Fringe was overrun. He assumed no one wanted to be the one to suggest it, they were hoping they could avoid it, and they'd kept quiet while they tried to pretend the horrible truth wasn't real.

The Tree was surrounded by a wall with a sturdy door, although it was left open. Riley had seen it before the meal with Eren. When they stepped through, once again, he felt a slight pulse that he couldn't explain. It wasn't like the energy he got from sex. It was peaceful and soothing. Even the complaining angels stopped bitching for a few moments, and everyone stared at the Tree.

It didn't look like something that had been there for centuries upon centuries. The branches and leaves seemed quite normal, and the grass under it was like any other grass. A flock of doves and a few crows burst from the branches. Several angels perched on the wall with mournful expressions, and some turned to fly away or climb down as if unable to bear the coming destruction.

"Have you seen it before?" asked the Commander.

"Once."

"Did you sit under it?"

"Erm, no."

"You should go sit under it or in the branches," said the Commander. "You can fly, so try it before we destroy it."

Riley flew to one of the lower branches near the trunk and perched on it while Buddy curled up near the trunk. The peaceful thrum increased, and he leaned against the trunk as he closed his eyes. Something told him that this magic was older than anything else, even the Tree itself, and guilt tugged on his brain. Once it was gone, they'd never be able to get it back.

The demons would take it, twist it, and use it for death and destruction. Whoever planted this certainly never had that in mind.

Since Orpheus must have given the twig he took from Lilith to Dade, his actions had resulted in a lot of death and pain farther down the line, and it had nearly killed the son he had tried to protect.

Riley would make sure it never harmed another, but he wasn't quite ready yet. He flew down to the Commander who was arguing with a small group.

"We'll repel the demons and make sure they never get their grubby hands on our Tree," said one complainer.

"You don't know that!" retorted the Commander. "We never thought they'd get past the Point, but they did."

"They haven't got another Nevyyn now!"

"The river could-"

"It's been strengthened now."

"We'd fight to the death for this!" another angel pointed at the Tree.

"We fought to the death to keep the Point from falling," shouted the Commander. "It still fell!"

"He's part demon, and he probably loves this." The first sneered at Riley. "You're probably laughing and hugging yourself on the inside."

"Go fuck yourself," said Riley. "If I didn't care about angels, I'd be happy to see the Tree used by the demons. Even if we lose this whole war, at least the demons will have to die for it and can't simply use a bunch of Nevyyns."

"It's being burned whether you like it or not," said the Commander. "Now get out or else."

The angels stomped out. One shot Riley a death glare, and he'd probably go tell all of his buddies how the nephalem loved destroying the Tree of Life. The Commander huffed and turned.

"I'm sorry about them. It's like burning a Church in their eyes. Worse actually. At least the Church is just wood and stone."

"I understand. Do you mind if I sleep under it and look through its memories?"

"Huh?"

"That's my power. I can lucid dream and see memories of the past."

"Oh. That's interesting."

"It might take a bit if you want to go do something else and come back."

"I'll sit and enjoy the Tree a little longer."

The Commander sat against the wall, and Riley went to lay down next to Buddy who licked his face before resting his head on the ground once more. Riley always carried a little bottle of rewek around just in case.

He found a fuzzy memory of two angels sitting on a branch and making out. They must have fallen in love here and made enough emotion. Riley focused on going back to the beginning and was sure he'd found it when he saw no tree but two people he didn't know.

They had their backs to him. One had black wings with a few silver feathers near the roots, and the other had red ones like Riley. He also had a set of huge red horns, and the other had black ones. For a moment, it was almost like looking at Eren and himself from the back, but of course, it couldn't be them, and Riley certainly didn't have giant red horns.

He eyed the tail on the first demon. It was black and segmented like a scorpion's tail, and it had a curved, sharp tip.

Oddly, the memory wasn't fuzzy at all. It was crystal clear, but there wasn't much to see. Riley slowly turned in a circle, noting the complete lack of *nothing.* Just black space, and he was standing on the edge of a patch of grass.

The black-winged demon tilted his head toward the other and kissed his cheek. “Plant the seed and create it, my little dreamer.”

The second knelt and pushed something into the dirt. It must have been awfully small since Riley couldn’t even see it. He was about to walk around them to get a proper look at their faces, but the ground started to shake, and he involuntarily took a step back.

Some of the dirt where the seed had been planted sunk downward. The two demons also stepped back as they held hands, and the first’s tail snaked around the leg of the second in a very Eren-like gesture.

The ground continued to quake as dirt sprayed up and out. Something black poked out.

“What the fuck is that?” yelled Riley.

From the ground, the head of a massive serpent rose. Its black scales rippled as it turned its head to look at the two demons with an eye as blue as sapphires. Huge fangs, each nearly as tall as Riley, glinted when it opened his mouth, and for a moment, he was sure it would eat the demons in one gulp.

The pair didn’t seem scared at all.

“Miðgarðsormr,” they breathed.

“Dream it,” hissed the snake. “When the next issss born and devourssss me, your realm will remain asss issss and connected. Your people will have sssafety from the other realmssss. What you do with thisss after issss up to you. The Tree issss the ssssymbol of my gift.”

The pair nodded as the snake rose further. The red-horned demon tipped his head back and closed his eyes. The air shimmered as the grass circle started to expand. Riley turned to see as it rapidly grew and turned into a field on either side. Above them, the snake opened its mouth, and its tongue flickered up. Blue grew from a spot in the air and expanded to create the sky.

Top and bottom spread until they met in the distance. Trees with lush foliage sprouted to the left and grew within seconds. Tiny wildflowers in various colors popped up in the grass. Fluffy white clouds drifted by one on one side.

Riley gaped at how rapidly everything had formed, and he got it then.

Miðgarðsormr lowered his head and sank down into the ground. One of his blue eyes seemed to fix on Riley before he disappeared. The dirt shifted to cover the hole he'd made, but something tiny and green poked up a moment later.

The green shoot snaked upward, and Riley realized it was the Tree of Life rapidly growing. Roots snaked into the ground to firmly anchor it as the truck thickened. Branches spread in every direction, and green leaves came to life. Black Wing made a faint gasping noise as the tip of his tail gently stroked the other's leg. Once the Tree was at full-size, Red Horn surveyed his creation with awe.

The entire realm had been dreamed with the help of the serpent.

"It's beautiful," said Black Wing. "I can't believe this was all in your mind."

"There's so much more. We must go see it all." Red Horn kissed his lover. "There's even snow in the north. I know you love snow."

Black Wing threw his arms around Red Horn, and Riley's eyes widened at their faces. There were differences, but there were similarities between him and Eren.

Each wore a gold ring on the fourth finger of their left hand.

As they drew back, Black-wing blinked his eyes, one purple and silver, and cupped Red Horn's face. "You are my everything."

"And you're mine." Red Horn had the same eyes as Riley.

They clasped their ring hands so the gold touched, and they vanished.

Riley woke up under the tree that was created ages ago all because one demon dreamed of a place where he, his lover, and the Fallen would be safe from the Flood and could live in peace.

Red Horn had created it with everything he and his lover would want. A paradise. It explained the different angle of the sun, the lack of rain, the occasional mist in some places, and the various plants and animals that didn't exist on Earth. Red Horn had wanted a place where winter never touched anything except some northern spot so that his lover could enjoy snow. Everyone had been meant to enjoy this realm.

Except everything had fallen apart at some time, leaving the Fallen locked in a war with no end. The demons would use the serpent's symbol to destroy and kill.

Those two demons wouldn't have wanted this. They'd roll over in their graves if they knew that the serpent's gift was used for death when it had been intended to represent life and a second chance.

He blinked at the branches as he tried to think if Red Horn had been a halfling. With the red, it was possible since nephalem had existed back then. He was like Riley, and he'd fallen in love with a demon similar to Eren.

Maybe it had been them.

After all, if the Abyss was real, it would explain Orpheus seeing so many kings and more than most demons. An ability of his must have been to be reborn over and over again while remembering past lives. It explained the hardness about his face. He wasn't just a demon forged by war in one life. He'd probably seen it dozens of times and made plenty of trips to Earth.

That explained his fascination with humans and why he didn't view them as pets. He'd seen a lot, remembered it, and had a different view of the human race over the course of centuries.

It was why Orpheus saved Uncle Grevin as a child and pulled him from the river when he'd almost drowned. He'd felt that Riley would have a good life among the humans even if other demons viewed them as inferior.

If the Abyss existed somehow, who was to say Riley and Eren hadn't lived past lives and that they simply didn't recall anything? Maybe that was why they had come together again with some sort of residual memory of the love they'd once shared. Riley couldn't quite make himself let go even though Eren was twisted and had done demented things.

And Eren, selfish and manipulative, said he *needed* Riley. He couldn't let go either. They'd fallen into their friendship so easily as children.

He'd saved the halfling from hurt, but he couldn't be trusted because he'd also caused him pain. The bad outweighed the good. If they had been reborn, any chance of them being together in this life was ruined because of their current circumstances.

Riley sat up and looked at the Tree. At least destroying it wouldn't ruin the realm. The demons wouldn't get to use Red Horn's creation to kill more angels. In fact, if he were alive right that second, he'd probably burn it himself to keep the demons from creating such a disgusting spell that caused so much death and pain and required agony to work.

The Commander gave him an expectant look when Riley came over. "What did you see?"

"Uh, nothing," fibbed Riley. He wasn't going to explain anything about what he saw. If Nyla heard any word about him seeing himself with a potential Eren in the past, it would likely make him look bad. She'd already had suspicions.

His gut said it was better if he just kept this to himself.

The Commander raised an eyebrow. "Nothing?"

Riley shrugged. "It was probably too long ago. I guess I can't see stuff that far back or maybe it wasn't emotional enough. Planting a seed didn't probably seem like that big of a deal at the time."

"Ah, that's true." The Commander seemed to accept it. Magic and abilities had limits after all.

They stood outside the wall as the Tree burned. Riley had touched the torch around the canopy, and they'd left it by the trunk. The blue fire engulfed the symbol of the serpent.

This was their realm to do with as they pleased, but he almost wanted to weep too as he watched the Tree of Life tip while the fire ravaged it.

Chapter Seventeen

The gold pentagram continued to glow after the demons finished fucking and eating their pearls, and Eren shoved away the one he'd used. The hurt expression didn't make him feel guilty. It just made him angrier.

No one around here had the ability to copy another's appearance, and it would seem strange if he'd wanted that. The lack of Riley made him pissed, and he'd already woken up on the wrong side of the bed that morning.

"M'lord, you liked me before," said the demon.

Eren had fucked him a few times a couple of years ago, but it had just been for pearls. He couldn't remember the demon's name now, and it didn't matter anyway. He had what he wanted.

"Would you stop staring at me?" Eren stood and swathed his cloak around himself.

"You gave me a kiss last time."

"So? If you're looking for one this time, piss off."

The demon's yellow skin flushed orange before he hurried off. All Eren cared about was the pearl for his shield. He and a few others would use it to rip a hole in the invisible barrier that ran along the length of the middle of the river. Angels could pass through with no problem, but demons would get bounced back. It stretched across the whole realm and up to one section of the Wraithlands north of where he and Riley had come out from. To the east, it simply went to the edge. Going around it wasn't an option.

Everyone knew that such a barrier had been created by foul magic and exactly what the angels had done to make it. Creating that barrier made the Nevyyn look like an innocent toy.

Despite its strength, such a barrier worked best with solid ground. The river would be its weakest point, and Eren was sure they could bust through.

He was more worried about what lived in the water.

The sun had risen a little while ago, and their base was bustling with activity. The walls of the Point still lay in ruins. Demons had stayed wherever they could, pitched tents, and made do since the town wasn't in good shape. Eren had taken a small stone house that was in pleasant condition except for the huge blood stains that remained on the wooden floorboards of its front porch. Someone unfortunate had died there.

Banna was waiting when he returned, although he told her she'd have to wait until he'd washed up. She gave a huff as if she was the demon Queen, and he had no right to demand she wait.

Just for the huff, Eren took his dear sweet time. Finally, he came out in his armor.

"If there are any children in Fringe, I want them," she said without preamble. "You need to give the order to the soldiers to catch any that might be left."

Eren raised his eyebrows. "I don't need to do anything, and you better watch that tone."

Banna tapped her long white fingernails on the wooden armrest of her chair as she narrowed her icy eyes. Her lofty tone, as if he would do as she said, made his blood boil. "It will help fuel the Nevyyns I can make. As we get closer to the end, we shouldn't hold back."

Eren marched over and planted his hands on the armrests, trapping her in the seat. He almost wished she'd do something so he'd have an excuse to kill her. Every day that he'd seen her around here, his hate had grown a little more. He knew damn well her obsession with finding children to torture and put in the Nevyyn had never gone away.

"Sometimes, I think you have the sickness."

"Torturing angel children doesn't mean I want to touch them," she sneered. "That's disgusting."

"What you want is also disgusting."

"I merely want fresh, young souls to help us win the war against those bastards. We're close to winning once and for all."

"You'll have any amount of Nevyyns with the Tree." He kept his eyes locked on hers. "We have prisoners to use. It'll work fine, and you don't need children at all."

"You know they're working on…things," she said with a suitably disgusted expression. "If they wish-"

"I don't care what the trash is doing. There are a couple of things demons don't do like using fresh young souls because we don't stoop to the angel's level. How dare you even ask me to sink to such a low."

"Hmm. To win the war, I'd say anything is fair game at this point. The quicker we end it, the better."

He slapped her and stood back. "Bitch. You better hope I don't hear anything about you. I don't care what you've done for us. You're trash and a disgrace to women everywhere. Even Eldhanna doesn't like you."

The woman who could kill and crush things with her hair was a vicious force to be reckoned with in battle. Her attitude could occasionally be cold and rather frosty like Banna's, but they didn't get along and were quite different. Eren had great respect for Eldhanna who always had an expression like there was a bad smell whenever Banna was nearby.

Her silvery cheeks grew darker as she flushed. "You might be the demon lord, but I'm the one winning this war."

"Remember who gave you the twig. I was the one that thought something might be possibly done with it. I might not be able to create spells, but I had a feeling one could be created with it."

"You only have that twig because Dade somehow got a hold of it," she retorted.

"I was still the one that gave it to you instead of letting it sit in a box like a useless trinket," he snapped. "Get the fuck out."

The look she gave him probably would have made a human piss himself. She stood and went to the door where her pet waited outside on his knees. The dead look in his eyes spoke of the life he had as Banna's plaything. He couldn't speak of it himself since she had cut out his tongue shortly after buying him.

The door slammed, and she was gone, but Eren had a feeling he'd have a problem with her later on. Torture was enjoyable, but she enjoyed it far more than most.

He had a battle to fight and win so he couldn't dwell on her all day. By mid-afternoon, they marched toward Fringe. Eren flew with a group as the massive army below trampled the grass and wildflowers. The spot where he'd eaten with Nyla was bare, of course, and they reached the river before it grew dark.

The boats had been carried or dragged along. Plenty of demons could swim, but the water would grow dangerous here. A massive cart pulled by a crag was quickly unloaded with the strong demon's help, and boats were taken to the water's edge.

Beyond the river, a loud bell was already ringing and alerting the inhabitants that an attack was coming.

The angels atop the wall looked tiny as they readied themselves. The hwachas, an idea stolen from humans and magically modified and powered, would be ready to go.

The demons wasted no time getting into their boats. Some were only big enough to hold about six or seven, and others were larger. Many would be destroyed, so they weren't fancy. The crag had to wait on the shore since his enormous, rocky body would probably sink a boat.

Eren got into one with a few other demons who would be aiding each other to break the barrier.

They couldn't see it ahead, but they knew it was there somewhere.

Rowers focused on their jobs while others at the front flung pebbles ahead. Eren looked over the edge and saw something smile at him with a mouth full of fangs. Anyone could swim in the river, and the inhabitants wouldn't bother them.

Until they smelled blood.

Eren saw a pebble hit the barrier which shimmered for a moment as it detected the demonic presence on the thrown object and instantly activated. The stone bounced off, and black cracks showed, although that didn't mean it was broken or weakened. Pebbles kept pinging off, and the shimmer and cracks helped rowers know they couldn't go past that point. Many boats started to hold back.

Eren's and two others kept going since they'd been farther back.

Being close to the barrier meant the hwachas could reach them now. Snaps sounded, and several hundred arrows that looked more like spears came flying from the walls. They'd go toward anything living, but the magic tracking grew less the further they went.

Metal shields went up, and magical shields activated. The arrows tore threw a few lesser ones. The arrows also did severe damage to boats depending on where they hit.

One narrowly missed Eren's boat and hit the one behind him. A scream sounded, and wood cracked as the boat collapsed. Eren glanced at the wreckage and saw red swirling in the water. A demon tried to cling onto a piece of wood, and he shrieked as something snatched him and dragged him under.

Ahead, a boat accidentally touched the barrier. It was barely a brush, but the boat was suddenly thrown into the air. Demons wildly waved their limbs and tails as they were tossed from it, and the boat hit another. A flier managed to catch one of the soldiers before he hit the water, but an arrow impaled them both a second later, and they landed with a splash.

Mermen were one of the abominations created by accident when an angel thought he could fertilize fish eggs and create an amazing new race of aquatic angels. They weren't intended to grow rabid at the smell of blood. One flew out of the water, propelled by his muscular tail. He landed on a boat and managed to tear a demon to shreds with his fangs and claws before the others could kill him.

"Fuck," Eldhanna muttered beside Eren as her hair grew. Woe betide anything that tried to jump into their boat.

Eren had his scythe ready, and he saw something break the water. It headed for their boat, but Eldhanna's hair lashed out and wrapped around it. Blood, guts, and other fluids better left unidentified gushed out as it was crushed. A merman popped up and tried to reach for her over the side of the boat, but Eren lodged his scythe in its skull a second later.

A second tried to grab his tail, which pissed him off beyond belief. He stabbed the pointed tip into the merman's mouth and down his throat. While the tail-grabber choked on his own blood, Eren yanked his scythe out of the unfortunate merman's skull as fish viscera from Eldhanna's kill splattered him.

The merman who had gripped his tail let go and sank into the water. Eren flicked the end of his tail as his boat neared the barrier.

A demon at the prow jammed a pole down into the river bed to hold them mostly steady. Three others pulled up right alongside them, and everyone who could create a shield instantly linked hands. One at the far end took an arrow to the face that knocked him right into the water. They still had enough. Other boats pulled up around them, ready to defend them if possible.

There were far more demons than monstrosities in the water, but they had caused enough panic. Eren caught a glimpse of a flier who was tackled by a merman as he jumped from the surface.

He had to focus, and he tuned out the screams and snarls behind him.

A great golden shield appeared around him with the Flower of Life symbols around it. The other's shields came up and overlapped without issue. It could create a perfect orb around the user, but he pushed it toward the center of the line of boats and forward. A merman face-planted on one of the shields and slid down with a wet squeak. The demons followed Eren's lead, and the glow in the center was almost blinding.

The barrier shimmered, and black cracks appeared at the touch of the shields. It blocked them from passing through, but the power was too much, and it started to warp inward as it struggled to contain the threat.

"Three," shouted a demon in the center. "Two. One!"

The demons exploded their shields outward. A great flash lit up the area, and the Flowers of Life intensely glowed and expanded. For a moment, Eren thought it might not be enough as the barrier stretched, and the black cracks expanded from the increased touch.

Grey and black sparks erupted as a massive rip appeared. A flier immediately shot through the gap, and a huge cheer rose.

The rip was at least fifty feet long. It bottlenecked their boats, and the hwachas were undoubtedly already being aimed right at that spot. Lesser shields went up, and Eldhanna's hair shot out toward a flock of arrows that came for their boat. Each was crushed and made useless. She let the splinters fall to the water as the boats started moving to the opposite bank.

They had broken the barrier, but they weren't anywhere near victory yet. Merman and nasty fish were still causing trouble. Curse that angel and his wretched experiments. Demon blood in the water would attract more who'd smell it and rush to the source, driven mindless by the odor and taste.

Eren's boat was past the barrier, and he itched to fly, but those arrows would grow more powerful the closer they got. Staying down was better. He shot a purple beam at a cluster of arrows and made them fall uselessly although they weren't broken.

His boat was suddenly tipped over so far, Eldhanna slipped into the water with a screech and a splash. Eren managed to grab her hand, and he spread his wings, ready to take to the air, but another merman tackled him and knocked him straight in.

The cold water shocked him for a second as he grappled with the merman and barely managed to keep its snapping jaws away from his face. For a moment, he couldn't tell which way was up or down as they rolled in the water. His soaked wings thrashed as he wrapped his tail around some part of the merman. He dropped his scythe and let lightning flow through his body. Hopefully, nobody else was too close.

The merman stiffened as the jolt hurt Eren too although not nearly as badly. Bubbles escaped his mouth as he quickly pulled it back, grabbed its head, and twisted it. The crack sounded dull underwater, but it worked.

He broke the surface with a gasp as he magicked his wings away. They'd be a drag at this point. Ahead, he saw a geyser of watery blood, and Eldhanna popped up. In the confusion and chaos, he didn't blame her for swimming straight for shore instead of looking for him in the chaos.

Some other boats had tipped. The merman and hwachas had done plenty of damage.

It didn't mean the demons were defeated. Not at all. Several fliers were heaving the crag across the river. Shapes raced up the shore, and fliers flew toward the walls to deal with the hwachas or die trying. Eren swam through the water and avoided the body of some demon that had been ripped in half. A stray wing minus the owner drifted by.

Getting to shore in one piece was his only goal now. Other demons that had been knocked into the water struggled in the same direction as boats were rowed. Eren tried to go to one closer, but a fleet of arrows destroyed it two seconds later. Wreckage blocked him from others, and most were to his left now. The shore was close. He could make it. Screams, snarls, and flashes of magic lit up the wall. The crag let out a roar as his carriers dropped him down.

Eren drew close enough to shore and felt ground under his feet. He hauled himself forward.

Something snatched his ankle and dragged him backward and down so fast, he inhaled water before he could think to hold his breath. Fouled with blood and the tang of pain, it filled his mouth as he choked and kicked. Teeth sank into his shin as if his greaves weren't even there. Eren's boot found its head as he jabbed with his sharpened tail. Resistance told him he was piercing flesh, but it wasn't letting go of him yet. His gloved hands scrambled along the sandy bottom, and he accidentally shot out a yellow blast by accident.

He had seconds before he was too weak. He aimed his palm behind him and sent out lightning.

The resistance loosened, although pain shot through his shin as he kicked and tried to reach the surface. Maybe he was already too late. Water filled his lungs, and his strength was already lessening. If anything else grabbed him, he'd be fucked.

He broke the surface and vomited water as he forced his body to keep going. It was all he could do. He had no other option. The ground was solid under him as he managed to crawl up the bank. He puked up more water and coughed as sat on his ass and looked at the gross head of the monster that had bitten him. Its sharp teeth were embedded in his shin, and its scales glinted. Damn pirbit.

He ripped it away with a snarl at the pain in his shin, and had to take off his greave and boot. He spit in his palm and rubbed it on the wound. It was a bit deep, and his spit worked better on shallow wounds. He'd need a healer later so it didn't scar, but this wouldn't slow him down. With his boot and greave back on, he stood, kicked the head away, brought his scythe to his hand, and made his wings reappear.

He shook off as much water as possible before he took to the air. The remaining weight from the dampness was an annoyance, but he'd be fine. He rose above the wall where the carnage was well underway.

Along the walkway, demons and angels fought. The gate had already been lifted, and fires burned farther in the city. Fliers swooped about as magic and arrows flew back and forth. A hwacha was thrown off the wall by a demon who looked like he ate nails for breakfast. Three chittering demons had taken command of one and were aiming it into Fringe.

Eren landed on the wall and attacked an angel at the same moment with a swing of his scythe. Black energy surrounded the blade, and the angel's wound started to rot once he fell. Eren left him there to scream and bleed as he jumped over the crenellation. He landed lightly with a couple of quick flaps to slow his descent.

An angel on horseback tried to attack him with a glowing spear. Eren hooked his scythe on it and yanked it away. The angel fell a moment later with the tip buried in his face. Eren jumped onto the horse which reared and lashed its many tails before it shot into a run.

Eren let it run. As it carried him through the streets, he killed any angel that was close enough. The demons were advancing and cutting down any they could. Ahead, he saw a cluster of angels that had formed a phalanx for protection. Demons were having trouble with it, although the phalanx wouldn't last forever. The angels knew they'd lose, and this was a last ditch effort to prolong their lives.

Eren was tired of the horse. It was only running in the hopes he'd get off, and it clearly didn't like him.

He gripped his scythe higher up, and the black energy vanished. He leaned over, sank the blade into the flesh of the horse's gut, and focused so a corpse spell would come from the tip. The phalanx was just ahead, and the angels at the front had expressions of utter terror as they held their pikes and spears level.

They could have the horse.

He jumped off. The horse ran into the pikes. Sharp metal impaled it as the angels at the front stumbled back from the force, although the overall formation remained intact. Eren had to give them credit for holding so well. They'd make any demon Commander proud.

The little burst spell Eren had also planted inside it was ruptured. Mixed with the corpse spell, it caused rotting guts and innards to fly out. With the magic still clinging to the blood and guts, they sizzled wherever it touched on the angel's exposed skin and started to rot their flesh. Panicked shouts rang out as it tried to eat through armor too, and Eren joined the rest of the demons as the formation started to fall apart.

Heads and blood flew. Eren ripped out an angel's heart for the sheer pleasure of it, and the tangy energy gave him a thrill, especially when he saw an injured angel on the ground turn light green with horror at the sight.

Eren's scythe ended his terror a moment later.

The angel army fought like hell, but the demons spread through Fringe like a plague. Homes and businesses burned. Blood ran through the cobblestones, and corpses littered the streets. The taste of pain was thick as screams rang out. Eren thought of nothing except his next target and killing them as quickly as possible.

A soldier who had pissed himself begged for mercy before Eren's tail shot through his throat. Blood dribbled from the angel's mouth as shock filled his eyes, like he thought his pleas would be answered.

Eren let the corpse drop there as he stopped to look around. Nobody else was fighting around him, although he could hear sounds from farther away. A few demons down his street hustled around a corner. While fighting, time lost all meaning, but it seemed that things were nearly over.

Many survivors would be slaughtered without a second thought, and any who would be taken prisoner probably wished for death.

As he strode down a street, he caught a couple of whiffs of sexual energy and knew some angels had suffered rape. Sex with an angel was considered to be pretty disgusting, but in wartime, rape happened. A survivor moaned and tried to drag himself along on the dirty cobblestones. Eren strolled by and stabbed the back of his neck with his tail. Ahead, he caught sight of Nez's blue hair and familiar figure near a group of healers that were dealing with some injured demons.

Those in command had congregated near a large guard house. Eren entered and found the cells filled with several angels who had been injured but wouldn't die yet.

Most were hogtied or bound in some uncomfortable way. Might as well get started on the torture now. All wore the collars with a nullify spell worked into it so they couldn't use magic.

"Please let me go!" one begged. "I never-"

A guard snarled and shot lightning through the bars to shut him up.

"M'lord, I have bad news," a Commander said over the angel's screams. "The Tree-the angels burned it."

Eren stopped dead in the center of the main room. "What?" he asked in a deadly quiet voice.

"I'm sorry, m'lord. It's gone."

"Do you mean a spell went awry and some fool burned it?" Eren would have the idiot whipped until the flesh fell from his bones.

"No, it was already burned," said the Commander. "The ashes are cooled. They did this before the battle started."

Eren stared at him for a moment. The angels burning the Tree was like a Priest pissing on a crucifix and then tossing it into a pile of burning Bibles that he'd lit himself. Unthinkable.

But of course, they'd done the unthinkable to keep the demons from having their precious tree.

"Someone must have bits or twigs of it. The angels think it brings luck."

"We're torturing a few for information in the basement, and others are searching bodies," said the Commander. "If anyone has one, we'll find it."

Eren went to look at the pile of ashes. The Tree had been surrounded by a wall, and torches flickered in the space as a few demons sifted through the ashes and tried to find even a small piece for Banna to use.

"Fuck." Eren went across the piles of ash and had to be careful to not slip on the uneven ground. Even the base of the trunk was gone. He stared at the center spot where it would have been and saw something red.

A feather. It was mostly blackened with soot, but the red was just noticeable. The demons must not have found it yet. Riley had surely been here. Eren ground the feather down into the ashes to hide the color and tried to calm his thumping heart.

What if he'd fought and been killed? Not that he likely knew much magic, but still. There weren't many red feathers around. What if he'd decided on his own to burn the tree? If he didn't have permission, the Queen might kill him for that alone. Riley had little reason to be this far south.

Nez came running as Eren headed for the city again. "M'lord! They found a child, and someone said Banna claimed it."

Eren stopped, and Nez almost quailed at the sight of his furious, glowing eyes. "She did what?"

"She took it. Like…to have, I guess. I don't know if she's done anything to the boy, but…you know how she is. Please don't tell anyone I said that."

Banna was above Nez, and she'd be furious if she thought some grunt was spreading rumors or talking ill behind her back. Still, shouldn't she have known that someone would tell if she took a child?

"Where is she?" asked Eren.

Ten minutes later, he kicked open the door to the house Banna had picked as her own for the time being while the army dealt with fires, injuries, and other things that were beneath her. Her pet jumped at the sound and went to cower in a corner with a little boy who seemed unharmed for the most part, although one side of his face was swelling near his eye.

Banna sat on a couch, not caring that blood had gotten on the fabric. She cradled a glass of grey wine in her hand as she glared at her lord.

"What the fuck do you think you're doing?" he asked.

"Nothing. I fought, and I'd like a moment to unwind before I clean up. I don't know why you're barging in here."

"That!" Eren pointed at the angel boy who had short, reddish-grey hair. Why his Father hadn't sent him away was a mystery. Perhaps he'd thought the angels would win and thought it safe.

Banna looked at the shivering boy as if she'd just remembered his existence. "Yes. That. He's my prisoner. I can keep him if I wish."

"We don't keep angels as pets, and I know you'll do something that's unacceptable."

"My chance at Nevyyn's is gone. I need a new way for a new spell if possible-"

Eren didn't even give her a chance to finish. His rage nearly blinded him. She probably never suspected that he would actually do anything to her despite his threats. But the smartest among their kind and the inventor of the Nevyyn wasn't untouchable.

His scythe flashed, and the blade cut through her neck like butter. She raised her hands as if about to use a spell, but it was too late. Her wineglass dropped and shattered as blood sprayed the walls. The head hit with a thump and rolled on the floor as the little boy buried his face in the human's chest.

"Bitch. I always wanted to do that."

He'd have the body strung up outside later as a reminder that no one was above Eren. Not even her. He marched toward the pair in the corner as he spun his scythe to make it disappear.

The pet probably wished for death and saw no point in living, but the child must have awakened something in him. The dead look was replaced by one of pure anger as Eren reached for the boy. The angel screamed, and the human grunted as he took a swing at the demon lord.

Ern grabbed his wrist and squeezed it so hard, pain flashed on the man's face. "Don't. You. Dare. I'm releasing the boy, so untwist your drawers, and let go of him."

It was easy to yank away the kid who collapsed in a heap of tears, snot, and wails on the floor. Devil below, he couldn't deal with a whiny child all day, and he didn't want to keep it here.

"Stop crying," Eren snapped at the angel. "I'm releasing you to go wherever. I have no use for a child, and I won't kill one either."

"You killed my Father!" The boy stood and flew at Eren with his fists waving. "He was sick in his bed, and you killed him!" He started pounding Eren wherever he could reach as he screamed incoherently.

The pitiful hits didn't hurt. Eren let the angel wear himself out until he stood there bawling with his fight drained away.

"I didn't kill your Father in his bed. I don't know who did, but you'll be free to go. Banna would have done things to you, but you'll be safe."

The human looked suspicious as the angel continued to sob.

"You have no Master now, so I'll give you to Nez," said Eren. "He's a nosexual, so he'll never fuck you. He has no interest, and he's not the type to torture you. He'll take care of you and probably yap your ear off. I'm sure you two can figure out a way to communicate by writing or with signs. It's either that or who knows who would buy you. Sound good?"

The human still seemed suspicious, but he ducked his head and nodded.

"Stay here until Nez comes to get you."

Eren carried the boy through the wrecked city and past where the Tree had been. The whole way, the angel cried, although he stopped when Eren set him down in the dark. Doges only roamed farther south and in the woods near demon territory along with other critters one didn't want to meet. Nothing frightening ran around here, and the next town, Fonest, was about eight hours by foot.

"Go on." Eren made a motion like the boy was an unwanted pest. "Scoot."

The angel blinked his faintly glowing grey eyes. "You're not going to kill me?"

"No." Eren bent down to peer at him. "There was a time when I wished someone could save me. No one did. Take your chance, child. Your death would bring me no pleasure."

The angel stared at him for a moment before he backed up.

"If the next town has already gathered its people and left, follow the trail," said Eren. "That many angels can't help but to leave one. If there are soldiers, they'll send you along with someone."

The boy ran and soon vanished from sight.

Chapter Eighteen

Riley learned that angel fire can consume things quite quickly, and the Tree turned to ash sooner than he would have assumed possible. Even the embers cooled and stopped smoldering faster than he thought. The Commander had walked away before it stopped, not enjoying the sight, and Riley leaned against the doorway in the wall.

"That's it, Buddy."

His drog looked up at him with sad eyes.

Thanks to money from Nyla, he had a small room in an inn to stay at, and he was up there before evening fell when he wondered if there was anything else to see by the Tree. He had focused on going back to the beginning, but maybe there was something else.

"Where do you think the serpent went?" he asked Buddy. "Is it somehow in the ground?" Buddy tilted his head. "You know what? Let's go ask someone."

He'd seen a bookshop earlier, so they left. The bookshop a couple of streets over was stuffy when the pair entered, and the angel behind the counter didn't seem awed or displeased to see a nephalem enter.

"Are you actually going to buy something or spend ages browsing? I want to go home soon."

Riley asked him if he knew anything about the names he'd heard in the dream, although he was pretty sure he butchered the pronunciation.

"Miðgarðsormr and Jǫrmungandr," the angel said in a lofty tone. "The names are rather interchangeable, but technically, Miðgarðsormr was the first, and Jǫrmungandr, the son of Loki, ate him. He is now the world serpent, but the names are still flipped sometimes. The world serpent connects the realms."

"How does that work?"

"I don't know. We don't actually know too much about Asgard. Both angels and demons have seen residents of that place in the past on Earth, but they usually don't like us that much. It's another realm ruled by gods. Well, they used to be seen as gods by some humans, but that was a long time ago. I don't think anybody worships them now."

Riley only knew a little bit about supposed gods like Odin and Loki. They were considered to be stories, and as far as he knew, they weren't even that popular.

"I used to have a book with a little about them, but I sold it years ago," said the angel.

"So...are there lots of realms?"

"There's supposed to be, but only a few are truly known. If you're looking to have a grand vacation, don't bother. You can't just go to Asgard or whatever. There are fairies that can make rifts to go to Earth and Asgard, but good luck finding one."

"What are fairies like?"

The angel rubbed his chin. "Kind of like angels and demons. They might have some animal qualities, but they're mostly human-looking. Humans wouldn't even be able to guess by looking at some. Their magic is different too, but I don't know that much about them beyond that. Besides, who cares about fairies? They've got their own realm, and they don't come here."

"The demons don't lure them to have exotic pets?"

"No. Their energy is too light."

"Is the world serpent in the ground?"

"Erm, he's midway between the realms, but I don't know that much about the world serpents beyond what I've told you. It's not like any of us will ever get to meet him."

"Well, that wasn't much help," Riley told Buddy after they left the shop. "Hmmm. Let's go see where the Tree used to be."

Riley grabbed his cloak and brought it with him, not that he needed it much. The weather was always pleasant and mild, but it was a habit from Earth that he hadn't entirely broken, and he'd need it now.

The space seemed empty, but not simply from the lack of the physical Tree. The pleasant sensation was gone. Wrapped in his cloak, Riley curled up on the ashes in the middle, trying to guess where the Tree had grown from. What if he could dream of this magic snake?

Some rewek helped him to sleep, and he tried, but he didn't get any results. He merely watched the same memory again, but he couldn't go before that. He went to his usual forest spot and tried to bring the serpent there, but he couldn't even do that. Maybe it was too grand for him, like trying to call on God. Riley didn't dare attempt that. For one, he was positive it was impossible, and two, if he could, God might be angry that someone tried to drag Him somewhere.

He considered trying to bring Loki or Odin to him, but if they were important beings, they might be pissed too. The last thing he wanted was beings from other realms trying to smite him.

He remembered Red Horn saying something about a snowy place to the north, and he wondered if anything interesting lay there. There had to be. It was something to ask Nyla about later. Maybe Red Wing and Black Horn had enjoyed mild weather but stayed up there sometimes since Black Wing had loved snow.

As usual, he brought up his dream version of Eren to fuck and feed. The fun thing about dreams was that if he wanted to be tied up, there was no prep work. He found the process of being bound enjoyable, but it was easier in a dream if he simply felt like getting to the main part.

He was about to finish when he woke up on the ground because Buddy was growling and tugging on his leg. It felt strange to be completely bound in rope and then wake up free on the ground with a raging erection.

Annoyance sparked for a second, but he knew Buddy wasn't being a dream cock blocker. Something had to be wrong, but when he looked around in the dark, he saw nothing amiss, although he was sure he could detect strange and faint noises.

"What is it?" he asked.

Buddy grabbed his leg and pulled again, so Riley stood and took off his filthy cloak. After leaving the courtyard, he saw what had his pet so frazzled.

Fringe was quite a ways off, but he made out a few beams that shot into the sky. Lightning bolted upward, and there was only one reason someone would be doing magic like that. Another bolt lit up the sky to one side and revealed a few moving specks that had to be fliers.

While he had been asleep and out of the city, Fringe had been attacked. Perhaps someone had gone to try and warn him but couldn't find him. They wouldn't guess he'd come here.

Dear God, if it wasn't for Buddy, and some demons came this way, they might have killed him first in his sleep and asked questions later. With his cloak around him, his crimson wings would have been hidden.

"Fuck..." he muttered.

Before he could even think of what to do now, he heard two young voices much farther off in the dark.

"We should help!"

"We're too young and I'm older, so you have to do what I say!"

"You're only hatched a couple of seconds before me!" The first sounded like he was crying. "They'll kill Father!"

"He'll live, and we can return after they win." The second sounded like he was trying to convince himself more than his sibling.

"Hey," called Riley, wondering why the hell these two were outside on their own.

The angels squealed in terror until they noticed him. Squinting in the dark, Riley was pretty sure one had spikes on his head.

"It's the halfling!" The second rushed to him, and the other followed.

On closer inspection, Riley saw that the first had spiked his short hair in clumps, but he didn't have time to ask about that. "What are you doing out here?"

"We're too young to properly fight, so Father told us to run. Some others have already left."

Of course, no one had checked the ruins of the tree or even looked since that was a shit place to hide. Both the angels looked almost exactly the same, so he guessed they were twins.

"We can heal minor wounds," said the first. "It's our ability, but we don't have many spells set, so Father said we had to go."

"We can come back later," the second said in a firm voice as his twin's lower lip wobbled slightly. "We'll catch up with the others for now."

"You can go fight!" the first pointed at Riley. "You can protect Father."

"I'm not very good at fighting," said Riley. "I haven't learned and set enough spells either."

"You're the nephalem everyone's talking about." The second glanced at Riley's wings and made a sound of derision as if he should have learned every spell possible and had them all mastered by now.

"You're supposed to be a great warrior," said the first. "But one of my friends thinks you're shit. I told him to shut up because he doesn't know anything, but he thinks he knows everything."

"I'm too new to be a good fighter, and I think Nyla would want me to haul ass," said Riley. "Come on. We better start walking."

"It's eight hours to the next town!"

"I can't fly you both." Riley could just imagine trying to hold them and accidentally dropping one. Whoops. Buddy could fly, but Riley was sure he couldn't hold a person on his back. The weight might be too much, and he would dare to try himself.

As they started hustling away, he glanced at the angels. Both were thin and had the look of teenagers who could eat all day and not gain a pound, not that they needed to eat. They couldn't have been more than eighteen or nineteen, and yet here they were as orphans now. Even though their Father had said they could return, Riley knew he'd just been saying that. Fringe was surely lost, and there wouldn't be anything to return too.

He tried to keep them distracted with talk, and he learned their names. The teens wanted to know why Buddy had a purple and silver eye.

Riley said his usual lie. "He was born like that."

"I don't think they can be."

"Well, he did. He's special, so I guess that's why."

Telling them that his pet had bonded with Eren wasn't a good idea, especially since it was Eren's fault their hometown was being destroyed right at that moment. Let them believe whatever they wanted about Buddy. They couldn't do anything. At least they weren't scared of him even though drogs weren't an angel pet.

The eight-hour walk felt like a three-day trek. Riley kept expecting something to jump out of the darkness and attack, but the twins said nothing was harmful around here. They didn't know how the demons got in. The barrier to keep out demonic scum was supposed to be pretty tough, but they had obviously figured out a way.

Riley didn't dare say it out loud, but some part of him couldn't help but worry about Eren. If he died, it would be better since the new lord wasn't even born yet. The heir probably wouldn't want his Father's old pet.

At the same time, if Fringe was taken, the demons were closer to winning this war than ever before, and they might actually manage it. They'd keep going even if Eren died. Why stop when they got this far?

On top of that, angels would die tonight. The twins probably guessed that too, and the one kept sniffling.

What would happen to Riley if the demons won? He'd helped angels and was partly one. They probably wouldn't be too kind to him. He couldn't live on the run for life because where would he go? With demons ruling the Fallen realm, they'd spread out, and he'd be screwed.

He needed to ask Nyla how the hell to get out of this place. He might have a better chance on Earth if she died, the angel's side was entirely defeated, and he somehow managed to live without being taken prisoner, although he'd have to mostly hide on Earth. He could conceal his wings, but if humans saw his eyes glow in the dark, they'd probably think he was the devil or something.

Riley wasn't as tired as the twins since he'd slept twice that day. The angels looked ready to lay down and fall asleep wherever, but that wasn't happening anytime soon. Fonest was a flurry of activity. All local patrols had been made to return, and they were prepping to evacuate the town. Riley didn't talk to anyone, but he had a feeling that everyone assumed that Fringe had already fallen.

Fonest wasn't set up for proper defense, and everyone on this side of the last wall would get behind it. Eren might as well already count the whole territory as his if Fringe had lost. After that, the demons would have to get past one more wall to get to Life City. Other towns, villages, and outposts around here would likely be smaller targets, but Eren would probably want to head for the Queen's home and butcher her as soon as possible.

The panic was palpable. Riley lost the twins in the crowd, and as he joined a random group preparing to leave, he heard an angel saying it was impossible to get past the river and the barrier.

"Clearly, they did so shut the fuck up!" snapped another angel.

Fliers had to stay grounded unless they were in the army. There was enough confusion on the ground, and they didn't need more in the air. Riley passed a house with the owner arguing that he couldn't leave his collection of books behind. He wouldn't have anything once the demons got here.

They had to give their name to a man on the road out to try and ensure they had everyone. One woman was sobbing that her husband hadn't come back from his foraging trip while the harassed-looking guy fluttered his elfish ears and said he'd get someone to go look for him. A red-eyed child clung to the woman's skirts and bawled.

Once they were on the road, Riley accepted the offer to ride on a guy's cart. His kid kept turning around on the seat to stare at him until the Father snapped at him to face front and stop gawping.

The raggedy line of angels stretched out on both sides, and it was only after a few miles when the fliers were allowed to take to the air and go if they pleased. Of course, some preferred to stay behind with friends or family who couldn't fly. As others spread out a bit, the noise decreased, although Riley could still detect the tension. These angels might never see their homes again, and the war that had been going for centuries might finally end with them on the losing side.

Riley took to the air after a bit, ready to head back to his sister, and Buddy followed. He heard a few gasps at the sight of the drog flying. Nyla probably already had the news via crow or she would soon. He didn't look forward to seeing her face.

She looked grim when he reached her tower after a few hours of flying to get to the next town where there was someone who could teleport.

"I know what happened," Nyla said as he entered her quarters. "I see you got out in time."

"I was trying to see if there were any memories around the remains of the tree. I fell asleep there."

"What did you see?" She perked up a bit as she sat on her couch.

He shook his head. "Nothing besides a pair of lovers having a smooch. I tried to go back to the beginning, but it didn't work."

"Maybe we're not meant to see the beginning. It would be like seeing God create the Earth. It's probably not intended for our eyes." She folded her hands in her lap. "I've already talked to the local Commanders. Spaces for refugees are being set up. It won't matter if the demons breach the wall…"

"Because it's over. I know." Riley side-eyed her as he knelt. He felt dirty and didn't want to sit on her furniture. Buddy flopped on the floor next to him. "You had to know this was a possibility if they got past the Point. Please tell me you've got something else."

She pursed her lips for a second. "I got word that they broke the barrier with combined shields. Powerful ones. We didn't know they could do that because they never got that far. The Point and its traps worked fine."

"Okay, but what about us now? Do you have some neat trick up your sleeve?"

"Another barrier before the wall here."

"We need something a little better than that. They'll just break that one too!"

"I know that!" she snapped. "We have a guy working on making a new type, but it's not perfect yet. It nearly is."

Whoever he was, he probably had angels fucking all day to collect magic. "All right. What's special about it?"

She bit her lip. "It's a secret."

"Even from your brother?"

"Just trust me."

Why couldn't she just trust him? She must have had lingering doubts. Maybe they had no special barrier, and she was trying to soothe him.

"All right. What if we fled to Earth? All of us? You, me, civilians."

"They'd come after us," said Nyla. "We can't bring the war there to Earth! We'd be sitting ducks after a while with no magic. Humans would be terrified of us and come after us. There's no way to hide all of us, and that would never work out."

"Can you tell me how to get out?"

"No."

"I should know this. I couldn't find it in the spellbooks."

"I'm not telling you," she snapped. "You'll leave me too just like Giasone did."

He gaped at her. "No, I won't!"

"Then why are you even asking?" she yelled. "Fringe just fell, and you're trying to figure out how to leave!"

"If shit goes down, and I happen to still be alive, I'd rather have a way to get out if possible. I'm pretty sure the demons won't be nice to me, and the last thing I want is for that obsessive bastard to get me. I'm not going to be a pet for him or any demon. If you die, and everyone else is about to cro-"

She leaned back and folded her arms. "I'm not telling you."

"Fine, don't tell me anything. Keep your brother in the dark because you think he'll run off and leave you. I need to go practice in case we get overrun so at least I'll have some kind of pathetic chance. Thanks a lot."

He ignored her hurt expression as he stormed out with Buddy following.

"She's so fucking insecure." Riley continued to seethe as he headed downstairs, but his anger turned to guilt.

She had every right to feel insecure. Her territory was slowly being devoured, and her best friend had already ditched her in her mind. No wonder she was scared Riley would run to Earth and take his chances there. It wasn't like they had even grown up together, so she was probably afraid that he didn't care that much about her. He paused at the bottom and considered going up to apologize but decided to wait. She was probably pissed now.

They both needed space, and he needed sleep.

After a hasty bath, he took a nap in the house and dreamed of Eren to fuck for energy. For some reason, he woke up with a headache that was solved with a few sips of liquid from a bottle in the privy room. Giasone had told him what the few bottles in the cupboard were for.

Apparently it didn't work for migraines or Eren would have it. Thankfully, it took care of Riley's headache, and he went into the backyard. Even though he had just fed, he felt hungry for energy. Fucking dream Eren should have been enough to satiate him. He'd even made it a long session with him tied up in an odd position, teasing, and edging.

How could he still be so fucking hungry? He hadn't felt like this before he went to sleep.

He told himself to get over it. Maybe it was because he wasn't actually having sex with anyone real. He was working on a minor fireball spell that was hard to pronounce, and he messed up sometimes, but it was growing easier. He shot them at the stone wall in the backyard.

It was hardly worthy of fighting with, and even a wraith would probably survive it, but he could work up to a better one. At least he could do fire spells unlike Eren who needed his scythe. The hunger grew worse, and he tried to ignore it. He'd just fed, so there was no way he could be that low.

Ignoring it did no good. He ran out of energy, and the spell wouldn't work without it.

For a moment, he stood there stunned that he'd actually run out. Surely, he should have had enough stored to keep going for a bit longer.

"What the fuck?" he swore, and Buddy who was snoozing by the backdoor lifted his head.

He fucked dream Eren every night even though that probably wasn't healthy. Still, he should have a good amount of magic unless feeding in his dreams wasn't giving him as much as he thought. Maybe he did need to go find someone to fuck in real life, but he didn't want to.

"Damn that bastard," Riley hissed under his breath as he paced.

What if he was like Nyla and had trouble collecting as much? They were siblings, and on Earth, people could inherit health conditions. Even though Riley had been born the natural way, and she came from an egg, that was possible, right?

He'd better ask, but first, he needed to apologize, and he did so after heading next door.

Nyla still appeared a bit miffed as she sat in her side office with a book that she was writing something in. "You just stormed out, and you don't know me that well. Why wouldn't you run off when everything is about to be ruined?"

"I wouldn't leave you. You're my sister. I don't have any family except for you. But if you die, and I'm still alive by chance, and everything is over or nearly so, I'd like a chance to get out."

"I'm still not telling you how to leave."

He resisted the urge to roll his eyes. She wasn't going to let that fear go. Giasone had probably sworn to be her pal forever. "Okay. Fine. Can we not be mad at each other?"

"I'm not mad. I'm wrecked inside because we might lose everything. Our history, our culture, our lives-" She flung her hands up. "We don't even know what happens when we die, and if we lose, does that mean God will continue to hate us?"

Riley was sure God wouldn't take them back even if they won, but he probably shouldn't mention that. "No ideas on the afterlife here?"

"There are theories, but that's all they are. Guesses."

"What about the Abyss?"

“Another myth. There’s no proof.”

“Maybe you’ll be reborn as humans.”

“That’s another theory, but we don’t know if it’s true,” said Nyla. “Maybe that would be a final penance that determines heaven or hell. But we might also just end up in a void.”

Or they’d be reborn as demons later. Nyla would definitely hate that, but who knew if it had happened already? Maybe some angels had died in battle, were reborn as demons, and went back to war against others they had been friends and lovers with.

There was no way to know for sure.

“It doesn’t matter if we’re reborn later because our current life is what’s important, and we might all lose that unless we can beat them back,” said Nyla. “I'll tell you about our barrier. You’ll have to come with me too because explaining it isn’t enough, but if it works, it could save us.”

“I can see it?”

“Yes. Come on.”

Chapter Nineteen

The stone room moved down for a long time. Riley was sure his night vision was a little better since that was inherent and didn't need energy. Nyla said his running out of energy wasn't necessarily a bad thing. He was still basically like a teenager, and sometimes, it ran out quickly. It was an annoying effect that occasionally popped up and usually wore off after a few weeks, but if it didn't, he could see the meditator again who could help.

"He'll touch my forehead again?" asked Riley.

"It's a little more complicated than that."

Giasone hadn't mentioned it. Maybe he'd forgotten, and if it was normal but something that didn't happen to everyone, Riley could see why. He figured it was like how some teenagers could eat all day and still be hungry.

"Do you have vials of energy I can use until I get through this?"

"Maybe I can get you some, but we're saving those for fighters for the most part right now. I'll see."

The room opened to reveal a blank stone hall. Nyla had said the guy who ran stuff here wouldn't like a pet running around, so they'd had to leave Buddy behind. He had a bone to chew on to keep him occupied.

"Oh, I meant to ask about farther north," Riley said as they walked down the hall. "Someone said it's snowy."

She squinted. "Yeah, but there's nothing there."

"Why is there snow? The weather's mild here."

"I don't know, but there's literally nothing there besides snowy plains, a forest, and a mountain. Trust me, plenty have gone to look before but there's nothing of interest. It's pretty."

"No one lives there?"

"We could since cold doesn't affect us the same as humans, but still...why not live where it's always mild? You'd need at least a coat there."

"The cold isn't that bad."

"Sure." She snorted. "You grew up used to having winter. I'll stay here, thank you very much."

He still wanted to go check out this place but not right at the moment. The hallway was pretty long, and they soon came to a door that opened on its own.

Riley found himself in what looked like an office with shelves and a desk covered in slips of parchment, books, and scribbled notes. The angel behind it had a head of reddish-blonde curls pulled back into a sloppy ponytail.

"Queen Nyla, you didn't say you were bringing visitors," he said without preamble.

"Red, this is my brother, Riley," she said. "Well, half-brother, but who cares?"

Red's mouth opened slightly and revealed his fangs. "You have a brother?"

"Long story, but yes. He's royalty. I'll tell you some other time, but I want to show him some stuff." Red frowned like he thought they couldn't trust Riley, and Nyla spoke again. "He's *fine*."

"All right, my Queen. Do as you wish. Nice to meet you, Riley."

"You too."

Nyla took him through another door and into a large room that had a few doors. Instantly, Riley tasted energy with a tang although it was still pleasant. Barred windows in the nearest door showed someone tied up and suspended from the ceiling with what looked like a sack over their head.

"Uhh...Nyla, what the fuck?"

"He's a prisoner."

"I thought you didn't torture prisoners."

"Of course, we do." She looked at him like was crazy for thinking that.

"I thought-"

"He committed a crime, so he'll suffer, but we don't have human prisoners. We don't get souls from Hell."

The ropes looked too tight, and the prisoner didn't move. Riley wondered if he'd been given something to sleep or keep him still.

"What the fuck," he muttered. "If someone did something dreadful, why not just hang them and be done with it?"

"Listen." Nyla walked up to him to point at his chest. "Don't be blabbing about this. Everyone knows it happens, and the energy is useful, but it doesn't mean we love the concept. I'm sure the hangman doesn't like hanging humans. He just has to do it to make sure the prisoner doesn't go out later and commit more crimes."

"Okay, but you could still just hang this guy if he did something so bad."

"And waste the energy?" She rolled her eyes.

He didn't dare ask if she liked the taste. Riley wasn't sure if that was normal, or if it was because he was a demon, and the fact that he was enjoying it twisted his stomach. He hated the sight of the guy trussed up like that. There was so much rope, he could barely see his skin.

He didn't want to look at the bars in the next few doors. He focused on the floor as he followed Nyla into a hall that curved left and opened into a room.

"The actual prison is elsewhere," said Nyla. "Red is a meditator, and he collects some energy here."

"You know, you told me a bunch of fucking angels were paid to make energy. You didn't mention this place."

"I didn't think you'd like the concept at first because it would probably seem too demonish to you."

Riley was afraid he'd see more torture. Sure enough, the next cage contained a mutilated man that looked dead as he hung from chains by his ankles. Riley had to turn away from the sight of blood and bones sticking out as his stomach lurched.

"See why we don't talk about this?" asked Nyla.

"You don't have to do this in the first place. Jesus fucking Christ. That's disgusting!"

"Yes, we do. Torture makes energy, and Red goes through quite a bit."

"Use energy from sex!"

"Believe it or not, it's not all quite the same. Not for what Red's doing." Nyla drew Riley through a door, and that room started to slowly move down too. "Listen to me."

He glanced at her. "I am, but I don't want to see more of this. It's disgusting."

She reached up and grabbed his chin in a surprisingly strong grip. "Get over it. You're royalty now, and what if something ever happened to me? The rest would need you, so you better suck it up."

"If something happens to you, I'll likely be dead too, and I'm sure the angels won't rally around some guy who didn't even grow up here." Riley moved his chin away. "Every single one of us might be dead soon."

"Not with the new barrier Red is working on. Everything we do is for the greater good. Do you understand me? Keeping the angels alive is for the greater good. Banna isn't the only one capable of creating stuff. Red hasn't had much success lately, but the breakthrough he recently had might be our lucky chance. Even with Fringe gone, we can still keep them back. What's the greater good?"

"Keeping all of the leftover angels alive?"

"And?"

"Us not dying?"

"Thinking of something smaller and more fragile."

"Ummm…" He was at a loss.

"Children."

"Oh, yeah."

"Ours live in a secret place, but the demons would slaughter them too. They'd eventually find it. Any chance of us repopulating would be gone."

The room paused, and the wall slid open, but Nyla didn't move to get out, so Riley didn't either. He remembered Eren saying he wouldn't kill children, and suddenly, he wasn't so sure if that was true. He'd probably just said that to make Riley happy since he was working on getting his pet in his good graces at the time.

He probably would order the children to die. Otherwise, they might have angels growing up and trying to start a rebellion if the demons ruled it all.

"Would you?" he asked.

"Would I what?"

"Would you have demon kids killed?"

"Of course."

He thought of Kyrian. "They're not bad yet. They're just little kids."

She frowned. "And how would you know?"

"What kid is bad?" He threw up his hands. "From what I saw of demon children who have been adopted, they're kind of like Earth kids. They skip rope and play with toys."

"What they are is already bred into them. They'll grow up, and letting demon kids live would be a mistake."

He wanted to snarl about how that was wrong, but the chances of her getting to win might be slim. "So what's the weapon? I haven't actually seen anything neat or useful yet."

"For the greater good, it's a shield that will cause severe agony to any demon that gets near it. It just has to be made big enough. No demon could even get close enough and be able to think straight to break it with another spell."

"Oh." Riley made a face. "Can't you make something to kill them if they get within a hundred feet? That'd be easier."

"You've been here long enough to know we can't just do whatever with magic. If that was the case, I'd snap my fingers, and the demons would all croak where they stand."

"True."

"Red's a meditator, so who knows what else he'll find? Maybe you'll get your wish. Now do you understand why we need energy from torture?"

"Yeah."

"For the greater...?"

"The greater good." He held back a scowl.

"Come on. You won't like this, but remember what it's for."

"Can I not see it? If it's more torture-"

Nyla had been about to step out, but she whirled to face him. "It's for *our* people, so deal with it. You're either with us or against us. Which is it?"

Was she still suspicious of him? Why was she so insistent he see this, like it would toughen him up or something? "You know I'm with you, Nyla."

"You might be part demon, but you better be all angel where it counts." She jabbed his chest, turned, and started walking. "Come on."

He followed her down yet another hallway to a door that she pushed open. Rows of cages lined an enormous room, and the bitter taste was like a smack.

Riley stared in horror. One angel who was on the floor and blathering to himself had what looked like whip cuts all over his naked body. His eyes had been gouged out, and he was missing fingers and toes. Another was screaming in a cage as he lay on what looked like a rack. His wrists and ankles were bleeding from the tight ropes.

That wasn't even the worst.

Riley wasn't sure if he'd be sick or not. He didn't eat anymore, but his stomach might throw up acid. The taste in here was foul and beyond wretched.

"Banna basically handed this to us," said Nyla. "Her Nevyyn caused some angels to go insane. They weren't close enough to die, but they were near enough for the transference to drive them insane. The pain was too much, and it cracked their minds. Torturing the insane creates energy that's a little different, and it's just right to fuel Red's spell."

He stared at her for a second and almost wanted to run out of the room. "This is fucking sick! These angels risked their lives, and this is how you repay them after they lost their minds? Are you fucking insane too?"

"It's for the greater good. It's them or it's the rest of the angels including the children."

"No! If a meditator can find ways to make more spells, then he can find a different way even if it needs pain. Torture rapists all day or-"

"Do you think we didn't try that?" She flung her arms out. "Insane angels was the key because their minds are so cracked from the transference of the Nevyyn, they're practically like innocent children now, but they're not children. Even a meditator can't always find the exact right way, so he's had to experiment, but this was it! This is how he'll fuel the spell that will save everyone else, including you."

"Fuck all of this!"

"Are you with demons or angels?"

"Angels, but-"

"There is no but," she snarled. "And you better prove it."

Prove it? With what? Did she expect him to sit and watch this all day? Either he'd throw up a lot of acid, or he'd grow a stomach of steel. Or he'd go crazy himself. That was more likely. How could Red stand working and dealing with this?

"Participate in something," she said.

"In what?" He shook his head. "I'm not doing anything to them."

"The torture chamber is in there." She pointed at a blank door to the side. "Red has a couple of guards to help since some of them fight when they're taken out of the cages. You can help him for a day, or you can fuck a child that we'll have brought here, make a pearl, and kill him afterward. A black pearl would be of great help to you because it's the most powerful energy source there is. If you ate one of those, you'd be filled to the brim with energy for weeks. It's even better than betrayal magic."

Riley's stomach flipped as his jaw dropped. There was no way she'd just said those words. No way. Even demons didn't view kids in such a light. Wordless, he shook his head.

"It will help us and prove your loyalty." She lifted her chin.

"I don't need to prove my loyalty," Riley managed to get out. "You're my sister-"

"You do," she said in a cold tone. "I'm sure Giasone told you a few things before he left. I don't trust you at all. I also know you weren't fucking him because he said so. You won't fuck anyone, but I bet you're letting Erebus up your ass in your dreams. Oh, I'm sorry. *Eren*. Your sweet nickname for the demon you still serve."

"I don't serve him! He betrayed me, and-"

"But I bet you wish he'd take you back," she snarled. "He'd make the betrayal all better. He's *sorry* for it. Or maybe that was all a lie too. An elaborate plan to get someone in here."

"The Nevyyn almost killed me! He couldn't have known anyone would save me, or that I'd even survive the initial blast. I told you I got out by accident."

"Either you do this or you have no place here."

"I'm not touching a kid. That's worse than anything demons do."

"Then help Red for a day if you can't stomach it."

"Fuck that! And fuck you!" Riley remembered Eren trying to tell him something about the angels, but Riley had walked away. He should have gone back to Eren. At least the demon lord didn't touch kids or expect anyone else to do that. "You clearly don't give a shit about me if you're asking this of me. This is beyond foul! I can't even describe-"

"It's these prisoners or a child for your life and the lives of our people."

Riley stepped forward. "I wouldn't touch a child if you put a sword to my neck."

Nyla moved toward one of the cages. "Then pick one of these. Giasone is alive, by the way. He got out just fine, and I had him hide somewhere. You spun me some pretty lies, but I might be able to forgive you if you do as I ask. You lied to me about what happened, and you've dug yourself in pretty deep, *brother*."

More cold dread formed in Riley's gut at those words. "He's not-"

"Oh, yes, he is." She smirked at his stunned expression. "We figured you'd die in the Wraithlands, but on the off chance you made it out, he stayed with me. He hid when you returned and came to see me. You fell for my sob act."

Giasone and Nyla had both played him like a fool. She knew he'd lied about things and left stuff out. There was no way she'd forgive him even if he did both things she'd asked. She'd use him, and in the end, he'd probably end up caged somewhere in here. It didn't matter what he did for her.

"You're a sick bitch." He marched up to her and pointed a finger at her face. "Absolutely fucking sick. The fact that you'd even think to create a black pearl and touch kids shows how utterly twisted you are. I'll tell everyone what you're willing to-"

She laughed. "Everyone knows about this. Black pearls aren't new. They were used to create the border around the Wraithlands. It's not something we brag about, but sometimes, it's done for the greater good."

"Fuck your greater good!" he shouted.

"Agree or else."

The angel in the cage behind her wasn't bound in any way, and he was simply curled up on the floor. The glazed look in his eyes said he was elsewhere in his head.

"You'd hurt your own brother who's done nothing?" said Riley.

"You'd lie to your own sister and serve a demon?"

"I don't serve any demon, and I had to lie to save my ass because Giasone filled your head with lies," he snapped. "I haven't been working for Erebus, and I definitely don't want to be his pet again. Do you think I want to spend my life being some demon's sex slave, especially after he showed his true colors? If I was working with him, I could have simply left after the Wraithlands. Everyone here would have thought me lost and dead."

Nyla narrowed her eyes. "We figured two things would happen. You'd either die out there because you don't have many spells for fighting."

Riley despised the energy in here, but it was still feeding the emptiness inside of him. Since the angel on the floor of his cage blinked, maybe he wasn't so lost after all.

“Or you’d dream and call on Eren for help,” she continued. “With him, he could probably get you out, and then, maybe he’d send his little spy back in.” She lifted her chin. “Sure enough, you got out. How do I even know if you’re my brother? You could have said anything. We don’t look *that* much alike, and those few red streaks in your hair mean nothing.”

“It’s not my fault if I take after my Father. Lilith *was* my Mother, and my Father did kill her, but I think he had a very good reason-”

“Oh, of course, your chosen side had a reason.”

The angel in the cage flicked his gaze to Nyla as his fingers twitched. Despite her trouble absorbing magic at the same rate as anyone else, she likely had plenty stocked. It wasn’t like she fought. Riley had very little now, but he didn’t need much. The angel sat up as he glared at Nyla.

She opened her mouth, but Riley was done. Done with her, done with this place, and done with the fucking angels. He used his recently set shove spell to drive her backward, and as soon as her back touched the bars of the cage, she yelled and stiffened as though shocked.

The angel jumped to his feet, reached his hands through the bars, looped them around her throat, and held her back. Both of them screamed as the lightning magic in the bars shocked them both, and the angel held fast with his muscles locked tight.

Riley ran.

He breathed heavily as the room moved upward. The lightning in the cages was likely meant only to torture and incapacitate someone if needed, not kill. Perhaps prolonged exposure would do it, but he had a feeling Nyla wouldn’t die. Not that easily. She’d mentioned guards somewhere, so he didn’t have long. Someone would be after him.

He wanted to free the others, but having a bunch of prisoners tagging after him wouldn’t end well for him.

When he came into Red’s office, the angel gave him a suspicious look. “Where’s Queen Nyla?”

Riley shrugged. “She said she had something she wanted to do.” He forced a smile. “I’ll be back later.”

“Oh?” Red didn’t seem to quite believe that, but if the halfling was here, everything must be okay.

“Yeah.” Riley widened his smile a little bit and thought about bashing the bastard’s brains all over the wall. How many people had he hurt? How many kids had he violated?

Like nothing was wrong, he strolled out.

As soon as he was free, he took flight. They were a little north of the city, but he couldn’t return. How many others knew of Nyla’s plans? How many others thought Riley was a traitor to the angels? There was no way she had kept this quiet. Giasone had been in hiding, but he must have known what Nyla planned to do today. If Riley agreed or refused her demands, either way, there would be no need to hide anymore. He might be at the house already, and returning could be a death sentence for Riley.

That meant he’d have to leave Buddy again, although if the drog got out, and he likely would, he'd come for Riley.

That night, he sat against the trunk of a tree in a small forest feeling more unsafe and alone than ever before. There was no one to help him, and he didn't even have Buddy to take comfort in. There was no one that he could go to for safety, and he had no idea how to get out of this hellhole.

This whole war was more than just two sides wanting land and power. Humans on Earth might go to battle for such things, but the demons knew what the angels did. Eren had tried to tell him, and the demons probably didn’t discuss it much because it was so disgusting. And if they all knew, why blather about it all day?

Just like the angels didn’t talk about it because they knew it was wrong in so many ways. They turned a blind eye to the reality and didn’t speak of such impolite things. Rather like how humans sometimes turned a blind eye and pretended to not know of terrible things or do anything about it.

At least the demons were honest in how they treated pets. They didn’t hide their humans and pretend that the concept of slaves didn’t exist.

No wonder Orpheus was so desperate for his son to have a life on Earth. Humans did bad things to each other, but at least whole countries weren’t in on child abuse even if only a few participated. It might have been lonely, but Camaday hadn’t been that bad. He could have had a decent life there. Better than here.

He stared into the dark as his eyes grew heavy. Nyla thought he was working for Eren, but he didn’t need the demon lord to go against her.

In fact, he could make her suffer all on his own.

He tipped his head back against the trunk. If he fell out of the tree while he was asleep, at least it wouldn't kill him.

Nyla wasn't dead. She didn't even seem hurt. No doubt, a healer had helped her from whatever damage she'd suffered from the bars. She seemed terrified when she saw her half-brother leaning against a tree trunk.

"What are you doing?" she hissed. If Riley didn't know her, she would have looked so innocent with her red hair hanging loose and her white, ankle-length nightgown. With her yellow wings completing the image, humans also would have thought her good and pure.

"You need to pay," he said.

"You can't kill me here."

"No, but I control everything," said Riley. "You can't hurt me, and you have no power here."

"I bet I can hurt you-"

"No, you can't because I said so."

Their surroundings changed to what he imagined hell to look like based on paintings he'd seen. Hideous red-skinned demons with pitchforks and horns danced around. A cauldron full of souls bubbled away in one corner while a demon poked at them with his pitchfork. Nyla made a face as she stepped back, but the small, cavernous room grew smaller. A few demons with forked tongues crept closer to her.

"I don't know what happens to our kind when we die," said Riley. "But I really hope that the Fallen from your side burn in Hell. It would be divine justice to let the Devil have you."

"You would do anything to win a war that's been going on for centuries," she hissed. "Someone found a way to give us a chance. Red's only serving the people. Our kind. Your kind."

"They're not my kind," said Riley. "Neither side is now. But even at the risk of your people, there is never a good enough reason to commit such an atrocity. Worse, the angels pretend it doesn't happen. You act like you're all so good because you don't use humans as pets, and you regret the Fall. Or I should say our ancestors did. It's all bullshit. You're taking something that's pure and good, and *defiling* it. Even Eren doesn't do that shit."

The demons crept closer to Nyla who shuffled away, but she bumped into another who let out a sick giggle. "Your creations don't scare me. They're not real."

One grabbed her arm, and she screamed.

"Your body will be fine, but I can still hurt you here," said Riley.

One of the demons thrust his pitchfork right into her gut. She let out an ear-splitting shriek as the tines emerged from her back. Blood blossomed on her white nightgown, and her legs buckled, but the demon held her up.

The energy was sour but delicious, like biting into a lemon cake and having the citrusy tang mingle with the sugar on his tongue. Riley wanted more of it, and it was nothing like the energy from the insane angels.

Plus, Nyla had no power here. No spells could harm him.

"I'm your sister!" she screamed.

"You don't care about your brother."

The demon in him gleefully fed on the energy until she was finally left to collapse in a bloody heap on the ground. And then he fed some more as he made the demons laugh and dance around her. The tortured souls climbed out of the cauldron and used their twisted, burned limbs to drag themselves across the floor toward her.

"Imagine suffering this several times a week," said Riley. "Every night before you go to sleep, you'll wonder, will Riley visit me tonight? Will he let me sleep? What will he think of tonight? You can stay up for a while, but you can't go without sleep forever. Your only salvation will be death or until your mind cracks just like those angels you have locked up."

He stepped closer and bent down to look at her. One of the souls dragged himself close enough to grab her head, and she let out a scream as she started to cry.

"If your mind completely breaks, I'm sure you won't taste good anymore. I'd simply kill you if I could now, but I can't, so consider this your prison sentence."

"I'll kill you for this," she spluttered through bloody lips.

"We'll see. This is your own fault."

He made himself wake up, and he knew that Nyla would wake up in her bed. She'd likely shriek and panic with the memory of the agony so real and fresh in her brain. She'd feel that her body was fine, no holes gaped in her gut, her wings were in one piece, and her hair was still on her head.

Maybe she'd feel relief for a few seconds. After all, whatever happened in a lucid dream didn't affect the body. But then, she'd remember that he could do the same again and again. He could punish her several times a week, and the mind could be affected over time because she wouldn't forget such things so easily.

Pain suddenly ripped through his skull. Riley almost fell out of the tree, and he had to grab onto another branch to stay upright as he gripped his head with his free hand.

"What the fuck?!"

It was just like in Eren's dream, but he was awake. How could this be real? Eren couldn't be nearby, right?

He took to the air and broke through the canopy, not caring about the branches that scratched him and tried to snag on his clothes. Once he was above it, he shot forward, fear driving him to get away even though he couldn't escape it. His wings strained with the effort as he flew. Something was lessening the energy he had managed to collect in the dream.

Something pulled on his mind, and the pain gave such a sharp jab, he faltered. The canopy below rushed toward him.

A last tug seemed to free him from the pain. Panic replaced it as Riley tried to regain control. Branches skimmed his body as he barely managed to stay in the air and head forward. Just like that, the pain was gone like it never happened.

The headache from earlier when he woke up made sense now. The pricks and tension he'd felt when he'd first met her and when he returned from the Wraithlands fell into place. It wasn't stress trying to give him a simple headache, and there was nothing wrong with his ability to feed or collect.

Nyla had been feeding from him.

Chapter Twenty

Eren leaned against the side of his bed on his knees as he gasped. Grandfather had fed from him for a few hours, leaving him in agony on the floor. It was over now, but he still shook and sweated.

He had energy left, but it didn't make him feel better. He fumbled in his bedside drawer for a bottle of rewek, took a few sips, and closed his eyes, waiting for the headache to recede. Thank God it wasn't a migraine because nothing helped those. He crawled onto the bed, stripped off his clothes, and lay collapsed on the bedspread, waiting for sleep to take away all of his thoughts.

With the end growing nearer, he wished he could find a permanent release. Winning this war wouldn't bring it.

His heart picked up when he found himself in a brightly lit forest with Riley.

"I'm not trapping you or doing anything like before," Riley said hastily, noticing his expression. "Why the fuck are you naked?"

"I went to sleep like this. Do you mind? It's not like you haven't seen it all before."

Riley rolled his eyes, and Eren suddenly had some plain trousers and a shirt. As long as Riley didn't terrify him, Grandfather wouldn't know this was happening since he'd said it was the fear that came through.

"Thanks," Eren said sourly. "So what? Did you come here to gloat at me or something? Yell at me for taking Fringe? Because I don't care."

"No. I don't care about Fringe. In fact, I'm glad you took it."

For a moment, Eren wondered if this was a trick. Riley looked away, and Eren noticed how worn out and exhausted he seemed. He had dark shadows under his eyes, his clothes were disheveled, and he looked like he'd slept in them. Had Nyla forced him to participate in their sickness?

"Riley, what happened to you?" asked Eren.

"You tried to warn me." Riley still wouldn't look at him. "I don't have anyone else to talk to. She showed me something and wanted me to-to do a bad thing. I escaped."

Eren suppressed the urge to wrap him in his arms. "I wanted to tell you."

"But I left. That's my fault."

"They're all like this. Maybe they don't directly participate, but they all know it goes on, and it's been like that since..." Eren vaguely gestured. "This realm was still pretty new when the war broke out."

"Why didn't you ever mention it before? You made it sound like this was a war that two monarchs would have over land and power."

Eren leaned against a tree. "I knew I'd have to betray you. You'd disbelieve everything I ever said at that point. Saying that the angels have molested and murdered the children of their own kind would sound like I picked the absolute worst thing, made up a lie, and fed it to you to make you hate them. Would you have believed me?"

Riley bit his lip. "No. Probably not. That would have sounded fake."

"Another thing is that you might have even started to suspect that demons do the same thing in secret. We don't because it's foul. But there is a reason I tried to get you before you went with them."

"And to have me back."

"Partly that, but I didn't want you with those beasts," said Eren. "I knew they wouldn't harm you or do anything right away. They'd make you feel at home, maybe let you get attached to someone, and they'd make you feel like you *belong*. Then they'd show their true colors. I'll do a lot to win this war, Riley, but I won't rape kids. To create a black pearl is...the greater good isn't always good enough."

"What you did was pretty foul."

Eren stared at the ground. "I'd take it back if I could. I just wanted the power to stop them. Even one new soul suffering like that is too much. We got past the Point, and the end grows nearer every day now."

"Were you going to use my ability against them and keep me a slave?"

Eren shifted. "I'd rather kill them, but I was thinking you could drag angels into your dreams."

"And torture them?"

"Yes, but if you couldn't bear it, I wouldn't have forced you. Even with the betrayal, I could only go so far."

Riley gave him a look like he didn't fully believe him. "I dragged Nyla into a dream, created some made-up demons like from paintings, and I had them rip her wings apart, tear her hair out, and stab her in the gut. It felt good, tasted good, and while that probably means some part of me is fucked up in the head, I plan to do it again. I want to drive her mad. She's not my sister anymore."

Eren's head snapped up. "What? Your sister?"

Riley's lips tightened for a second. "Yeah. I found out some things. Lilith was my Mother. The demon, Orpheus, was my Father. I don't know how they came together or why he slept with her, but here I am. Lilith had me in the Wraithlands so no one would know."

Eren took a moment to absorb that info. "Maybe she tricked him into thinking she didn't engage in such practices, or that she didn't want to. Even if it's a known and accepted practice on the underside, not everybody does it. Just like not every demon wants a human pet. Why do you think some angels desert? It's not always because the war itself scared them."

"Maybe she did, but he killed her, and took me away to Earth. He-" Riley stopped.

"What?"

"It doesn't matter."

Eren narrowed his eyes at the halfling. He knew something about why, he just wasn't saying it. Of course, Eren shouldn't have expected total trust.

"You could come to me."

"I can't trust you either. Not really. You jammed a knife into my heart, and I still can't get it out. You want to win this war so badly, and I see why now, but you're also willing to go to great lengths and hurt others that you shouldn't hurt. Even though you won't hurt kids, you might snare me again and betray me so you can have another special pearl."

"I won't-"

"You say you won't," said Riley. "You also said you didn't want me to fear you, and that you didn't want to hurt me. Both happened, and you can't go back and undo that." He turned away as his wings sagged. "I don't have anyone now. "

The words were like knives in Eren's chest, and he knew that feeling all too well. He didn't have anyone either, not even Riley.

"You're not human at all, so I shouldn't have had you for a pet. Our culture keeps those with human blood, not angel. Why do you think we don't have angels on a leash?"

"Because you'd get a spell to the face if you tried to fuck them," said Riley.

"There are ways to suppress magic. We could put them in a cage and do what we like in them. And we have collars for demon prisoners."

Riley turned to him. "A human is so much easier."

"You know your Father, and he didn't reject you. It sounds like he wanted to protect you. You could get citizenship and be one of us. The people would have to trust you. That might be a little more difficult, but they'll listen to me. You wouldn't have to see me. You could start over and live your life here…without me."

Hope flickered on Riley's face, and for a moment, it brought Eren joy. Despair smothered it because he'd be betraying Riley all over again.

"How do I know if you're lying to me?"

Eren threw up his hands. "Do you want a contract in blood?"

"Yes," Riley said instantly. "You'd die if you go back on your word."

"Fine. I can do that. If you want us to sign one, I'll write it up."

Riley thought for a few seconds. "If you'll do that, I can give you info on something. You won't be able to simply march ahead with the army and into Life. They're setting something up, and I don't think you'll be able to beat it so easily."

"There's been talk about that," said Eren. "Banna wasn't the only one capable of meditating and learning new spells. She was just the best and smartest we had."

"Was?"

"I took her head off." Eren smiled. "It was so satisfying. The little bitch stole an angel child and defied me. I released him."

"You-you killed her? The creator of your great weapon?"

Eren bared his fangs. “The bitch was probably considering a black pearl since the Tree was destroyed. I won’t win a war with those. Have I not made that clear?”

“Okay, I get it.”

“What’s their plan?”

Riley shook his head. “I want the contract first. No contract, no info."

Eren sighed. “Fine. You’ll have it. You should meet me somewhere. How about where the Tree used to be?”

Riley narrowed his eyes. “How do I know you’re not fucking me over right now in some way?”

Eren knew he deserved it, but every ounce of distrust was like another twist of the dagger. “I guess you don’t, but even if I took you prisoner, do you think that would really work in my favor? You could drive me mad in my sleep like you plan on doing to Nyla. I have an army behind me and years of fighting experience, but you’ll always have more power than me with your lucid dreaming.”

Riley looked away. “That’s true. We’ll meet at the Tree. Or the ash pile I should say.”

“Are you okay *right now?*” asked Eren. “I don’t know where you’re at, but are you safe? I could come get you.”

“No, that’s all right. Getting out is easier than getting in, remember?"

“Yes, but they'll be specifically looking for you. The angels didn't know I was in there.”

“No, don’t take that chance. Besides, I just need a bit. As for the contract, I want full citizenship, full rights, and full protection. I want to be able to get a job later, and I want to be paid for the info I’ll give you. It’s not to simply suck money from you, but I’m completely broke right now, and I haven't even got a spare pair of drawers. I want a bit of a safety net. Also, I want the contract to say you can’t hurt me or take me as your pet.”

“Done.”

“I’ll meet you in a week.”

Riley didn’t say anything else before he cut the dream. Eren didn’t remember other dreams, but he awoke on his bed in the morning. For a moment, he stared at the covers as his eyes stung.

He’d rather be stuck in the tomb for a whole year than do this. A lifetime. Eternity. Anything if it meant sparing Riley.

The whole week was torture as each day seemed to speed by. The army wanted to push on, but Eren held them there by saying he had business to do. They didn't argue. Soldiers gloated over their kills and were eager for the upcoming battles.

Everyone kept saying this was the beginning of the end. They would finally know peace in the realm, and they had been the ones who helped to bring it about.

Grandfather would torture the information out of Riley so they could get past any spells, use him against Nyla and the angels, and then he'd use Riley against Earth. Everything Grandfather wanted was also so close.

Everything Eren wanted would be destroyed and tainted. There was no peace for him.

When he waited in the courtyard where the ashes occasionally swirled up in a light breeze, he had a contract written up.

He thought his heart would beat out of his chest when he noticed Riley's form coming. The only thing he loved landed on the top of the wide wall, and Eren rushed up to meet him. They could have a few precious minutes together.

"You don't look so good," said Eren. "I mean-"

"I know, I look like shit." Riley rubbed his face.

"Are you hurt? Did anyone bother you on the way out?"

"No. I've been hiding out and staying away from anyone. I managed to evade all patrols. Thank God, I don't have to eat. I've tortured Nyla every night, and I think it's working because I have to wait until later to get her. Last night, she didn't sleep at all."

"Ah. She's staying up later, and now she'll hope to catch snatches of sleep when you're awake."

"Yeah. I don't think she enjoyed being torn to shreds by wild doges."

Eren couldn't help his nasty smile. "I wish I could have seen that."

Riley made a face. "I hate her, but…doing this isn't really me. Before, they wanted me to do something like that to your army, but I refused. I said I didn't have it in me to torture someone every night. Now I know I don't have it in me to do this to dozens or hundreds."

Eren glanced away. That's exactly what Grandfather wanted him to do. "She fucked you over and asked you to do something vile. I wouldn't feel guilty."

"I'd rather just kill her for real and be done. Do you have the contract?"

Eren pulled out a roll of parchment. "Yes, here. You can look it over."

Riley accepted it. While he read it, Eren studied him. What he'd give to have Riley under him one more time. Or even if they could just have one day together without sex. Anything for more time.

This likely wouldn't work.

Riley nodded. "All right. I guess I cut myself and sign it with blood, correct?"

"Exactly."

"Do I have to say a spell or do something for a blood contract?"

"No, the blood is automatically binding," replied Eren. "I have a quill, and you can use my dagger."

"What if I decided I wanted to change something for any reason whatsoever?"

"We'd have to void that one by writing that word in our blood. Both of us would also have to take a side to tear it. A new one could be written up. But first..." Eren hesitated. "Can I have a last kiss?"

Riley sighed, and for a moment, want flickered on his face. "Can we just sign this and be done with it? Then we can move on to other things. We're done, Eren."

"I know you don't want me. I'm just asking for a final kiss."

Riley huffed, but he stepped forward a little too quickly as if he couldn't wait to kiss Eren. The touch of his lips was fleeting like he was afraid to have it last, but Eren grabbed him, and with his still greater strength, he held Riley's body against him.

Riley tensed, but his lips parted easily, and a second later, he had his arms wrapped around Eren. The feel of his torso scorched his as he snaked his tail around Riley's waist, further pinning him, and he reached down to grab his ass with both hands.

"Fuc-" Riley managed to get out.

"Don't talk," Eren mumbled against his lips.

For the first time, Riley reached up to grab his horns near the base, and Eren growled. Riley probably hadn't even figured it out yet, but that was only something two demons in love would do. The touch, feel, and pleasure of the moment was so insane, that if Riley told him to bend over and take his cock, he might actually do it. He broke off the kiss with the intent to bite Riley's neck.

He seemed to realize that because he let go and jerked back. "That's enough. Don't bite me. You don't own me, and you're sure as hell not marking me."

"You're hard." Eren eyed the bulge in his trousers.

"I'm fine. Give me the dagger." Riley held out his hand. "I shouldn't have given you a kiss."

Eren's tail lashed. The moment was so close. "Here."

Riley took the proffered dagger and knelt to smooth out the parchment. "Hold that, will you?"

Eren pinned it down so it wouldn't curl up once more. His heart pounded as he tasted Riley on his lips, and he watched the halfling cut his palm. It was shallow, but enough blue blood welled up.

"Honestly, this is rather disgusting."

Eren held back a snort at Riley's distaste for such things that bothered no one else here.

Riley dipped the tip of the quill into his blood and signed his name. The blue glinted in the light of the sun, and it was a bit rough with the texture of the stone, but it didn't matter. "There. Here, do you mind healing it?"

Eren took the dagger, but he didn't cut his own palm. Instead, he placed it by his feet before he bit his hand to make his blood flow. With his free hand, he gripped Riley's wrist to hold it steady as he dribbled his blood onto the wound. They locked eyes as a sheen of sweat broke out on Riley's face, and Eren continued to hold his wrist.

"You're creeping me out," He tugged his hand away and swiped it on his dirty trousers. "Sign it. If you don't mind, I'd really like a bath soon that doesn't involve a cold dunk in a stream."

"I'd give you anything," said Eren.

"Then sign."

Eren remained crouched. Riley put out a hand to steady himself as his eyes grew glazed.

"I'd give you anything if I could." Eren stood as Riley's eyes snapped up to his face. He knew. "You have no idea how much I love you, and how much I wish things could be different."

"Eren-"

"I didn't want you as my pet. I wanted so much more. I wish I'd truly told you before that I love you. I love you more than anything, and I have since I was a child. I didn't want to leave you. Every day, I thought of you and wished I could return. I didn't want to betray you, and I don't want to do this now." Eren, who had faced armies ready to kill him and didn't shake, started to tremble. "I'm sorry."

Riley shifted and fell back on his ass. The poison in the dagger would make him sleep for a little while. He'd never even suspected. He had no idea what was written in invisible ink on the parchment either. Invisible ink was child's play, but Riley, so inexperienced about this world, hadn't suspected.

"I'll sign the contract." Eren quickly snatched it and crouched a few steps away.

"Eren, you fucking bastard." Riley's voice shook as his eyelids drooped. "You can't have me. It negates the contract."

"There's no rule that a citizen with full rights can't be taken somewhere or have something done to them. It says *I* can't physically hurt or own you."

"You have to sleep sometime. Even you can't stay awake forever. I'll never fucking kneel for you anyone again, you bastard. I fucking hate you! You sick fuck! What did you put on that dagger?"

Every word from Riley's mouth was like another stab. Eren bit his palm to make more blood well up, dipped the quill in, and signed the contract with his blood before he licked his palm to heal it.

"You're a fucking traitor!" Riley's limbs were sluggish, and his wings sagged as he tried to lift them to flap. Realizing flight wouldn't be an option, he tried to crawl away along the top of the wide wall like he still had a chance to escape.

Eren stuffed the contract in his pocket, tucked the quill up his sleeve, and replaced the dagger into its leather sheaf on his waist. Riley nearly slipped off the edge, but Eren grabbed him.

"Let me go!" Riley tried to push on him even though his movements were growing weaker.

"I'm sorry." Eren hugged him close and kept him upright.

"You're not." Tears streamed from Riley's eyes which he couldn't seem to open now, and he tilted his head, still trying to get away. "I trusted you! You were supposed…to protect me. You promised..."

The last bit came out mumbled, and Eren broke down as he felt Riley go limp against him. Eren buried his face in the halfling's shoulder.

"I'm sorry, Riley. I wish you were on Earth with your husband. I wish we'd never met. I wish you were simply a human. You'd be so much happier because I destroy everything I touch."

Riley didn't reply as the havar poison made him sleep, but the dagger still twisted as Eren sobbed into the nephalem's shoulder. A demon would be out for longer with havar, but the tiny dose surely wouldn't last long with Riley's angel blood. Still, it was enough. As he supported the nephalem, he reached for the cord around his neck.

When they appeared in front of the cave, he didn't move for a bit as he held Riley against him. He stared at the yawning black mouth and almost considered leaving because if this didn't work, they might both be dead in a few hours. If that happened, Eren's child would be left to carry things on. He hadn't wanted that, but he also couldn't simply sacrifice the one loved to save his unborn heir.

If Eren took Riley to Earth, Grandfather would never give up. He'd send Bellim to track him down once more. Even if he didn't, Grandfather would surely see his plans come to fruition before Riley's lifespan was over. He couldn't hide forever, and he'd be punished for fleeing. Eren would already be dead for such a betrayal, and he wouldn't be able to save the halfling then.

This was their only chance, and it was a pisspoor one.

Eren laid him on the ground, took some rope from his pocket, and tied his wrists together in front. Afterward, he stuffed the contract into Riley's pocket, picked him up, and took a shuddering breath.

Riley awoke as the room moved down. Eren had him on his feet and upright. Hugging the limp body to himself, he was so terrified at the dark space and what awaited, he didn't even fully register the movement at first.

"What-what are you doing?"

Eren curled his tail around Riley's waist. "Shh."

"Let me go!"

Eren's terror was more overwhelming. What if the room stopped, and they were both stuck there forever? He'd be trapped with the one he loved most who hated his guts.

He almost tripped in his haste to get into the hall as he tugged the nephalem along.

"This isn't the children's place. What is this? Eren, what the fuck are you doing? I will never be a slave again. I swear to God, I'll drive you insane! I'll drive your whole army insane! You can't keep me awake forever-"

Eren hugged him close, ignoring the hate. Riley twisted and tried to jerk at the rope, but Eren crushed his body close. "I'm sorry. I wasn't lying. I do love you."

"FUCK YOU! You're a fucking liar! Just fucking kill me and be done."

"Please, just do what you're told for now anyway. It'll be easier."

"Fuck you!"

He tugged Riley toward the door, ignoring the way he tried to be dead weight, dig his heels in, and twist.

"About time."

Riley only paused in his struggles as he heard the voice after Eren dragged him into the cavernous room. The table wasn't set with dinner, but two glasses of wine sat on the pristine cloth. Grandfather sat in his usual spot, and Riley's breathing picked up as he took in the man, the wraiths in the shadows, and the table.

"What are you doing? Eren? Please! Tell me what this is!"

Eren dragged him closer, and Grandfather stood. "Drop him."

Eren placed Riley down on the floor. The nephalem instantly tried to get to his knees to start crawling away, but Eren placed a boot on the halfling's chest to hold him down.

"I said to drop him," Grandfather said coldly.

"Shouldn't I treat your offering with a little more respect?" Eren tilted his head. "I wouldn't take your possessions and drop them on the floor."

"Who the fuck are you?" spat Riley. "I'm not fucking you. I'm not doing anything you want."

"Shut the fuck up," Eren yelled before his eyes caught something on the floor. "Grandfather, what is that?"

Grandfather smirked. "Bellim spell-killed him."

"Why? You only have two wraiths now."

"That's enough. The pearl helped him."

That meant the wraiths might grow smarter with the consort out there, not that he had time to sit and worry about that right now.

"What the hell, Eren?" yelled Riley. "You let him fuck you? I'm not going to be anyone's toy."

Eren kept his gaze away from Riley. At least the hate and fury were genuine. No one could fake that. "We don't fuck."

Grandfather approached, crouched, and pushed away Eren's boot. The eagerness on his face was sickening, and Eren was tempted to grab his head and snap his neck. Not that it would work. "Riley, you're going to work for me. I will fuck you if I please later on, but I have far greater plans."

"I'll drive you mad in your sleep. I'll torture every demon in the army. I'll-"

Grandfather grabbed Riley's hair and yanked him into a sitting position. "I know what you're capable of, and that's why I want you. You're going to help me destroy the angels. Wouldn't you like that? If you help me, you'll be the third most powerful being in the realm and on Earth."

"I'm more powerful than you," snarled Riley. "I'll drive you all insane."

Grandfather grabbed his neck. "I'm not something you can defeat. I'm far greater than you despite your ability. If you behave, you'll have untold power. The angels will fall to us."

"And then what?" Riley managed to get out with his head bent back and a hand at his throat. His eyes flicked to Eren who quickly looked away in shame even though he remained upright and tried to keep his body fluid and at ease like this didn't bother him.

"Earth is next. Eren will rule it for me in general, and if you behave, I'll let you have a small portion of your own. You'll enter the dreams of Kings and Queens and those close to them. If they refuse to kneel, you'll torture and break them bit by bit. Every single nation will soon fall and bend the knee to me."

Lies. He'd never let Riley have anything. Even if the halfling didn't break, Grandfather would never trust one with such a power.

Riley stared at the beast holding him as the pieces seemed to fall into place for him, and he looked to Eren as if still hoping for some shred of humanity. "Eren, you can't be serious-"

Eren forced his voice to be cold. "We're very serious. You'll enter the dreams of rulers, and you'll make them bend the knee in real life, or their sleep will be agony until they die or go insane. That's the only mercy they'll get. Once everyone knows that not a single person is safe, I imagine they'll fall in line quite quickly.

You'll also be a good tool to stop any rebellions that might pop up."

"The humans will team up-"

Grandfather laughed as he shoved Riley back onto the floor. "Even if every single human gathered in a great army with the best weapons and armor, and the brightest came up with a plan, we'd still crush them. Some will resist, but they'll be under me. They're weak compared to a demon."

Eren tacked on a smirk. "Earth will be our playground. Now be quiet, Riley. If you're smart, you'll do as he says. I don't think Grandfather wants to hear your prattle." He ignored Riley's incredulous look.

Grandfather turned to him. "Eren, fuck your pet."

"I can get someone else later."

"Do it now."

"You're not fucking touching me," Riley snarled at Eren.

"I had my fun with him," said Eren. "Besides, I can get a new pet from Earth later. A nephalem's ass is the same as any other. Since I have a battle coming up, I'd like to have my full ability ba-."

Grandfather got in Eren's face. "I'm not asking you to fuck him. I still doubt your loyalty with your talk of kindness. Did you think you had me fooled? Fuck your childhood friend. I'll take the pearl once you're done. And no, you can't have your ability back yet."

Eren struggled to keep his expression composed and his tail from lashing about. "I did what you asked, and you agreed I could have it back once you had Riley."

"No."

"You promised me you would when I brought him."

"Do you think I'd be that stupid when your loyalty is in question?" Grandfather chuckled.

Eren tilted his head. "I've done everything you ask, and you said my rewards would be great. I'm only asking for one thing because it's mine, and I could use it for the fights ahead."

Grandfather narrowed his eyes. "You got this far without it. Maybe if you fuck him, I will."

Hardly. Eren had suspected he might refuse, and that left one option.

"And now, you're stalling," said Grandfather. "Everything you have, including your life, is because of me, and when I command, you obey. Fuck him, or else. You'll be spending time in the tomb later."

"Fine."

Riley tried to scoot away on his rear. "No! Get away from me."

Eren stepped closer, grabbed his arm, and pulled him to his feet.

"Eren! You can't do this! Let go of me." He tried to be deadweight, but that didn't work against Eren's strength.

"Stop struggling. You're only delaying it."

Riley kicked at him, and even spit. Eren barely avoided it before he forced Riley over to the table.

"If you hurt me-the con-"

Eren clamped his hand over Riley's mouth as he bent him over and pinned him down. "You never know when to shut up. You better not talk so much with Grandfather."

He was about to whisper something, but the sharp tip of a dagger on his back made him freeze. Would Grandfather simply kill him even if he obeyed now that he had Riley? Calan would take over the army, and they could go forth without Eren.

Technically, Grandfather didn't need him at all anymore now that he had Riley. The two remaining wraiths could deal with the nephalem and keep him imprisoned. He didn't need Eren to take over Earth either. Once the heir was born, Grandfather would use him too because Calan had no choice but to obey the terms laid out. Family or not, Eren meant little.

"Make it quick, boy," said Grandfather.

"I'm not into fucking with a dagger at my back."

"You better get used to it."

Eren reached around Riley to undo his belt while he kept his hand over his mouth and used his weight to pin him. The sob Riley let out nearly broke him right then as he pretended to fumble with the buckle. There was no way out of this that would keep Eren alive, but in the end, at least he'd keep the promise that he made so many years ago when they were boys in the forest.

"Run," Eren whispered against the halfling's ear as he let out a tendril of poison from his forefinger. Even with his terror, Riley seemed to hear as he tensed.

"Hurry up," snapped Grandfather.

Scaring or pinning Riley down didn't count as breaking the contract. Even bringing him here technically didn't count since

Eren had caused no physical harm yet. Riley jerked as the poison touched his stomach, and he made a strange noise that seemed more out of shock than anything else.

The contract was broken.

Searing pain blossomed in Eren's heart. He released Riley's mouth and yanked on the rope binding his wrists just as Grandfather drove the dagger in.

"I knew you were weak! I-"

The wraiths fluttered forward to aid their Master. They only hesitated when Eren summoned his scythe, and they saw the blazing fire on the tip.

"You can't kill me!" Grandfather snarled as Eren danced sideways with his weapon raised. The dagger fell out of his back and hit the floor with a clang.

Eren knew his scythe wouldn't do shit against Grandfather. He'd already tried to kill him at the age of seventeen when he'd learned of his ability and kept it a secret. Despite being at the top of his age group, he hadn't known everything or thought things through.

Riley had a chance to run now, and with the contract in his pocket, he'd be safe. In the desperate hope that he'd be able to somehow save Riley at some point, he'd given him everything.

"Riley, run!" Eren swung at Grandfather as a distraction. The shield, one that no one else could do, appeared in front of Grandfather. His scythe hit it, and the sound of metal on metal sounded even though the shield was made of glowing purple energy. Purple sparks flew, and Grandfather laughed, clearly thinking his descendant was beyond foolish to attempt this again.

The two wraiths started to move around the side, and instead of running, Riley lunged.

For a moment, Eren's panic was absolute. He thought only death would fully undo the things that had been done to him, but a shadow grew by his boots as blood ran from his mouth. He knew he was as good as dead, and that must have been enough to let him have this much of it back.

The shadow, blacker than ink, grew as tendrils snaked along the floor. The wraiths wouldn't die from it, but it was enough to make them pause for a moment. Grandfather's shield faltered a second later as he stumbled forward.

Riley drove the dagger in deep and twisted it. Eren, terrified out of his mind in the moving room, must not have felt him slip it from his sheath, and he hadn't wiped off the poison from earlier.

Grandfather roared as it sank into his back. It wouldn't kill him, but the wound would weaken him. At that moment, one of the poison strands lashed around his ankle under the grey robe he wore, and he vanished. The dagger hit the stones, and Riley mumbled something as he lunged for it even though it wouldn't do anything against wraiths.

He wasn't dead. The top of the tomb shuddered slightly, and he knew Grandfather had gone to hide and rest. The tendrils headed for the wraiths, but Eren stumbled as his legs shook. When he coughed, blood splattered on the floor. The shadow vanished, and he couldn't make it come back. He was too weak.

"Riley, r-run."

Chapter Twenty-One

Like Riley was leaving him here now that he understood a couple of things. He grabbed Eren's arm and started hauling him toward the doors. With the sight of their prey fleeing, the wraiths lunged. Eren stopped, turned, and threw his scythe. It arced toward them with the flame on the blade leaving bright blurs as it went. They jerked to the side to avoid it, and the few extra seconds it bought them worked as Riley dragged Eren toward the doors. The demon lord's scythe flew back to his hand.

When they made it into the hallway, Riley noticed a horned woman standing in the room, although she was grey and transparent like a ghost or a spirit. She hadn't been there before. Riley didn't have time to wonder, and he slammed the door. For whatever reason, the wraiths hung back and didn't seem so intent on following anymore

Eren had already made his scythe vanish, and he moved his hands to do the lock spell. The hall lit up, and the cavernous room was sealed.

"It's locked," he whispered. "We can get out. They...can't. I don't think they want to leave Grandfather. He won't come out."

Riley turned away from the doors. The sight of Eren with blood running from his mouth and the way he shook made his stomach twist as panic made his limbs go weak for a moment. "Eren, heal yourself!"

Eren wiped at the blood on his chin as he stumbled back. "Not here. The magic's too oppressive."

With the way Grandfather had spoken and acted, it was clear Eren was under his control. A lot of things made sense now, but Riley didn't have time to deal with it. Eren looked like he was dying which he was supposed to do after breaking the contract, but he must have had a way around it.

Riley didn't feel anything oppressive in here but hope blossomed in his chest. Eren always had a way around things. Manipulation was his number one talent, so of course, he wouldn't die by breaking the contract. His healing ability was likely far stronger than Riley thought. He dragged Eren toward the doors to the moving room. As the wall slid up, he noticed the woman was gone,

"I'm sorry." Eren's bloodied lips brushed Riley's cheek as the room started to move up. "I had to. He's used me since I was a child, but I wanted to protect you-"

"You did." Riley clutched him, wishing the room would hurry up. "You protected me. Please tell me you'll be fine once we get out."

"Yes. I wanted to-"

"You can tell me when we get out. I need you to be okay first."

"No more lies after this."

"No more," agreed Riley.

Fear wormed into the hope in his chest. Eren couldn't seem to stand from the way he held onto Riley, and a tremble ran through his body as he dragged in wheezy breaths.

He couldn't even walk out of the cave on his own. Riley had to hold onto him as they went out. The sunlight hit them, and Eren fumbled for a cord around his neck to press on a gold disc.

In a blink, they were in a field.

"The city's behind you," Eren gasped.

"Heal yourself!" The sight of more blood running from Eren's lips, down his neck, and all over his shirt blew away the last bit of Riley's hope.

Had he lied?

"I can't. It was one last lie. I'm sorry."

Riley stared at his face, pale and with red streaked across his mouth and chin. "I've seen you heal yourself with your spit. Do it! Use a spell! Something!"

"Not for this. It's in my-my chest. The contract."

"You protected me! You got me out! Come on!"

"There's no second chance when you break it. I just wanted you out, and I didn't want to die in there. There was no other way because I couldn't hurt you like he wanted." Eren's fingers brushed Riley's. "Please, forgive me. Everything."

Panic raked across Riley's guts. "Then I'll get you to the city." A healer had to be able to do something. There had to be a way to fix this and get around a blood contract.

"Not everything can be healed."

Fuck that. Riley was about to fly with him, but Eren seemed to find the strength to hook an arm around his neck as his tail curled around his leg. The image of his face blurred with tears. He wasn't lying this time. He hadn't found a way to word the contract so that he'd somehow escape death and perform the ultimate manipulation.

That little spot of raw, burning pain on the skin of Riley's torso had been enough.

"You can't die," he whispered. "Please, fight it. Something-"

"I'm tired." Eren seemed like he was having trouble focusing his eyes on Riley's face. "I can't fight anymore. If the Abyss is real, we'll see each other again, all right? I'll find you, and I'll love you better. I…promise."

"No, Eren, please!"

For a fleeting moment, Eren's arm tightened like he was desperately trying to hang on for a few more seconds. "He's not dead but weakened. Look at the contract…it's…it's…"

His tail went slack and dropped as his eyes seemed to lose their luster.

"Eren, I love you. Please…"

The demon lord went completely limp, and his arm slipped away. Riley held him up, willing him to move. He couldn't be dead. He had to move, speak, and somehow get better.

"Please, please, please. I love you. You can't die! Damn it, Eren! Wake up!"

The demon lord had no pulse. His tail didn't curl around Riley's leg, and his head remained tipped back as his blank eyes looked at nothing.

"EREN!"

Riley sank to the grass with the demon in his arms as he sobbed. How could he simply die like this? Riley remembered wishing death upon him, and all the nasty things he'd said. He hadn't meant them, not deep down, and Eren had loved him if he'd gone this far.

He'd said a demon always keeps his promises, and Eren had fulfilled the one he made in the woods years ago. He'd kept Riley safe even at the expense of his life. His words on the wall by the Tree's ashes had been real. He'd always loved Riley, but that thing had a hold on him somehow.

Exactly why or how was a mystery, and at that point, Riley didn't give a fuck. Every cruel thing Eren had done had been because something else had been pulling the strings the whole time. Every glimpse he'd given Riley of his inner feelings had been true.

He remained there as the sun slipped lower, unwilling to release the body. Eren's face was peaceful in death with no strain around his half-closed eyes and no snippy or snarky reply about to come from his lips. Riley would have razed Hell to the ground if it meant he could hear a single word from the demon's mouth. How could he wait until another life?

The Abyss.

If the Abyss was real, could Riley somehow reach it? Was it a place he could get to in a lucid dream? Maybe he could find Eren like that? If he could drag people into his dreams, that meant he had their soul in a way, right? He couldn't harm their bodies with it, but what if there was a way to get someone out of a dream and into their body?

Or maybe he was grasping at nothing in his desperation.

The Fallen realm had been dreamed by Red Horn, so maybe the Abyss had been dreamed and made real by him. If souls got out of it to be reincarnated, there had to be a way for Riley to bring back Eren.

He was a citizen now, so he could go to the city. No one would try to make him their pet or kill him for his angel side.

He gently lowered Eren onto his back. The demon lord had left the contract in Riley's pocket and said to look at it. It was rumpled, and at the bottom, both of their signatures had been signed. As the light hit the parchment, he noticed something off.

Eren had said to look at the contract.

Riley held it up to the sun and noticed faint marks in the blank space between the terms of the contract and their signatures at the bottom. What the fuck had he truly signed? He couldn't make it out.

Eren might not have found a way to cheat death, but he'd had something up his sleeve to keep Riley safe in the long run. He didn't understand everything that happened in the cave, and he needed Eren back first. They could figure out the rest afterward.

And this time, Riley wasn't leaving him.

"It'll be me that finds you this time," he whispered to the body.

The courtyard was quiet as he landed in it with Eren's body. He didn't see the twins, and he headed right upstairs to put Eren on his bed. Watching him lay there in the dim light made Riley choke up again. Eren's eyes didn't glow anymore, and even his scent was nearly gone.

Riley had wished to see him dead, but now he wanted to take it all back. He wanted to take back every cruel word he'd ever said to the demon lord. Eren had still loved him despite everything.

A bottle of rewek was in the drawer, and once the door was shut and locked, he drank some.

"He'll be back when I wake up," he whispered to himself as he got into bed and put an arm over Eren. He wasn't warm anymore, but he would be soon.

In the forest, Riley focused on Eren and drew him in. He almost cried with happiness as he saw Eren standing before him again. His purple and silver eyes glowed, and he was wearing the same clothes, but they appeared clean and weren't rumpled. No blood marred him, and he wasn't deathly pale. They locked eyes for a second.

"Don't call on me again," Eren said before vanishing.

Riley made a frustrated noise. The hell he wouldn't! He brought Eren back again and spoke in a rush.

"I just have to figure out how to bring you back-"

"Don't call on me again." Eren vanished.

"What the fuck?!"

Did Eren not want to come back? He'd said he was tired, and he probably meant life in general. He'd known only war, and Grandfather had been using him. That must have started in childhood since Eren had vanished from the woods. Maybe it even started before that. Maybe bringing him back was selfish, but he couldn't let things end like this. Eren had only done what he felt he needed because his choices had been few.

Riley sniffled and tried to bring his Mother. Nothing happened just like last time. He tried with Father, wondering if he'd get the same response, but Father didn't appear.

What was different now?

Riley took a deep breath and tried to bring Uncle Grevin, but the forest remained empty except for him. Perhaps it didn't work on humans. Weren't they supposed to go to Heaven? Maybe that was why. Eren had said demons didn't get to go to Heaven or Hell because neither side wanted them. But if Father had appeared once, why wouldn't he now?

"What if…" He focused on Eren's Father.

A man with the same horns, eyes, and hair appeared, but his face was a little different, and his hair was shorter. It wouldn't take a genius to figure out who he was.

"Don't call on me again." Dade vanished.

Riley bit his lip and wondered if the demon that Eren had called Grandfather was actually his real relative or if that had been a different term. It didn't make sense for a past ruler to live in a cave like that. Why wouldn't he be on the throne? He hadn't exactly looked well, but why make an old family member live out there?

When Eren's Grandfather appeared, he didn't look like the demon in the cave. One eye was silver, but the other was a dark blue, and again, he had similarities to Eren and Dade, although his hair went far past his shoulders.

"Don't call on me again." Eren's real Grandfather vanished.

That demon in the cave certainly wasn't Dade's Father. He had two different eyes, black hair, and wings, so maybe he was somehow related.

If three dead people could be brought in, but they vanished, that must mean their soul was somehow alive. It was *somewhere*. For those who couldn't, they must have been reborn or maybe they passed on to Heaven or Hell for whatever reason.

Father had mentioned seeing more than most. Eren said no one was reincarnated, but he didn't believe in it, and how would he know for sure if he didn't remember past lives? Father must have been rare if he remembered. Mother might already be reborn, but she was someone else, so she wouldn't remember being *Lilith.*

Father might be reborn too. He could be a baby right now among the demon kids, although Riley wasn't sure if he'd remember the past right now if he'd just hatched.

It didn't matter. Riley took a deep breath as he brought Eren back and quickly focused on bringing him out while he closed his eyes. He had no idea if this was working, but it was all he could think of.

When he woke up, the demon lord's body was still.

"Eren?"

Riley sat up and blinked as the sluggishness gripped his brain. He put a hand on Eren's chest, but it didn't rise, and the demon didn't move.

"Eren, please..."

The demon remained cold and silent, and Riley let out a choked noise of frustration and rage. There had to be a way to bring him back. He wouldn't accept this. He dipped his head to Eren's chest as his throat tightened.

"This is fucking bullshit! You have to-"

"Riley!?"

"Why human sad?"

Riley almost jumped out of his skin. Fuck. The twins had heard him. The parchment in his pocket rustled as he practically flew off the bed and nearly tripped. His heart pounded as he exited. The twins stood in the sitting room with shocked expressions as he shut the door and stood in front of it.

"Riley nephalem?" Nagorth whispered as Eedwa's mouth fell open to show all of his rotted teeth.

"Uh, surprise," Riley said sarcastically as he rubbed his face. "Er-why don't you go downstairs-wait! Is there a way to make a message invisible?"

Eedwa managed to close his mouth as Nagorth tilted his head. "Secret?"

"Er, yeah."

"Invisible ink?"

"How would you read something if it was written in that?"

"Water make see," said Eedwa. "Any liquid. Water best."

"Oh, okay. Go bring me some water."

"Why blood?"

Riley stupidly tried to wipe off his dirty shirt. "I-I had a little accident, but I'm fine now."

"Where Lord Erebus?" asked Nagorth.

"Um, there's some stuff going on. Go get me water."

The twins looked at each other as they seemed to consider the request.

"Riley…nephalem? Lord Erebus know?"

"Of course, he knows. Look, it's a long story, and I really don't feel like explaining it right now."

The twins continued staring at his folded red wings.

"Water? Remember? Hurry up." Riley made a shooing motion.

The twins scuttled for the door, and he heard Eedwa whisper. "Bet he still silly."

"Like human."

"Same Riley."

"Lord Erebus love."

"Ass still tight."

They snorted as they hurried off.

He shooed them off again once they brought water. In the office, he laid out the parchment and patted it with a wet cloth. Sure enough, the words became visible and turned grey. Eren had written them in the space between the original contract and their signature. Anybody who grew up here would probably be wary of such a possibility, but Riley hadn't thought twice about it. Like a fool, he could have signed anything. Hell, if Nyla had ever thought of such a thing, she could have tricked him into signing some bullshit.

Riley scanned the words in Eren's neat script and thought he must have misread them. Surely, the stress of today had addled his brains, but when he read them again, his heart started thumping. Eren had gone a step further to ensure Riley's safety.

Why this? It was insane. How could Eren think this was a good idea in the event that he died and Riley lived? What if Eren had died in that room, but Riley hadn't been able to get away from Grandfather? This surely would have doomed him.

Unless it had been another way of saving Riley in case they didn't make it out. In fact, it probably would have been a mercy if Riley had died there. Grandfather wouldn't have been able to use him to take over Earth.

What else would break this? Being away too long? If he brought Eren back, that would surely negate it safely, correct?

Either way, Eren had intended to keep his promise in more than one way. The words blurred as Riley pushed away the parchment. Even if he didn't know Grandfather, a lot made sense. His migraines were likely a response to stress in some way. When he left at times, it had probably been to see Grandfather.

That night he'd gotten into bed while shivering meant he must have gone to see Grandfather. Perhaps Eren had been told then that he needed to lure Riley into love and security for betrayal magic. He hadn't been cold like he'd said, and he'd never been able to say a word because another blood contract likely kept him silent.

He'd probably also been punished for not raping his pet, and that's why he had returned with a migraine that one morning.

When he'd said they could own each other, he'd meant it in his heart, but he hadn't been able to promise it because Grandfather wanted Riley. Eren had wanted a future with him, but he didn't see how it could be done.

His unborn heir would likely be used. If Lancefs signed blood contracts, who knew what was in it so Grandfather would have another to control? There was no way he would have risked Eren dying in war without someone else to lord it over.

Eren had left his desk drawers unlocked. Riley dug through them and found old documents relating to the war, and things involving taxes. He'd never thought to ask, but of course, the demons must have paid taxes to him. Someone else must have taken care of that for him since he'd never mentioned it, and nobody ever came to the Hall with it. A few of their rather plain gold coins lay forgotten at the bottom of one drawer.

Riley hoped to find a note or something explaining more, but it didn't seem that Eren had left him anything. He'd have to make decisions on his own now. He looked through the shelves, wondering if Eren had a secret compartment somewhere. Maybe the contract with his Lancef was in there.

All he found in one corner was a raggedy book with the corner of a piece of parchment sticking up. It was so small, Riley nearly missed it, and he pulled out the book to open it. The parchment was folded up small, and it was stiff and yellowed like it had been there for ages.

Riley carefully unfolded it. Eren hadn't been lying when he'd said he'd loved Riley since they were children.

The drawing appeared old, it was clear a child had done it considering the wobbly lines and the crookedness. Besides, he couldn't imagine Eren doing this as an adult.

Two little stick figures stood in front of a house and held hands. A stick cat and a puppy stood by them. The faded ink was black, and no color marked the black dots of their eyes, but it was clear the one with a tail was Eren. The other must have been Riley.

His eyes stung again, and he pictured Eren as a little boy, trapped under Grandfather's thumb and not allowed to see his best friend anymore. Perhaps he hadn't even been permitted to speak of Riley, but he'd drawn this and kept it, putting into a picture what he really wanted even though the words probably would have killed him or caused him to be punished.

Riley didn't know what else to do with it after he folded it up, so he placed it back in the book. He had to let the demons know something, and he might as well get it over with.

It was night, but a fake command from Eren worked. The twins relayed it out and came to get him when they said everyone was there. Riley sent them down and said to wait. The twins obeyed.

He remained on the couch for a moment to steel himself before he went into the bedroom to grasp Eren's limp hand. Even though the demon couldn't hear him, he spoke anyway.

"I'll do this because you wanted it, but I am going to bring you back. I'm not going to wait for another life to love you. I love you now in this one, and when I bring you back, that thing you called Grandfather is never going to get his hands on you again. Somehow, we'll have that future that you wanted."

When he entered the Hall, it was packed with the citizens of Hell City, and the crowd spilled into the street. Not everyone would hear him, but the gist could be relayed. The demons clicked, spoke, growled, muttered, and many gasped at the sight of Riley with his red wings. Clearly, they had been expecting Eren.

A few who looked particularly astounded might have remembered him from his pet days when they thought he was nothing more than a cambion. Riley remembered he hadn't changed or washed up. He let his wings spread out. Dirty nephalem or not, they better accept Eren's wishes.

He heard the word "nephalem" whispered a few times as he sat on the throne. Despite his old, usual spot being quite close, the room looked so different from Eren's point of view. The demons stared at him as they waited for something to happen.

Riley tried to make his expression firm like he knew what he was doing. That's what the demons expected from Eren, and he tried to emulate that as he lifted the parchment and raised his voice.

"With this contract signed in blood by me and Erebus, I am now Lord Riley and the ruler of the demons."

To be continued in And In-Between (An M/M Demon Angel Romance)

Other works by Julie Mannino

For info on the latest books, including queer fairy tales, fantasy, M/M, and M/X romance, sign up here for the Newsletter.

Jack's Day (Jack's Reign Book One)
Chloe's Purpose (Jack's Reign Book Two)
Eado's Birth (Jack's Reign Book Three)
Leon the Lion (Jack's Reign Side Novel)
A Royal Obsession

The Grey Wolf

M/M Tippy the Knight An Erotic Short Story

LGBTQIA+ Loki's Price
M/M Angel Devil A Thrall Short Story
M/M Thrall A Novel of Alternate Earth

LGBTQIA+ Finley's Way
M/M The Hunted

M/M Secrets
M/M Secrets II

M/M Promises

M/M Valentine (An Asexual M/M Fairy Romance)

M/M Lessons (An MM Dark Academia College Romance)
M/M Lessons II (An MM Dark Academia College Romance)

M/M A Touch of Innocence (A Demisexual M/M Fairy Romance)
M/M A Touch of Savagery (A Demisexual MMM Fairy Romance)
M/M Roth's Present (An MMM Fairy Romance)

M/M As Above (An M/M Demon Angel Romance)
M/M So Below (An M/M Demon Angel Romance)
M/M And In-Between (An M/M Demon Angel Romance)
M/M Desire (An M/M Paranormal Romance) (The Fallen)
M/M Azriel (An M/M Angel Nephilim Romance) (The Fallen)

M/M Prince of Pain I (A Dark M/M Fairy Romance)
M/M Prince of Pain II (A Dark M/M Fairy Romance)
M/M Prince of Pain III (A Dark M/M Fairy Romance)
M/M Prince of Pain IV (A Dark M/M Fairy Romance)
M/M Prince of Pain V (A Dark M/M Fairy Romance)

M/M Mine (An M/M Prison Romance)
M/M Yours (An M/M Prison Romance
M/M Ours (An M/M Prison Romance)

Alternate Earth Tales-Queer Fairytales

M/M Little Red Riding Hood
M/M Cynric Ella
M/X The Piper

Printed in Poland
by Amazon Fulfillment
Poland Sp. z o.o., Wrocław